D1710899

BARTHOLOMEW

MARK LAGES

authorHOUSE®

AuthorHouse™
1663 Liberty Drive
Bloomington, IN 47403
www.authorhouse.com
Phone: 833-262-8899

© 2022 Mark Lages. All rights reserved.

No part of this book may be reproduced, stored in a retrieval system, or transmitted by any means without the written permission of the author.

Published by AuthorHouse 03/16/2022

ISBN: 978-1-6655-5482-4 (sc)
ISBN: 978-1-6655-5481-7 (e)

Library of Congress Control Number: 2022905028

Print information available on the last page.

Any people depicted in stock imagery provided by Getty Images are models, and such images are being used for illustrative purposes only.
Certain stock imagery © Getty Images.

This book is printed on acid-free paper.

Because of the dynamic nature of the Internet, any web addresses or links contained in this book may have changed since publication and may no longer be valid. The views expressed in this work are solely those of the author and do not necessarily reflect the views of the publisher, and the publisher hereby disclaims any responsibility for them.

CHAPTER 1

CAKE AND CANDLE

My name is Rick Harper, and the cake is for me. Everyone is here because it's a big deal, because it's not every day you get to celebrate your sixty-fifth birthday. Sixty-five is the magic number—I can start collecting Social Security, and I get to go on Medicare. I quit my job at Wiley & Associates. My golden years are on the horizon, and there isn't a cloud in the sky. There's plenty of sunshine and lots of vitamin D. I smile. At my age, I'll take all the free vitamins I can get.

We are outside, in our backyard. It is around one in the afternoon, and Pamela has placed my cake on the patio table. There is a single candle poked into the top of the cake, and Pamela lit it before bringing the cake to the table. With icing in cursive, it says *Happy Birthday, Rick*. One candle representing sixty-five years—sixty-five years of experiences, loves, hates, successes, resentments, wins, losses, arguments, agreements, pleasures, pains, good fortune, and bad luck all distilled down to a single burning candle on a cake. Everyone sings happy birthday, and I blow the candle out. I tell everyone I made a wish, but I didn't really make one.

Let me tell you about our group. Obviously, Pamela, my wife is there. So are our two sons, Nate and Zach, and their better halves, Emily and Mary Ann. My mom is there, all ninety-plus years of her—not sure of her exact age. My dad died of a heart attack four years ago, but he is there in spirit. My brother, Ralph, and his wife and kids are there. My aunt and uncle are there, and so are two of my cousins and their three kids. John Wiley, my former boss, is there with his wife, and two of my friends from work showed up. There are a few neighbors and friends, including Jeff Anderson, who I've known since high school. Jeff got divorced three years ago, but he brought his girlfriend along. She's twenty years younger than him, if you can imagine that. That about covers it, well, except for one very important guest. The invisible guy. He is the guy no one but me can see or hear, seated in the lounge chair near the pool. His name is Bartholomew.

More about Bartholomew in a minute.

"You're a free man," Mr. Wiley says. Pamela has just handed him a plate with a slice of cake.

"In a way, I am," I say.

"What are you going to do with yourself?" my uncle asks.

"I've thought long and hard about it."

"And?"

"You guys are going to laugh," I say.

"Tell them," Pamela says. She is still slicing cake and handing out plates and forks.

"I'm going to write poetry," I say.

"Poetry?" my uncle asks.

"I want to be a poet."

My mom is listening, but she doesn't say anything.

My aunt asks, "What do you know about poetry?"

"Next to nothing," I say.

"Interesting," Mr. Wiley says.

"I didn't know you were a poetry fan," my uncle says.

"Who's your favorite poet?" my cousin asks.

"I don't really have one," I say.

"Someone must have inspired you," my aunt says.

"He doesn't even read any poetry," Pamela says. "We don't own a single poetry book."

"No?" my uncle asks.

My mom laughs. She is amused by this conversation, but she still says nothing.

"I used to write poetry when I was in high school," my cousin says. "Mostly about boys."

"I probably won't be writing about boys," I say.

Everyone laughs.

"Have you written any poems yet?" my uncle asks.

"I've written a few."

"Quite a few," Pamela says.

"Ah, so you've already started," my cousin says.

"What are they about?" my high school friend, Jeff, asks.

"All kinds of things. Things that interest me and get my attention. Curious things. Weird things."

"Are they any good?" my uncle asks.

"I don't know," I say. "Like I said, I have no idea what I'm doing. For me, poems are like puzzles. Putting all the pieces together in the proper order. Choosing the right words. Assembling them. For me, it's like designing a house, and I've had plenty of experience with that."

"True enough," Mr. Wiley says.

"Maybe it's the architect in me. I've spent a lifetime working as an architect, putting all the pieces together, making them all work as a whole. Maybe I see poetry as an extension of that, but with no clients, building departments, or contractors. Just me and a blank computer screen, and a keyboard that responds to my moving fingers. Just me. I don't have to please anyone other than myself."

Everyone is quiet for a moment, thinking and eating their cake.

"You should write songs," my aunt says.

"That's where the money is," Jeff says.

"I don't know anything about music."

"You don't have to know anything. A musician can put all your words to music. You just write the lyrics. You know, like Bernie Taupin. Elton did all the work, and Bernie made a fortune. The dude is rich."

I look over at Bartholomew. No one can see him, but I can. He is shaking his head and laughing.

Bartholomew knows.

"I'm not trying to get rich," I say. "I just want to write some poetry. I've spent my whole life working to earn a buck. Enough with the bucks, already. How much money do I really need? I want to do something for myself. Something I truly love. Something that makes me want to get up in the mornings."

"But you want people to enjoy your poems?" my aunt asks.

"Of course he does," my uncle says.

"Maybe," I say. "Maybe not."

Okay, I should probably now explain who Bartholomew is. I'm not sure when he first came into my life. I was very young. My memories go back as far as when I was about five years old, but no further. When I was five, Bartholomew was already a good friend. He was as invisible then as he is now. He was my childhood imaginary friend.

It isn't unusual for children to have imaginary friends. He was someone I could turn to at will. He was someone who liked me no matter what I did. He was loyal. And best of all, he gave me sound advice. He didn't give me the sort of advice my parents gave me. He gave me a kid's advice, inspired by the logic only a child has, delivered to me in a way only a child could deliver it. I trusted Bartholomew, and I knew he would never lead me down the wrong path.

My first memory of him? First, let me explain something to you. Life was different when I was a child. My older brother and I didn't get put in time-outs. When we did something wrong, there was a good chance we'd get a thrashing. My dad used to make us pull down our pants, and he would bend us over his knee. Then, with a leather belt, he'd whip our bare behinds five to ten times while we screamed bloody murder. I hated being whipped! I'm not sure other kids carried the same fear with them as I did, but I was terrified of that belt in my father's hands. Just the thought of it was nearly unbearable. Granted, I think I only got whipped three or four times—and it was likely that I deserved it—but the fear! At the age of five, I had yet to be whipped, but I'd seen my brother get it more than once.

My father's belt ensured that I behaved myself for the most part. But I was a kid, and behaving myself wasn't always in my repertoire. Kids are kids, right? I had my moments, such as the time I broke my dad's study window. I was five. It wasn't intentional, but it was definitely belt-worthy. I was in the front yard one Saturday morning with my baseball bat, whacking rocks from the rock bed. It was fun, and I was enjoying myself. Strike one, strike two, and a home run! Mom and Dad had told me to stay out of the rock bed. It was a rule, but rules don't always register with five-year-old boys.

One of the rocks I hit flew off the bat sideways—a foul ball, if you will. It flew sideways off the bat and smashed right into my dad's study window. *Crash!* The window was broken, and the rock was now sitting on my dad's study floor. Dad was not in the study, and no one heard the noise.

Enter Bartholomew. "You've got to get out of here," he said. "Do something in the backyard. Put the bat back in the garage, get to the backyard, and pretend you were always there. If your parents find out you were playing in the rock bed and broke your dad's window, all hell is going to break loose."

"What should I say?" I asked.

"That you were in the backyard all morning. That some other kid must've thrown the rock through the window."

"You want me to lie?"

"Do you want the belt?"

"No, no," I said.

"Then, yes, you should lie. You must lie. You were never in the front yard!"

Bartholomew was right of course, and I took the bat and put it back in the garage. Then I snuck to the backyard around the side of the house, and I played with my Tonka trucks. It wasn't so bad. I liked my Tonka trucks. I made a noise with my mouth that sounded like engines.

After about an hour, Mom came out through the patio door and told me it would be lunchtime soon. "I was wondering where you were," she said. "I thought you were out front."

"I've been back here all morning," I said. Lying to my mom? What could be worse? I'll tell you what could be worse. It would be feeling the wrath of my father's belt slapping the soft flesh of my bare behind!

Well, we had lunch. Me, my brother, Ralph, Mom, and Dad. Bologna sandwiches and Fritos. Dad had a pickle spear. Dad always had a pickle with his sandwiches. Don't ask me why. I hated pickles with a passion, and it twisted my mouth up just watching him eat the darn things. One day, I would be a dad, but I swore I wouldn't eat pickles with my sandwiches. It would be a cold day in hell.

Hell.

I'd learned all about hell in Sunday school class. That's where I would be going if I didn't behave myself. That's where I would be going if I broke my parents' rules. That's where I would be going if I whacked a rock through my father's window, and that's where I would be going if I lied. Me? I didn't want to go to hell, but I kept the lie up. When Dad found the broken window and the rock later that same day, he showed me the damage. "Were you in the front yard this morning?" he asked.

"No, sir," I said.

"He's been playing with his trucks in the backyard," Mom said.

"Jesus," Dad said.

"Who do you think did it?" Mom asked.

"Kids," Dad said.

"It was probably Bobby Richardson," I said. Why not? Bobby was a troublemaker. He was always getting into hot water. Add a broken window to the list, and it wouldn't matter to Bobby.

"Probably," Dad said. I knew my dad didn't like Bobby. No harm done.

"No way to prove it," Mom said.

It was wrong to blame Bobby, and I knew it, but it was either that or be on the receiving end of my father's leather belt. Bartholomew knew. He always knew the right thing to do. Better Bobby than me. Besides, Bobby *was* a rotten kid. Breaking someone's window was right up his alley, and blaming him for the broken window only substantiated what my father already knew. There were always a few kids like Bobby, kids who were troublemakers.

Thank God for Bartholomew.

My first inclination had been to tell my parents the truth, but my invisible friend had talked me out of it. My imaginary friend saved my hide!

Bartholomew disappeared from my life when I was seven. Mom and Dad knew about him, and they told me it was time to grow up, time to abandon my childish fantasies. And I *did* want to grow up. I wanted to grow up in the worst way. There was no formal goodbye. There was no last hug or shaking of hands. I just let him go. It was time, and I moved on.

That was the last I heard from him, until a year ago, on my sixty-fourth birthday. I went out to dinner with Pamela to celebrate, and while we were waiting for our salads, I got up to use the restroom. When I entered the restroom, a man was washing his hands. I stepped to the urinal, and the man turned off the water, dried his hands, and left the room. I was by myself when my friend showed up. At first, I didn't recognize him. He was no longer a kid. He stepped up to the urinal next to mine, and he unzipped his pants. We looked at each other.

"Do you recognize me?" he asked.

"Do I recognize you?"

"That was my question."

"Not really," I said. "Should I?"

"It's been a long time."

"A long time for what?" I asked.

"A long time since you've seen me."

I looked, but for the life of me, I could not tell who he was. Although, his face did seem familiar. "You seem familiar to me," I said. "But I'm sorry."

He laughed.

"Bartholomew's the name," he said.

"Bartholomew?"

A man then entered the restroom, and I turned to look at him. The man peered at himself in the mirror for a moment, and he combed his hair off his forehead with his fingers. He came toward the urinal next to me, and when I turned to look, Bartholomew was gone. Just like that, he had vanished! As the man took his place, I zipped up my pants and flushed the urinal. I washed my hands at the sink and returned to the table with Pamela.

"Are you okay?" she asked.

"I'm fine," I said.

"You look like you've seen a ghost."

"Do I?"

CHAPTER 2

THE MAMA DUCK

You're probably wondering, "Why now?" After all these years, why would Bartholomew suddenly have come back into my life? Was I regressing back to my childhood? Was I going crazy? Was there something wrong with me? These were the questions I asked myself, for it wasn't just an idle fantasy. I saw him and heard him in that restroom. Bartholomew was real!

The second time I saw Bartholomew as an adult, I was at home and in my den. This was shortly after I saw him at the restaurant. It was early in the morning, and Pamela was asleep. By early in the morning, I mean *really* early. I had recently been getting up at about two every morning. I had been using these early-morning hours to work on my poetry. I would get up at two, and I would write until seven. Then I would take a nap until around ten or eleven, and I would arrive at the office after lunch. I'd been working half days during my last year at Wiley & Associates. Mr. Wiley said he didn't mind. He told me I was welcome to keep up the half-day schedule as long as I liked, but I told him that I was retiring in a year on my sixty-fifth birthday. I told him my mind was made up.

Bartholomew showed up in my home office at about three in the morning. I had already finished my first cup of coffee, and I had just gone into the kitchen to brew a second. I sat down at my computer in my den, and I placed the hot coffee on my desk on a coaster. I had been putting the finishing touches on a poem, a poem about my current life, and the title of the poem was "Here I Am." I wouldn't call it a happy poem, an uplifting poem, or an optimistic poem, but it was honest.

Here I Am

Computer on my desk,
A rug on the floor,
I think of what it means:
Life at sixty-four.

Where did all the time go?
And just what have I done?
What have I accomplished?
So, was it any fun?

I used to be a kid,
And then a strong young man.
I have been a winner;
I've been an also-ran.

Struggled to pay my bills,
And counted my profits.
Bumbled my way through life,
And survived by my wits.

I'm all over the place.
Who in the heck am I?
I could ask myself how?
I could also ask why?

A man should have a thread
That he can call his own,
But me? I have nothing.
Can you give me a loan?

Pin the tail on the
Donkey. Ha, I am off
By a mile. I am hard
Where I ought to be soft.

I am mean as a bear,
And sweet as a humming
Bird. I am nothing at
All; I should be something.

Don't you think a man should
Know who he is? My life
Is like a sore that won't
Heal, like a nagging wife.

Every day I live, I
Look forward to the fall
Of the curtain. Can't wait
For the end of it all.

There will be no applause,
And no one will stand, shout,
or cheer. But this nightmare
Will be over and out.

Roger that.

Finally, no more lines.
No more pretending to be
Someone else, anyone but
My lost and lonesome me.

Yes, it was an odd little poem, and like I said, it wasn't exactly happy. Or encouraging. Or optimistic. But it was honest, and it expressed the way I felt when I wrote it. I had the poem up on my computer monitor when Bartholomew appeared in my room, and he stepped to my desk.

"You again?" I asked.

"What do we have here?" he asked, looking at the poem on my monitor.

"It's a poem," I said.

"You're writing poetry?"

"I am," I said. "I enjoy it."

"Do you mind if I read this?" Bartholomew asked.

"Be my guest," I said.

He read the poem, and then he sat in the armchair adjacent to my desk. "You're up so early," he said.

"It's my writing time."

"You think clearer in the morning?"

"I do," I said.

"Interesting poem."

"Did you like it?"

"Not really. I mean, it was pretty good as far as poems go, but it was also kind of depressing. Do you really look forward to dying?"

"Often I do," I said.

Bartholomew stared at me for a moment, and then he said, "You and I need to talk."

"About what?"

"About you, of course. You and yours."

"You want to talk about me and my family?"

"I want to talk about you and everyone."

"Everyone?"

"Everyone and everything."

"That could take days. It could take weeks. Heck, it could take months."

"I've got time," Bartholomew said. "That's the one thing I have plenty of."

Everyone and everything? Before we went any further, Bartholomew wanted to know more about me. He asked me to tell him ten stories from my life, and I agreed to this. I would do my best to be honest. Of course, whenever one is talking about himself, there are bound to be inaccuracies and distortions. It's easier to be objective when you are looking at someone's life from the outside in, rather than from the inside out. That's the truth, but I would try to be objective.

Why ten stories? Why not nine? Why not eleven? Why not twenty? Because, as Bartholomew told me, ten was a nice, round number. Ten was a human number. Ten fingers, ten toes. Ten. It was the most convenient number, a sensible number. Sixty-four years of living on this earth, and yes, I would come up with ten stories. To describe me. To describe my life. One little story for each digit on my grubby human hands, told in no particular order, told as they popped like Chinese firecrackers in my sixty-four-year-old mind. Bartholomew listened to the first story patiently.

I told Bartholomew the story about the duck. I remembered that day. I had gone to the store to pick up some groceries, and I was on my way home in my car. I was listening to the radio as I drove, and I remembered the song they were playing. It was "Stairway to Heaven" by Led Zeppelin, and it sent me back to my high school days. We used to listen to this song over and over at my friend's house. It was on just one of the four albums that he owned. Over and over, we listened, and I still didn't understand the lyrics. It was something about a greedy lady, but what the heck half the lyrics meant, I had no idea. "And the forests will echo with laughter." What laughter? Why is everyone laughing? I didn't get it. Not at all. But I loved that song. It had to mean *something*.

Anyway, I was listening to "Stairway to Heaven" and driving home with my groceries. I wasn't speeding, but I wasn't exactly driving slowly. There weren't any other cars around. As I approached the intersection where I would be making a left turn, I drove into the shadows of a large oak tree. It was a sunny day, and the shadows speckled the road. Then it happened. In the speckled shadows, a mother duck and five or six little ducklings were crossing the street. I hadn't seen them, and by the time I reached their procession, it was too late to stop. It was awful! There was nothing I could do, and I ran right over the mother duck. I looked in my rearview mirror afterward, and I could see the little ducklings scampering about in a panic. Their mom was as flat as a pancake! Flattened guts and feathers and bones. Jesus! They were just minding their own business, and along I came in my three-thousand-pound automobile. My heart sank.

During the days that followed, I couldn't get the image out of my mind. The hysterical little ducklings! The horror! I wondered what happened to the ducklings. Could they even survive without a mom to lead them around? I had brought them the worst kind of tragedy imaginable. Me and my car. Me and the "Stairway to Heaven." Me and my trunkful of groceries. Me, Rick, the murderer, maker of orphans!

That was years ago. I've always wondered why that event had such an impact on me. I am bothered by it every time I think about it, and to this day, I still think about it. Obviously, I still think about it. Why else would I tell Bartholomew about it? Why would I include it in my ten stories?

Every time I thought about that day, it made me feel bad about myself. I'd tell myself that it wasn't my fault, but it didn't make me feel any better. Ducks. Who cares about a handful of stupid ducks, right? But I cared. Bartholomew listened to this story, but he didn't say much. He did point out that it wasn't my fault.

"How about another one?" he said.

"Another what?" I asked.

"Another story."

"A happier one?"

"It's up to you."

"I can tell you a funny story. A story about my son Zach. Nate was also there, but the story is about Zach."

"Go ahead," Bartholomew said.

I decided to tell Bartholomew the steak story. I think Zach was about fourteen at the time, which would've made Nate seventeen. We were in Palm Springs on the three-day vacation. Zach is now thirty, so it would've been about sixteen years ago. We used to take three-day vacations to Palm Springs. We would usually go there during the summer months, off-season, when the rates were lower. It would be in the hundreds, but it was a lot of fun. We spent tons of time at the swimming pools and lots of time in the air-conditioned restaurants. Eating, playing in the water, and maybe playing Monopoly in our motel room. Or maybe watching a few movies together. We always enjoyed ourselves, and our boys were still young enough not to hate being with us.

One of the restaurants we decided to go to was Sam's Steakhouse. It was supposedly world-famous. At least that's what all the billboards said on the freeway. I wasn't a big fan of steakhouses since they all seemed to charge a lot of money for relatively small pieces of meat, but Nate wanted to go to Sam's. He believed all the hype on the billboards.

Nice atmosphere. I'd give them that. The waiter was kind of stuffy, but I ignored his demeanor. I was there to have fun. When it came time to order, Pamela ordered a filet mignon. Nate ordered the tomahawk, and Zach ordered a New York steak. I ordered a porterhouse. I was looking forward to my meal; I hadn't had a good porterhouse for years. We all ordered our steaks medium rare, except for Zach. He ordered his steak rare. I didn't say anything. I guess I should've said something. I just figured Zach knew what he was doing.

Well, when he brought out our steaks, everything looked fine. The cuts were a little small, but I expected that. Then, when Zach cut into his New York, he dropped both hands to the table. "Look at this thing," he said.

"What's wrong with it?" Pamela asked.

"They didn't cook it."

"It looks cooked to me," I said.

"But it's all bloody on the inside!"

We all looked at his steak. "Didn't you ask for it rare?" Pamela asked.

"I said rare, not raw."

"What did you think rare meant?" I asked.

It turned out that Zach thought rare meant rare, as in unique, uncommon, or hard to find. Rare should've been a good thing. In Zach's mind, rare had nothing to do with cooking time. We all had a good laugh, all of us except for Zach.

"What are you?" Nate asked. "Some kind of idiot?"

"Go to hell," Zach said.

"Language," Pamela said.

"Do you want to send it back and have them cook it more?" I asked. "They can put it back on the grill."

"No," Zach said. I thought he really did want to send it back, but he was also embarrassed. And sending it back would mean he didn't know what he was doing.

"You can send it back," Pamela said.

"No, it's fine."

Nate laughed. "That's about the stupidest thing I think I've ever seen you do."

"Shut up," Zach said.

Poor kid. He really was embarrassed, and I felt bad for him. And I suddenly felt guilty. Pamela and I should've taught him this years ago. But we'd been to so many restaurants, so how could Zach not have known what rare meant? All those years, and all those meals, and he had no idea what we were talking about when we ordered steaks. It was funny. But it also demonstrated what a lousy dad I'd been. Why hadn't I taught him?

And what other vital everyday knowledge had I carelessly deprived him of because of my negligence?

"It wasn't your fault," Bartholomew said.

"Of course it was my fault," I replied. "When you're a parent, your kids depend on you to show them the ropes, to teach you to throw a baseball, to teach you how to ride a bike, to teach you the difference between right and wrong."

"You don't think Zach knows the difference between right and wrong?"

"Well, he knows that," I said. "I *think* he knows."

Bartholomew smiled and said, "It's about time for Pamela to get up."

"It is," I said, looking at the clock.

"I'll see you later."

And then, just as abruptly as he had first appeared, he vanished.

Chapter 3

A Laundry Room

Pamela climbed out of bed at seven, and by this time, I was ready for my nap. I got comfortable on the couch, and I turned on a recorded episode of "Star Trek." It was not one of the newer ones; it was one of the originals. There's nothing like an original episode of "Star Trek." Great stuff. Very creative. These were entertaining stories that make you think. I would watch the show and probably fall asleep halfway through.

It was sort of weird, wasn't it? Talking to Bartholomew in my den? I can't say that it bothered me, even if it should have. I mean, seriously, I was a sixty-four-year-old man, way too old to be talking to an imaginary friend. At my age, you're fodder for psychiatrists and mental hospitals when you have conversations with people who don't exist. It isn't exactly a sign of good mental health. What would they call it? A psychosis? A case of schizophrenia? I didn't know. What the heck did I know about psychiatry? I knew about as much about psychiatry as I knew about molecular biology, but I *did* know one thing. I knew I would be best served by keeping my conversations with Bartholomew under my hat. It would be kept a secret. I wouldn't share this situation with anyone else—not even Pamela.

You know, they say there's one thing you can count on with secrets: that they don't stay secrets forever. So be it. If the secret ever did get out, I figured I'd cross that bridge when I came to it.

Anyway, I pulled a blanket up to my chin and watched my "Star Trek" episode. I remember most of them, but this one didn't seem familiar. Kirk, Spock, and McCoy were walking through the halls of a castle. There was a black cat. There were cobwebs. There was also a dungeon. I fell asleep and tumbled into a dream. I tend to dream vividly when I take my morning naps, and this dream was no exception. But there was a difference in that this dream woke me up. I had only been asleep for about twenty minutes before I opened my eyes and sat upright. "Jesus," I said under my breath. "So much for my nap!"

I could remember the entire dream, which is unusual for me. Usually, I can remember only bits and pieces of my dreams, but this one I could recall in detail. In the dream, I was tagging along with Kirk, Spock, and McCoy as the ship's resident expert in architecture. They wanted my opinion of the castle. Specifically, they wanted to know if it was real, and they wanted to know what exactly an earthly castle was doing on a planet so far away from earth.

"It certainly seems real enough," I said, looking around. "Right down to the cobwebs. Right down to the stonework."

"But what is it doing here?" Kirk asked.

"I should take some pictures," I said.

I had a camera with me. You would think it would've been some space-age contraption, but it was my old 35mm camera that I owned when I was in college. I needed film for it, and we continued to walk until we came across a retail area. There were restaurants and stores, and I found a drugstore. All of this inside the castle—weird, right? But it seemed perfectly normal in my dream, and I stepped into the drugstore to see if they sold film. Sure enough, they did. The clerk was a middle-aged Asian man with a pointy nose and crossed eyes, and he put both hands on the counter and looked at me. "What can I do for you?" he asked.

"I see you sell film here," I said.

"We do," the man said.

"I'd like a couple of thirty-six-exposure rolls, please." I opened my camera and saw that there was an undeveloped roll of film. I removed the roll and held it out to the man. "I'd also like to get this roll developed."

"Is it twenty-four or thirty-six?"

"It's twenty-four," I said.

"Ah, it figures. We don't make much money developing twenty-four-exposure rolls."

"How much will it cost me?" I asked.

"I'll have to check." The man pulled a binder out from under the counter, and he began to thumb through the pages.

"What's that?" I asked.

"It's our price list."

"I see," I said.

"Is this going to take all day?" Kirk asked. He was standing behind me, growing impatient.

"I need film," I said to Kirk.

"That's logical," Spock said. He was standing beside Kirk with his tricorder.

"Ah," the clerk said. "Here we go."

"How much?" I asked.

"What are your photographs of?" the clerk asked.

"I don't remember," I said. "What does that have to do with anything?"

"I need to know."

"I don't remember what's on the roll. It's been months since I used my camera. They could be of anything."

"Of crimes?" the clerk asked.

"Of crimes?"

"Did you photograph any crimes being committed?"

"I don't think so," I said.

"Naked women?" the clerk asked.

"No," I said.

"There's a big difference in price. In fact, now I'm not sure if I can even sell you the film."

Well, you get the idea. The dream made no sense at all. It was one of those dreams where you're frustrated at every turn. I don't remember if I bought the film or not. If I did buy it, I don't remember taking any pictures. It was a long dream, and I won't bore you with any further details. Suffice it to say that near the end of the dream, we were in the castle's dungeon. We were all in shackles, and a man with a black hood was about to torture us. I was to be first, and the man grabbed me by my wrist. He jerked me away from the others, and the jerking motion woke me up. I wasn't sweating, but my heart was beating like a timpani drum. I walked to our bathroom to shave, shower, and get ready for work.

Work.

I have worked at Wiley & Associates for twenty-four years. I am one of John Wiley's top designers, or so he tells me. Truth is, I think he tells this to all of his designers. I can't even count the number of projects I've been responsible for. Wiley & Associates has been around for years, and

I *have* played a significant role in its success. We are very good at making our clients happy. Does that make us great architects? I'm not so sure about that. Regardless, I've kept myself on track. I'm pretty good at reading people and figuring out what it will take to please them.

Things were so much different back when I was a college student studying architecture. I had long hair. I had a beard. I smoked cigarettes like they were going out of style, and I drank four pots of coffee per day. I knew what I wanted to be—I wanted to be an artist. Pleasing people was the last thing on my mind, and all I cared about was designing great buildings and prompting people to say, "He's a genius!" That was me, the genius. I would astonish the public, and I would set trends. Back then, I was just a kid, but I was alive! I had dreams, visions, goals, and a lot of self-confidence. I knew I would get my way. In my heart and soul, I *knew* it.

So, what happened? Now I was a people pleaser, chained to my drafting table, churning out mundane, people-pleasing house designs like a computer churns out information. Input and output. That's what I'd become, a processor of architectural mumbo jumbo and stale ideas. I couldn't remember the last time I was really excited about one of my projects. It would've been years ago, when I was just beginning, before I was old and experienced enough to know where I was headed. Every day, I drove to work and labored in my office. It was a nice office, with books and doodads on the shelves. I had a radio and a coaster for my coffee cup. My diploma hung on the wall next to some photographs of the houses I'd designed. I was acceptable. I had made an acceptable career out of mediocrity.

When I arrived at the office that morning, the "Star Trek" dream was still fresh in my mind. It was like I couldn't quite wake up all the way, like I was still half in a dream and half at work. I poured myself a cup of coffee and brought it to my table. The coffee helped. I had a meeting scheduled with Ned and Sylvia Waterhouse. I had been working with them to design their dream home, to be built on a lot they had purchased in Newport Beach. God knows what they paid for the lot. These people were loaded and new to the game of having money. Ned had just sold his computer software company for some amazing sum of cash, and he couldn't spend the money fast enough.

I'd been working with Ned and Sylvia for several months, trying to nail down a floor plan that would meet their needs. I thought we had come up with a final design, and I had sent my drawings to the structural engineer. But yesterday I got a call from Ned, and he said we had to meet as soon as possible. He said Sylvia was having second thoughts about the location of the laundry room, that they might want to move it near the bedrooms. Right now, it was off the kitchen area. Moving the laundry room would require some significant reworking of the plan. It figured. Just when you thought you had someone pegged down, they sniggled out from under with another change.

We met in the conference room, and I spread out the floor plan so we could all look at it. Ned let Sylvia take charge of the meeting.

"It can't be that big of a deal," she said.

"It depends on what you want," I said.

"She wants the laundry room moved," Ned said. "Seems simple enough to me."

"I understand you now want it by the bedrooms?"

"Can it be done?" Sylvia asked.

"Of course it can be done," Ned said, nodding his head like he knew what he was talking about.

"Let's take a look at what we have," I said. I looked over the floor plan. It was a good plan. I'd spent so many hours on it, getting everything just right. But now the laundry room. Where in the world would I put it? It was always *something* with clients, especially clients who had money.

"My friend Erin Parker just had her house built," Sylvia said. "They've been living there for six months. She put her laundry room off the kitchen, and she told me it was a big mistake. Now she has to lug her laundry clear across the house from the bedrooms to the laundry room. She's the one who brought it up when I showed her our floor plan. I think she's right. We should've put the laundry room near the bedrooms. Do you think I'm right?"

"Of course you're right," Ned said.

"It can be done either way," I said.

"Someone should've pointed this out to us. We put it near the kitchen because that's where it is in our current house. We never gave it much thought."

"I understand," I said.

"Can it be done?" Sylvia asked for the second time.

Ned nodded his head again. "Of course it can."

"I was thinking of putting it here." Sylvia pointed to a spot on the plans.

"I can't just *put* it there," I said.

"No?"

"I mean, I'll need to redesign the bedrooms to make it fit. And the bedrooms will be smaller."

"The bedrooms can't be any smaller," Ned said.

"Or maybe we can make the bedroom closets smaller?"

"That won't work either," Ned said.

"We need the closets," Sylvia said.

Like an idiot, I stared at the floor plan while Ned and Sylvia stared at me. They were waiting for me to say something encouraging and architectural. They were waiting for me to come up with some great bulb-over-the-head idea. The truth was that I didn't see how we were going to be able to move the laundry room without totally redoing the entire floor plan. It wasn't just your ordinary laundry room. It was big enough to park a car in because Sylvia had wanted it that way. "Nothing worse than a laundry room that's too small," she had told me. "I need room to move."

"This is going to require some time," I said.

"How much time?"

"I don't really know. It depends on how things work out."

"Make it happen," Ned said.

"I already sent the plans to the engineer."

"Call him. Hold him off."

Jesus. What was I supposed to do? I got on the phone immediately and called the engineer. He was out in the field, so I left a message with the firm's receptionist. "Tell him not to work on the Waterhouse project," I said. "The floor plan is going to change."

"Was that so hard?" Ned asked.

"Hopefully he hasn't got to it yet."

"I don't expect to be charged extra for this," Ned said. "You should've advised us about the laundry room to begin with."

"Yes," I said.

"We've been counting on you."

"I understand," I said.

Well, Ned and Sylvia left my office, and I met with Mr. Wiley to give him the news. Needless to say, he wasn't happy about this turn of events. He had only allotted so much of my time for the design of this project, and we were already over budget. And now adding the laundry room change, he'd be lucky to be breaking even. "I don't know what to say," he said.

"I'm sorry about this," I said. "But I can make the changes on my own time, if that helps."

"You don't have to do that."

"But I want to," I said.

"I'll leave it up to you."

And that's exactly what I did. I came in early each morning for several days, and I worked on the project on my own time until I got the laundry room where Sylvia wanted it without sacrificing any of their other needs. I felt like a putz. Working for free and having made such a mistake. And it was a mistake, wasn't it? No, I wasn't a mind reader, but, yes, I should've explained the benefits of having a laundry room near the bedrooms and not clear across the house near the kitchen. I was the architect. It was my job. Even though Ned was a pain, he was right to throw the problem into my lap. He had every right. I should've known.

It was interesting, me, with all my years of education and experience as both a young man in school and a seasoned architect. I knew so much. Yes, I knew a lot. I knew all about the history of architecture down through the ages, the way it had twisted and turned to meet the ever-changing needs and desires of humanity. I knew all the styles, a giant palette of architecture paints and colors available to each and every modern-day designer. I was an expert. So, what style did you want your home to have? I was a master of them all! There was Classical, Neoclassical, Greek Revival, Industrial, Bauhaus, Victorian, Craftsman, Cape Cod, Tudor, Art Deco, Modern, Brutalist, Contemporary, Beaux-Arts, Colonial, Mediterranean, Prairie, French Country, Ranch, and on and on.

I also knew who all the great architects were. There was Vitruvius, Filippo Brunelleschi, Leon Battista Alberti, Andrea Palladio, Sir Christopher Wren, Daniel Hudson Burnham, Antoni Gaudí, Louis Sullivan, Frank Lloyd Wright, Walter Gropius, Ludwig Mies van der Rohe, Le Corbusier, Alvar Aalto, Philip Johnson—just to name a few. When I was younger, I had immersed myself in their work. I studied their philosophies. I put them all on pedestals, and I read all their books. To say that I was inspired by their efforts was the understatement of the century. More than anything, I wanted to be the next architect added to the list. I wanted to make my mark. I wanted to be revered. I wanted *my* name recorded in the history books. Then, as with most of us, it happened. Then the winds of reality blew through my life, day by day, and year by year.

Ugh! Now, there I was, a sixty-four-year-old man with a wife, a job, two sons, and a mortgage. There I was, working for free. There I was, in all my glory, foiled by a laundry room.

CHAPTER 4

MEXICO!

It was a week before I saw Bartholomew again. I thought he'd appear sooner, but he didn't. I liked talking to him, and I found myself wanting to see him. But just as when I was a child, Bartholomew had a mind of his own. He came to me when he felt like it—and not necessarily when I wanted him. When he did finally show up, it was early in the morning again. I was in my office on my first cup of coffee, in the middle of writing another poem. As I was looking at my computer monitor, Bartholomew materialized to my left, out of thin air. He was standing and smiling at me.

"Still at it?" he asked.

"I am," I said.

"You're serious about this poetry thing?"

"I don't know if I'd say I'm serious," I said. "I like doing it. I'm not so sure if I want to be serious. I was once serious about architecture—and look where it got me."

"You seem to have done okay."

"That's a matter of opinion."

"You haven't been successful?"

I stared at Bartholomew for a moment, and then I said, "I'm disappointed."

"Disappointed with what?"

"With what's become of me."

"I see," Bartholomew said.

"Goals, dreams, and *thud*."

Bartholomew smiled. I think he thought it would make me feel better. "Have you come up with a third story?" he asked, changing the subject. "You told me about the duck and Zach's steak. What's your third story?"

"I do have a third story for you."

"Go on."

I decided to tell Bartholomew about my attempted trip to Tijuana. It took place about twelve years ago, and I was in my early fifties. First, you have to understand that I was not a big drinker, but that afternoon was different. I'm not exactly sure what came over me. Maybe it was like Pamela later said. Maybe I was just having a midlife crisis, going out and getting good and drunk, acting like a crazy man, the rest of the rational world be damned.

Pamela was out of town with our sons that day, visiting her parents in Oregon. I told her I was too busy to go, but that wasn't really the truth. I just didn't care much for her parents, and they didn't care much for me. So, what would be the point? Besides, it would be nice to have the house to myself. I took them to the airport on a Friday morning, and when I got home, it was lunchtime. I made myself a bologna sandwich and poured myself a scotch and water. Ha! Drinking in the middle of the day. Try doing that when the wife and kids are around. There were now no rules. I was as free as a monkey in a tree!

I finished my sandwich and poured myself another drink. And then another. The next thing I knew, I was watching TV. I don't remember what I was watching. Maybe a game show, or maybe a soap opera. I felt overcome with a burning desire to *go somewhere.* Have you ever had that feeling, like you've just got to get out of the house and spread your wings? The house was suddenly a prison from which I had to make my daring escape. True, I was by myself, but it felt like my family was there, staring at me, disapproving of my drinking, looking down on me for watching TV in the middle of the day. I loved them, sure, but enough was enough! I got my keys and wallet, grabbed what was left of my bottle of scotch, locked the front door, and climbed into my car. I turned on the ignition and cranked up the radio.

I drove around for about fifteen minutes with no particular destination in mind with the bottle of scotch between my legs and my radio blaring. Then I thought, *Why not go to a bar? Any bar will do.* So, I drove out to the Newport Peninsula and found a little drinking establishment along Balboa Boulevard. I don't know the name of the place. It didn't matter. It was perfect! It was a rundown little beach bar half full of people. What a dive—it was the perfect place to have a few drinks. I stepped up to the bar, and the bartender asked what I wanted. She was a rough-looking tattooed gal, and about a hundred pounds overweight. But she had a nice smile.

"Scotch and water," I said.

"Got it."

"Make it a double," I said. "And give me a bag of potato chips."

She poured the scotch and water into a glass, and she slid it in front of me. Then she grabbed a small bag of chips off the rack on the wall and placed it next to my drink.

I reached for the chips. "Perfect," I said.

"Anything else?"

"I'm good," I said, and I brought my drink up to my lips. Just as I took a sip, a lady sitting a couple stools away smiled at me. She looked too well dressed to be in a bar like this, and I wondered what she was doing there.

"Taking a break?" she asked.

"From what?" I said.

"From work. From whatever it is you do."

"I guess you could say that."

"What do you do for a living?"

I was a little drunk, and I felt mischievous. How boring would it be for me to say I was an architect? An architect? Who cared? Instead, I said, "I'm a gambler."

"A gambler?" The lady smiled. She liked this answer, and I liked giving it to her.

"Sports," I said.

"You bet on sports?"

"I do," I said.

"How interesting. Do you make any money at it?"

"It's a living," I said. "I like it. I place my bets every morning, and then I do what I want with the rest of my day."

The lady laughed. "My name is Nancy," she said.

"I'm Rick," I said.

"I've never seen you in here before."

"First time for me," I said.

"I come here every Friday afternoon. I only work half days on Friday, and I like to come here to end my week and start my weekend."

"What do you do?" I asked.

"Escrows. It's boring."

"I see," I said. "Can I buy you a drink?"

"Sure," Nancy said.

I got the bartender's attention. "One more for Nancy—and another for me."

"Got it," the bartender said.

Nancy and I talked for a while, and we had several more drinks together. She seemed to like talking to me, but the more we talked, the drunker I got. I could tell I was beginning to slur my words, and I was surprised that she didn't notice. Or maybe she did notice. Maybe she just didn't care. We talked about all kinds of things, but mostly about sports. She was a big Angels fan, and I told her I'd made a lot of money betting on them. This was a lie of course. Then we started talking about Mexico. I have no idea how we got on this topic, but suddenly I stood up from my barstool. "You know what?" I asked.

"What," Nancy said.

"I'm going to Mexico!"

Nancy laughed. "How are you going to get there?"

"I'll drive," I said.

"You probably shouldn't be driving."

"No?"

"In fact, you should probably have April call you a taxi."

"April?"

"The bartender," Nancy said.

I laughed and said, "You're on a first-name basis with her? April, you say?"

Nancy made eye contact with April, and April came toward us. My radar suddenly went off. I quickly realized that if I wasn't careful, these two women were going to talk me out of my car keys. *Fuck that*, I thought. *I want to go to Mexico!* I paid my bill and left April a nice tip.

"Where are you going?" Nancy asked.

"I told you," I said.

"Sir," April said. But before she could finish, I was out the front door and on my way to my car.

I climbed in. I still had a little scotch left in my bottle on the passenger seat, and I drank it down. I turned on the ignition, and the car started up. And the radio was blaring again. "Look out, Mexico," I said. "Here I come!"

Was I irresponsible? Yes, I was. Was I criminally negligent for driving while having had so much to drink? Yes, that too. But you know what? I was drunk, and I didn't care. I was tired of being responsible, and I was tired of obeying the law. Pamela and the kids were out of town, and I was going to have some fun. It would be a two-hour drive to Tijuana. Off I went. I'll bet I was speeding the whole way. My car was going eighty, and my mind was racing a million miles per hour.

I made it to San Juan Capistrano, and then the engine sputtered and stalled. I pulled the car over to the shoulder of the freeway and rolled to a stop. "What the hell?" I said. Then I looked at the dashboard. I noticed I was seeing double, but I could focus well enough to see that the gas gauge was on empty. I had run out of gas, and I hadn't even made it out of Orange County! I picked up my scotch bottle, but there was nothing left in it. *Damn!* I thought. *Of all the rotten luck.*

I pulled my wallet out of my back pocket, and I fumbled through it for my AAA card. Then I called the number on the card with my cell phone.

The lady said that they would send someone to help me within the hour.

So, I waited, listening to the radio. Cars were whizzing past me—all those people who *had* gas. It seemed like three hours, but it was only forty minutes until the AAA tow truck arrived and pulled up behind me. There were two people in the truck: a man about my age and a kid who appeared to be in his late teens or early twenties.

The kid stayed in the truck.

The man got out and approached my open window. "Out of gas?" he asked when he arrived.

"Yes," I said.

"Let's get you going. I brought a five-gallon can. That should easily get you to a gas station."

"Five gallons is good," I said. I didn't exactly sound sober. I could tell that I was still slurring my words.

"Been drinking much?" the man asked.

"A little," I said.

"You really shouldn't be driving."

"I think I'll be okay."

"We should get you home. Maybe you should sleep it off. You really shouldn't be driving."

"I'll be okay," I said again.

"We'll take care of you."

"Take care of me?"

"Hand over your keys. I'll need your keys before I pour in any gas."

"My keys?"

"I don't want you taking off."

"Fine," I said. What choice did I have? I needed the gas, and I had no other way of getting it. I was stuck. I removed the keys and handed them to the man.

He went to his truck to get his gas can. He poured the gas into my tank, and then he took the empty can back to his truck. He opened his truck door and talked to the kid in the passenger seat. The kid then climbed out of the truck, and the two of them approached my open window.

"This is Teddy," the man said. "He's my nephew. He likes to come along with me."

"Nice to meet you, Teddy," I said.

"You're going to ride with me, and Teddy is going to drive your car. You can tell me how to get to your house, and Teddy will follow us."

"My home?"

"We're going to take you home. Are you married? I'd like to talk to your wife."

"She's out of town," I said.

"Ah, I see. So, when the cat's away."

"Something like that."

"Anyway, we're going to get you home. Where do you live?"

"In Irvine," I said.

"Good, five gallons ought to handle that."

I was still pretty drunk, but the excitement was gone. *Mexico? What was I even thinking?*

It was embarrassing, being taken care of by this man. He was a good man. "Is this part of my AAA service plan?" I asked. I was trying to be funny.

"Just one guy helping another," the man said.

"Okay," I replied.

"Let's get you home," the man said, and we hopped into his truck.

The man gave his nephew my car keys, and Teddy climbed into my car. "Name is Eddie," the man said, reaching to me for a handshake. I shook his hand, and then he started up his truck. And off we went with Teddy following behind us. We drove all the way to my house, and by the time we reached the house, it was a little after six.

"Make yourself some dinner and then see if you can't sleep it off," Eddie said.

"Will do," I said. "And thank you." I was feeling sober now, even though I was still drunk.

"Promise you'll stay put?"

"I promise," I said.

"Take care of yourself," Eddie said.

His nephew handed me my car keys and then climbed back into Eddie's truck.

"Bye," I said.

I stepped into the house through the front door. God, I felt like such an idiot. Idiot, idiot, idiot!

Bartholomew listened to this entire story. "You're lucky you didn't kill someone," Bartholomew said.

"Kill someone?"

"Drinking and driving."

"Yes, there's that," I said.

"It's interesting."

"What's interesting?"

"That you would choose this story to tell me. Why this story? What does it say about you? What does it tell me?"

"I don't know."

"Are you happy?"

"Am I happy?"

"That was my question."

"I suppose I am," I said. "I mean, what really does it mean to be happy?"

"The stories you're choosing to tell me imply that you're not happy at all. There is an unsettling sadness to them. A kind of hopelessness. A kind of everything-I-do-comes-out-wrong anti joie de vivre."

"Come again?"

"You get down on yourself a lot."

"I've only told you three stories."

Bartholomew laughed. "That's true," he said.

"I have some good ones."

"I'd like to hear them."

"Fine," I said, and I thought for a moment.

"Well?" Bartholomew said.

"I feel like I'm being put on the spot."

"That's because you *are* being put on the spot. I'll give you a few days. Let's see what you come up with."

"You're going to leave again?"

"I can't hang around here forever."

"But you're going to help me, right?"

"Help you?"

"Yes," I said.

"Maybe I'm going to help you to help yourself."

"Whatever you want to call it," I said.

"Yes, whatever," Bartholomew said. Then his eyes twinkled, he smiled, and he vanished.

Chapter 5

Ribbons and Trophies

Was I happy? That was what Bartholomew asked me, and you know what? I wasn't sure how to answer him. What exactly was happiness? Was it smiling all the time? Was it looking forward to each day? Was it a good sense of humor or maybe just general contentment? Was it knowing that you were a good person? Abe Lincoln said, "Most folks are as happy as they make up their minds to be." Do you think this is true?

Bartholomew did not return for a month. During that time, I wrote my poetry in the mornings as usual and worked at Wiley & Associates in the afternoons. In the evenings I watched TV with Pamela. Sometimes we'd read, but usually we'd watch TV. Our routine was the same, but *was I happy*?

It was interesting. I was sixty-four years old, and in all those sixty-four years, I'd never really asked myself this question. Was I happy? Happiness always seemed like sort of a superfluous pursuit, outside the realm of what was really important in life. And what was really important? I guess we all learn things like this from our parents, don't we? We learn what to pursue and what to ignore. Listen, I don't mean to blame my parents for my current state of mind, but they have had a lot to do with it.

I should tell you a little about my dad and then a few things about my mom. It was primarily their parental hands that molded me into the man I am today. They were good people. There was never any question about this. They had strong and admirable morals, and they did their best to raise me to understand that there was a difference between right and wrong. Do the right thing. Be kind to others. Try to be understanding. Don't be selfish. Do unto others as you would have them do unto you, and so on. We went to church every Sunday, and we took the sermons seriously. Mom and Dad didn't necessarily believe in a literal heaven or hell or in a Garden of Eden, but they did believe in loving your fellow man and doing right.

Dad was a businessman. He was successful and respected. He got his college degree at Stanford University, and he worked his way up the ladder, eventually becoming the CEO of a Fortune 500 company that manufactured office supply products. Boring, yes, but lucrative—we lived well, and for the most part, I can say I liked my childhood.

But here was the thing. My father expected a lot from me as a child. "Life is all about achievement," he would tell me, and he meant this from the bottom of his heart. The good thing about Dad? He never required me to pursue one thing over the other, and he let me find my own way in life. But he did demand excellence. Coming in at second place, or third place, or any other place other than first was not acceptable—the blue ribbons and first-place trophies were all that mattered. I was never encouraged to cheat or do anything outside the realm of proper behavior, but I was encouraged to win. By my skills, by my wits, and by my best efforts. "Always be the best," Dad would say to me. "Be the best, and the rest of your life will fall in line."

I didn't mind this. It was fun to win, and Dad was right. I took everything I did seriously, and my efforts would often pay off. Did I experience any anxiety? Of course I did, but I believed this was a sign that I was doing the right thing and was headed in the right direction. As a child, I wanted to please my dad. There was no doubt about this. And I knew what it would take to make my dad's list of worthy human beings: the people he talked about, the people he admired, and the people he loved. These people did what had to be done to achieve. These were the people who deserved respect and adulation, the winners, the first to cross the finish lines.

Mom wasn't much different, although her domain was all her own. She was in charge of my schooling. She once told me that, "All you have to do to get a C is crack open your textbook." What did this mean? It meant that Cs were unacceptable. It meant that Bs were tolerable, but that the A was the unquestioned goal. She helped me. She tracked my homework. She made sure I studied for my tests, and she assisted me with my projects. No child of hers was going to fall into that dreaded going-nowhere category of the average student. I was special. My older brother was special. She made sure the two of us were among the best students in the school.

During his last two years in high school, my brother, Ralph, resisted. He let his grades slip. He said he didn't want to go to college. I remember that, and I felt sorry for him. Fool! I never did understand him, and I still don't get it. He had everything going for him. What was he even thinking? He told Mom and Dad he wanted to work on cars and that he didn't need straight As or a college degree to become a car mechanic. I didn't envy him. Like I said, I felt sorry for him. He seemed to be giving up, and I think Mom and Dad felt the same way. But more about Ralph later.

Dad was thrilled when I was accepted to UC Berkeley. I had the grades, and I had the SAT scores. I immediately declared a major in architecture because the field interested me. "It's where art meets reality," I said to Dad, and he liked this idea and told me he was sure that I would do well. He was so proud. He was so sure I would make a name for myself, like another Frank Lloyd Wright. He bragged to all his friends about me. I was only eighteen, and I already had a lock on life. A promising future was on my horizon, and just as Dad believed in me, I believed in myself.

I did well in college. It was like the clouds in the sky had cracked open, and a whole world of information was pouring into my young life. So much to learn, and so much to know! This was probably the most exciting time in my life, and I took full advantage of it. This was also when I met Pamela who, back then, was just a girl in an elective classic literature class. God, she was beautiful. And smart. And sweet. I got up the nerve to ask her out for coffee, and the rest is history. We got married when we were seniors, and as of now, we've been married forty-four years. Asking her to marry me was the best decision I ever made in my life, and despite how I sometimes complain about her today, I still love her now as much as I did back then. It's a different kind of love, but it's love. As they say in baseball about some home runs: it was a no-doubter.

Pamela has always been right behind me. She's been my cheerleader and lover. She supports me, and she cares for me. She never did start up a career of her own, though she certainly could have. Instead, she simply wanted to be a wife and the mother of our children. She has no regrets. I know this because she told me so.

But it's funny, isn't it? It's funny how we both fell into what I now like to call "the flat years." I think we all fall into them. Most of us, anyway. The flat years. The amazing thrill of college is in the rearview mirror, and we have said our vows and slid the rings on our fingers. It's onward down the highway of life. Not that it doesn't have its wonderful moments, but compared to what we were accustomed to, it is *flat*. Like Paul Simon sang, "An endless stream of cigarettes and magazines." Except it's an endless stream of baby diapers, nap times, stuffed animals, toys, job promotions, salary raises, mortgages, kids' sporting events, school projects, report cards, electricity and gas bills, credit card balances, overdraft charges, doctor appointments, Christmas trees, turkey dinners, vacations to Hawaii, car payments, insurance claims, and the occasional cocktail party. Whew! It makes me tired just thinking about all of it.

What happened? The answer is pretty simple. *Life* happened. I'm just coming to realize it now. My dad, bless his CEO heart, realized it years ago. And how did he handle it? He fell into a long and gnawing depression. He would never admit to this if you asked him, but all the signs were there. After I got married, and after I got my first job, I began to notice it. I think he saw me falling into the same routine his own life had become, and I think it broke his heart. No more children's baseball games. No more report cards. No more college, and no more marriages. And for him? I think he realized that he had reached his apex. Office supplies was all it was ever going to be. Office supply decisions. Office supply financial statements. Office supply stockholder meetings. Balancing the ball of his office supply business life on the tip of his nose, performing for the crowds, and slapping his hands together.

Depression is an awful thing. It's one thing to feel it yourself, and wholly another to see it consume someone you love. I never did talk to Dad about his state of mind. I just didn't think it was my place to do so. Maybe I was wrong, and maybe I should've said something. But I didn't. I just let it go on and on over the years like the sun rising and falling, and I assumed that Mom was doing everything she could. She loved my dad. I had no reason to believe she wasn't doing her best to help him. Perhaps if I'd been doing more with my own life, it would've provided him with a spark of some kind, something more to live for. More blue ribbons and more trophies.

Dad died of a heart attack when he was in his eighties. He had lived a reasonably long life. As I already told you, Mom is still alive. I was calling her once a month to chat, and she always asked what I'd been up to. I'd tell her. I think she liked hearing about my life, but it was nothing like the old days. Routines were routines, and jobs were jobs. And diversions were diversions. Seems I could have been telling her about any responsible person's life in America, and it would have suited her just as well. I will miss her when she finally dies.

Now I knew what I wanted my fourth story for Bartholomew to be about. It would be about my parents. I would tell him about the talent contest in middle school. This exercise in cruelty was to be held in the school gymnasium on a Saturday night, about a month before Christmas. Kids in the school were encouraged to sign up and show off their talents to an audience made up of other kids, parents, and teachers. Trophies for first, second, and third place would be awarded to the best acts as voted on by a panel of teachers. How did these teachers get on the panel? I had no idea, but there were five of them. Who said that they had any qualifications to judge talent? I guessed that they did. I figured I had a slight advantage; I had one of the teachers in my English class, and he seemed to like me. I got good grades on his assignments, and I behaved myself in class. But as to the other four teachers, I knew next to nothing about them. And they didn't know me.

It was Mom who wanted me to sign up. There were openings for ten acts, and they held auditions to fill the open slots. Only the best ten talents were to be allowed to perform in the contest. I guess it made sense, but can you imagine the nerve? Telling a child that he or she wasn't good enough to be in the show? I didn't think much of this at the time since that's precisely what they did in school. They judged you. They gave you grades. They told you when you were and weren't good enough. Now that I'm an adult, I can see the cruelty that I couldn't see as a child. For a child, it was to be expected, just standard operating procedure. Of course, teachers and parents had an unassailable excuse—they would say they were preparing us for the world.

So, I showed up for the audition. Mom was with me, but Dad was at work. There was a large crowd of kids there. Some of them were obviously scared, and some were eager to perform. What was my talent? The piano of course. For the past several years, Mom had me taking lessons to broaden my horizons, to make me a more well-rounded person. I kind of liked it, and I kind of didn't. I didn't like learning and practicing, but I got a kick out of playing the pieces I had mastered. We decided that for the talent contest I would play Beethoven's *Sonatina in G Major*. My audition came up between the baton twirler and the magician, and I played the piece flawlessly. Everyone applauded when I was done, which made me feel good. It was a successful audition, and when they posted the list of the ten kids who would be in the show, my name was on it.

Then came the show. Christ, there must've been a couple hundred people there, seated in the gymnasium, in the bleachers and on fold-up chairs. And me? I was suddenly terrified. I'd never played in front of such a large collection of people. My hands were shaking, and my stomach was turning. A girl named Claudia Myers was to perform in front of me, and she would be singing "Close to You" by the Carpenters. Mrs. Gilbert would be playing the piano to accompany her singing, and I remember watching and listening to Claudia. She was pretty good, and when she was done, she got a hearty reception from the audience. Would they like me as much? I had no idea.

Then it was my turn. The truth was that I just wanted to crawl into a cave and die. Why did I sign up for this? Why was a torturing myself? What the heck had I even been thinking? But I mustered up all the courage I could and walked to the piano, sat down on the stool, and tried to pretend I was in a room by myself. But that didn't work. I could hear people adjusting their weight in the creaky fold-up chairs, clearing their throats, and coughing. All their eyes were upon me! And suddenly I felt like I was in a dream, and it was not a pleasant one.

I played the piece.

I wish I could say that my performance was flawless, but it wasn't. It felt like my timing was off. And worse yet, I hit five wrong notes. I was butchering Beethoven. Ludwig was surely turning in his grave.

When I was done playing, the audience applauded politely. I looked at all the faces, and most of them were smiling. But were they smiling because they enjoyed my performance or because I had done such a lousy job? Ugh! One of the worst days of my life, to be sure. I stood up and walked back to my chair at the side of the stage. I sat next to Claudia, the singer. "Good job," she said. I think she could tell how upset I was. She was trying to be nice. She was a nice girl.

My act was followed by a boy named Joey Sanchez. Joey was a juggler—and a pretty good one. His act was definitely a crowd-pleaser. I watched him. He juggled balls and bowling pins. He didn't make a single mistake.

The results of the contest? Joey got third place, and Claudia got second. First place went to Henry Acre for his stupendous magic act. He sawed his sister in half, and then he put her back together. Then he made her disappear. He also made a large bouquet of flowers appear out of thin air. It was all routine magic show stuff, but he was quite good at it. And the kid had a great personality—sometimes that's half the battle. The audience ate it all up. And so did the judges.

Dad drove us home in his car when the show was over. He wasn't angry that I had won nothing, but he was disappointed. And so was Mom. They were quiet until Dad finally broke the silence and said, "I counted five mistakes."

"That sounds about right," I said.

"Were you nervous?" Mom asked.

"A little," I said.

"I liked that magic act," Dad said.

"The juggler was pretty good too," Mom said.

"Takes a lot of practice," Dad said.

"They were good," I said.

And that was the end of my career as a pianist. My piano teacher was a nice lady named Miss Andrews. I'd been working with her for several years, and she taught me a lot. But some things are meant to be, and some things aren't. I remember my last lesson. Mom told Miss Andrews that we were going to stop the lessons, and Miss Andrews said, "I'm so sorry to hear that."

"We need to move on," Mom said.

"Was there something I could've done better?"

"You were fine," Mom said. "We just don't think Rick's heart is in it. Music, I mean."

"I understand."

"But it was a lot of fun," I said. I suddenly felt sorry for the woman.

"You *were* making progress," Miss Andrews said.

"I was," I said.

Mom removed her wallet from her purse. "How much do we owe you?" she asked.

CHAPTER 6

YARD JOB

When Bartholomew appeared in my den again, I told him the story about the talent contest, and he laughed. Then he asked, "Has anyone ever talked to you about distorted thinking?"

"I don't even know what that means," I said.

"Aha," Bartholomew said.

"Aha what?" I asked.

"Aha, I didn't think so." Bartholomew laughed again, and I'll be honest—his laughter annoyed me a little.

"Am I supposed to know what you're talking about?" I asked.

"I guess not."

"You guess?"

"I haven't seen you since you were seven years old," Bartholomew said. "How should I know what you've heard or haven't heard? We're just getting to know each other again."

"Fair enough," I said.

"Do you consider yourself to be a perfectionist?"

"I haven't really thought about it," I said.

"Perfectionists are very unhappy people."

"Are they?"

"They set high standards for themselves. They set lofty goals for themselves, often unrealistic, often unreachable. Then they set out to reach those goals and meet those standards, and the next thing you know, they're miserable because they realize something. They realize that they're just human beings. They're not gods, and they're not perfect. They may be good at one thing or the other, and heck, for a period of time, they might be the best. But there's no way a human being can ever be the best at everything all the time. They have flaws, chinks in their armor, and flies in their ointment. It's all a part of being a human being, being imperfect."

"And you think I'm a perfectionist?"

"I think you participate in perfectionist thinking."

"Meaning?"

"Tell me about your brother," Bartholomew said, changing the subject.

"I thought we were talking about me."

"I'd like to talk about Ralph."

"Ralph is Ralph," I said. Seriously? Why did Bartholomew even want to talk about him?

"Is he still a car mechanic?"

"He is," I said.

"Does he plan on retiring? He's older than you."

"I don't think he'll ever retire. He probably can't afford to. He never has made all that much money."

"Maybe he's made more than you think."

"It's possible. To tell you the truth, I don't know how much he makes. But he's lived with his wife in the same crappy house in the same sketchy neighborhood ever since they got married. And he wasn't able to put either of his kids through college. They both had to take out student loans and work their way through. If he's been making a lot of money, he's been doing a great job hiding it."

"Do you think your brother is happy?"

"You'd have to ask him."

"But I'm asking you."

I thought about this. "You know what?" I asked. "I think he is. In his own sort of dumb, bumbling-through-life sort of way, I think he's happy as a well-fed pig."

"And you would rather be miserable?"

"Who says I'm miserable?"

Bartholomew laughed and said, "I've asked you to tell me ten stories about yourself, and the first four were about your failures. You told me about your failure to stop for that poor mother duck. You told me about your failure to teach Zach how to order a steak, and your failure to behave yourself while your wife trusted you and went out of town. And your failure to get along with her parents, and finally—your failure to perform at a school talent contest. If I was to judge your happiness based on the stories you've been telling me, I'd say that no, you're not a very happy person. I would say that deep down inside, you dislike yourself for not living up to your high standards. You think that setting high standards is making you a better person, but all it's really doing is shining a light on your flaws. And it's making you unhappy."

"That would be your opinion."

"That's true."

"You asked me about Ralph. I said he was happy, but I wouldn't want to be Ralph for all the money in the world. What has he done with his life?" I was being defensive, but I was speaking to an empty room. Bartholomew had vanished again. There was no warning. No indication that he was going to leave. Just *poof*, and he was gone. Pamela then walked into the room, and I looked at the clock on my desk. It was six-thirty, and I looked at my coffee cup. It was empty. Where had the time gone?

"Who are you talking to?" Pamela asked.

"Talking to?" I asked.

"I heard you talking."

"Did you? I guess I was reading my poem out loud. You know, to see how it sounded."

"What time did you get up this morning?"

"Around two," I said.

"That's too early."

"I'm going to take a nap," I said. "In fact, I think I'll do that right now."

"Make sure you're getting enough sleep."

"I am," I said.

"It isn't good to miss your sleep."

"No," I agreed.

Bartholomew was gone for a week this time. During this week I thought about the things he'd said to me. I also thought about Ralph, the happy car mechanic. Ralph, who probably never would be able to retire. Ralph, who lived in a neighborhood I wouldn't be caught dead in unless I was looking for someone to fix my car. I decided to tell Bartholomew a tale about Ralph for my fifth story. It would be a story about Ralph and me, not just about Ralph. After all, that was what Bartholomew said he was after—stories about me.

I would tell him about the yard job. That's what Ralph called it—a yard job. We were in high school; I was a freshman, and Ralph was a senior. We didn't do much together in those days. Three years difference is huge at that age, and honestly, Ralph wanted very little to do with me. As I told you before, Ralph had lost interest in doing well in school when he was a junior, and when he was a senior, his disdain for school was even worse. Me? I was the good kid. I took school seriously, and I always got good grades. While Ralph was over at his friends' houses working on cars, I had my nose in my schoolbooks, cranking out homework assignments.

Mom and Dad treated me kind of like a baby. They were much more protective of me than they were of Ralph, and I think they actually felt if they had kept a closer eye on Ralph during his younger years, he wouldn't have turned out so rebellious. Mom used to tell Ralph, "You should be more like your little brother." Ralph would just poke his finger down his throat and pretend to vomit. I didn't like it when he did this. I mean, I thought Ralph was a fool for doing some of the things he did, but he was my brother. My older brother. And I wanted him to like me.

Anyway, it was on a Saturday night in spring when Mom and Dad drove to Fresno to attend the wedding of one of my dad's best friends' sons. The friend was Jack Carlson. Dad had known Jack since college. The wedding was to be held in the afternoon, and a big reception was planned afterward. It was important to my dad to be there. It was a big deal. Since the event was all the way up in Fresno, my parents would not be home until the early-morning hours, and they were concerned about leaving me alone in the house. I was fourteen, but like I said earlier, they kind of treated me like a baby.

Mom wanted to be sure there was someone with me, and she enlisted my brother to look after me.

"Aw, Mom," Ralph said.

"It's just for one night."

"But it's a Saturday night."

"We don't think we should leave Rick alone in the house," Mom said. "What if something happens?"

"What's going to happen?" Ralph said.

Mom finally got Ralph to agree to look after me. It was funny. I don't think either Mom or Dad trusted Ralph any further than they could throw him, but they left him in charge. It turned out to be a big mistake. Heck, *I* could've told them it was a mistake. I think I would've been better off without Ralph, but I guess parents are blind when it comes to their kids.

There was a party that night at Julie Elliot's house. Julie lived about eight houses down from us. The Elliots had been paying Ralph and his friend, Abe, to do yard work for the past week. Ralph did the work because he was saving up to buy a better car. Dad could easily have bought him what he wanted, but he wanted Ralph to "learn the value of a dollar," and he made Ralph work and earn the money himself. Ralph enlisted the help of Abe, and the two of them had been cleaning up the Elliot's large backyard—which was a mess—and they'd been stuffing all the debris into cardboard boxes that Mrs. Elliot had retrieved from the local grocery store. By the time of the party, they had filled about eight boxes with dirty weeds, dead leaves, and trimmed branches.

It was eight when my parents called the house from the wedding reception to check up on us. They told Ralph they would be calling, to be sure he answered the phone. I heard Ralph talking to Mom when she called. "Yeah, yeah," he said. "Everything's going fine. Abe is over. We've been watching TV while Rick does his homework. Everything's fine." Then Ralph hung up and smiled. "Okay, little brother. You're coming with us. Put on a jacket and comb your hair. We're taking you to Julie's."

I knew about the party. Julie's parents were out of town, and Julie had invited half the high school. It was going to be a big party. In fact, it was also my first party. I'd never been to a high school party before, but I figured I'd be safe. I figured Ralph would look after me. I knew they'd have beer at the party, but I didn't plan on drinking any. I wondered if anyone I knew from school would be there, but I knew it wasn't likely. The party was for older kids.

When we got there, the front doors were open. The music was loud, and the house was filled with kids. All of them were holding red plastic cups.

"Beer is in the kitchen," one of the kids said to Ralph.

I followed Ralph and Abe into the kitchen, and a keg was sitting in the middle of the kitchen floor. In fact, there were two kegs. One was active, and there was another to replace it when it went dry. Kids were filling their red cups with beer, one after the other. They were talking and laughing. They were smoking cigarettes. They were having such a good time. I felt out of place, but the truth? I was thrilled to be there.

"Are you Ralph's little brother?" an older girl asked me.

"I am," I said.

"He's cute," the girl said to her friends. Then, to me, she asked, "Where's your cup?"

"My cup?"

"There's plenty of beer for everyone."

"Get him a cup," another girl said.

The next thing I knew, I had a cup of beer in my hand. I'd never even tasted a beer—let alone had a full cup of it in my hand.

Ralph saw me, and he laughed. "Go easy, little brother," he said.

I went easy on the beer, but it didn't take long for it to go to my head. I felt strange. I also found myself becoming very talkative. I was talking to kids I didn't even know, kids who were older than me. "You're Ralph's little brother, aren't you?" they'd ask, and I would nod my head. "Far out!" they would say. These kids were a lot nicer than I'd expected. They actually seemed glad that I was there, drinking with them, partying on a Saturday night.

It was fun.

About an hour or two passed, and Ralph and Abe were drunk. They were laughing and stumbling, looking for me. When they did finally find me, Ralph said, "We're going to blow this joint. Finish off your beer, little brother. It's time to go. Abe has to be home by eleven."

"Okay," I said, and I finished off what was left in my red cup. I said goodbye to the girl I'd been talking to, and we left the house through the front door. But we didn't walk on the path to the street. Instead, Ralph walked across the lawn and around to the side yard. Abe followed Ralph, and I followed Abe.

"Where are we going?" I asked.

"Just follow us," Ralph said.

It was dark outside. We walked through the open gate and finally to the back of the house. I could still hear the music blaring from inside, but there was no one in the backyard. There was a swimming pool, and alongside the pool were all the cardboard boxes of debris Ralph and Abe had scraped up from the yard during the week. Stacks of boxes, all stuffed to their tops.

"Geronimo!" Ralph shouted.

"Geronimo?" I asked.

"Me an Indian—me now get even with white man."

Abe laughed.

Ralph walked over to the boxes, and he did something that took me completely by surprise. He picked up one of the heavy boxes, took it to the pool, and turned it upside down, dumping its contents into the water.

"Holy shit!" Abe said.

"Let's dump all of them!" Ralph exclaimed. He picked up another box and took it to the pool.

Abe joined in and picked up a third box.

"Come on, little brother," Ralph said.

"Me?"

"Little Indian boy. Let's get even with the white man."

I laughed.

Ralph could be funny. And I was half drunk, thinking, *What the hell? Why not?* I joined in and picked up a fourth box. The next thing I knew, we were dumping one box after the other into the pool. God what a mess! The leaves and branches were floating on the top, and the dirt was sinking to the bottom.

Finally, Ralph dumped the last box and said, "We better get out of here."

"No shit," Abe said.

"Do you think someone saw us?" I asked. I was laughing when I asked this.

"They're all in the house," Abe said.

"Hurry, let's go!"

The three of us ran. We sped to the side of the house and finally to the front yard. Then we slowed down as if nothing had been going on. We walked to my brother's car and climbed in. We were all still laughing.

"They be cleaning that mess up for weeks," Ralph said.

Ralph drove Abe to his house across town. After dropping off Abe, we returned to our house. "You can't tell anyone about this," Ralph said.

"I get it," I said.

"Not even your best friend."

"I know," I said.

Ralph then looked at me and laughed. "God, that was fun, wasn't it?"

"Fun," I said.

The next morning, I was so racked with guilt that I could hardly look my mom in the eye. What had we done? Why did we do it? What if someone saw us? It was horrible, and I never wanted to drink again.

Mom thanked Ralph for looking after me, and he said to her, "What are brothers for?" When he smiled and winked at me, it turned my stomach.

Chapter 7

My First Poem

It was a month and a half before Bartholomew would come back to see me. While I waited for Bartholomew to return, I visited my mom at her house. I wanted to see her, and I wanted to check up on her. She was in her nineties, not exactly in the prime of her life, and I was worried about her.

It wasn't that long ago that I had taken away Mom's car keys. In my opinion, she was too old to drive, and I didn't want her to get in a wreck. She put up a fight, but she finally acquiesced. It was a kind of a milestone, losing the ability to drive her car around town. It marked that time in her life when she was no longer able to function without someone's help. Cleaning the house. Going to the grocery store. Fixing her own dinner. It was all becoming a little too much for her to handle on her own. I talked with Pamela about it, and she agreed with me. Something had to change. I went back to see Mom and tell her what Pamela and I decided, and she listened patiently. I proposed that we sell her house—and that she come and live with us.

"Not a chance," she said.

"You need help," I said.

"I'm not going to move into your home. The last thing you need is some needy old woman living with you."

"We really wouldn't mind."

"It's not going to happen," Mom said.

I'm not going to get into all the gory details. Just know that the time had come: my mom was no longer capable of living on her own. She did need help. She did need to move out of that big house, but I'll be honest. It was a relief that she turned down our offer to have her come live with us. The truth? We only offered because it was the right thing to do, but we really didn't want her living with us. Was this selfish? Maybe it was, but there was another alternative: we could move Mom to an assisted-living facility. She could have her own room, a room small enough for her to easily maintain. And she could make some new friends and take part in their community activities. And there would always be people on call to help her out, and they would cook for her, clean for her, and help her with her hygiene.

I ran this idea past Mom, and at first, she wasn't too thrilled with it. But the more we talked, the closer she came to agreeing that things had to change. If she wasn't willing to move in with us, this was the next best thing.

"We'll come visit you often, and you'll never be alone," I said. "It'll be like going to summer camp. Do you remember when you were a kid, going to summer camp? If you keep an open mind, I believe you will be a lot happier there than you are here. It'll be a whole new phase of your life."

Mom sighed.

I did my due diligence and looked all over Orange County for the right place to put Mom. She had plenty of money, so she wasn't really on a budget, and I would put her in the best place I could find. I decided upon a development in San Clemente. It was near the ocean and built on a large piece of property. The grounds were amazing, with trees, flowers, paths, a couple swimming pools, and rolling green lawns. The building itself was also very good, although it was kind of a cross between a nice apartment building and a hospital. They had a cafeteria, a formal dining room, several recreation rooms, a library, a dance floor, and a music room. The place was huge, yet it also had an intimate feel to it. There was only one opening, so we had to act fast. Pamela and I signed a hundred papers and wrote a check, and the next thing we knew, we were moving Mom in.

What to do with her house? That became the question. It was easy to put the house on the market for sale, but what would we do with all the things inside that Mom and Dad had collected over the years? Pamela and I took a few things. Ralph also took some stuff, but there was still a ton of possessions left over. It was gut-wrenching, emptying the big house—all those memories, and all those years. We hired a liquidation company that specialized in emptying houses, sorting through the valuables, selling all the good stuff, and disposing of the rest. The price they offered for the valuables was cheap, but what was I supposed to do? Hold a massive garage sale? I signed a contract with the liquidation company, and two days later, they backed their trucks up to the house. They must've had twenty workers, and they worked fast. In no time, it seemed, the house was empty.

"I hope we've done the right thing," I said to Pamela. We were standing in the driveway, looking at the empty house.

"We have," she said.

"It's such a drastic step."

"Your mom will be much happier, and she'll have people to look after her."

"Jesus," I said.

I thought back to just a few years ago. It wasn't all that long ago when Mom was so fiercely independent. Back then, I would never have imagined putting her into a senior citizens facility for her own good. The woman was a human dynamo, and there was no stopping her.

"She'll be fine," Pamela said.

"I hope so," I said.

The next time I saw Bartholomew, it was on a Saturday afternoon, and Pamela was gone running errands. She would be gone a few hours, so Bartholomew and I would have plenty of time to talk. It was noon, time for my lunch. I made myself a roast beef sandwich on sourdough bread and poured a large glass of milk to go with it.

"Are you ready to tell me your fifth story?" Bartholomew asked.

"I am," I said.

"Well?"

"It's about my brother and me."

"A story about Ralph?"

"Yes, you asked about him. I figured you'd enjoy hearing a story about me that involved him."

"Go on," Bartholomew said.

I told him the story about the yard job and how we dumped all the yard debris into the Elliots' swimming pool.

Bartholomew laughed at the end of the story and said, "Kids do stupid things."

"I still feel guilty," I said.

"To this day?"

"Yes," I said. "I feel bad every time I think about it."

"It *was* a pretty rotten thing to do."

"It was."

"Had the Elliots ever done anything to hurt you?"

"Nothing," I said.

"Did you like them?"

"They were a nice family. Everyone liked them."

"That makes it even worse," Bartholomew said, and then he laughed again.

"You think it's funny?"

"Don't you?"

"Not at all," I said.

"You're taking yourself way too seriously. Don't you even want to be happy?"

"This is about happiness?"

"It's all about happiness. Life is about happiness. It's the goal, the objective, the pot of gold at the end of the rainbow. It's illusive, baffling, and seemingly untouchable. Yet I promise you, it is there, and it can be had. Let me ask you something. Do you enjoy being unhappy?"

"I hate it," I said.

"But you think of yourself as a realist?"

"I suppose I do."

"You're honest with yourself?"

"I think I am. Sometimes I think that may be the source of my unhappiness."

Bartholomew stared at me for a moment and then said, "Be honest with this incontrovertible fact—you are a human being. You are not perfect. You never have been, and you never will be. You're going to make terrible mistakes, and you're going to make bad decisions. You're going to hurt people, and you're going to hurt yourself. You're going to be pigheaded, selfish, prejudiced, cruel, greedy, envious, callous, and shallow. You're going to disappoint your wife, your parents, and your kids. You're going to be mean and disrespectful to strangers. You're going to vote for the wrong candidates and argue in favor of the wrong causes. You, Rick Harper, are going to be a rickety, convoluted mess. The question isn't what you're going to be; the question is how you are going to deal with it. Are you going to beat yourself up—or are you going cut yourself some slack?

Are you going to frown, stew, and incapacitate yourself with guilt—or are you going to laugh?"

"Laugh?" I asked.

"Laugh at the absurdity of it all. Laugh at all the clowns. Laugh when they fall on their faces. And most importantly of all, laugh at yourself and your own foibles because you may be the funniest clown of all."

Why poetry? You know, I thought long and hard about it, about what I was going to do when I turned sixty-five and quit my job at Wiley & Associates. What was I going to do with my time? I knew I wanted to escape architecture, the *business* of designing buildings. That's exactly what was wrong with it, right? It *was* a business, and I had become a businessman. That was never my intention when I got into the field. I had wanted to become an artist, and now, here I was, in my sixties, still practicing the mind-numbing routine of maintaining an inventory of ideas, optimizing returns, providing customers with what they wanted, and bending over backward to please these customers. I was not an artist. I was a glorified shopkeeper.

I thought of painting, but I'd tried this years ago as a hobby and learned that I had no aptitude for it. Same with music. I had tried to go back to playing the piano, but the aptitude was just not there. I needed something that I could be good at. It occurred to me that writing novels might be fun, and I had started working on a couple of them in my free time when I was in my late fifties. But I couldn't stick with it. I think the furthest I got was the third or fourth chapters before I ran out of steam. I would grow bored of my own stories, which I determined was not a good sign. Then I thought of poetry. It was quick, fun, intriguing, and aesthetic. It was like designing little houses, but without the city building departments, without all the codes, without the customers, without budgets, and without all the greedy and inept beer-guzzling contractors.

Poetry.

It was perfect, right? And I really did enjoy it, picking all the right words and putting them together into little literary buildings and landscapes, conjuring up images and thoughts in my readers' minds. Honestly, I had no idea what I was doing, but that was half the fun of it: exploring uncharted territory and challenging myself to learn along the way. I've saved all the poems I have written since starting. My first poem? It was about poetry. It was about my newfound love, about the unknown. I titled it "A Letter."

A Letter

Pen to paper,
You in my thoughts,
What should I say to you?
And what should I not?

You could love me
The way that I'll
Love you. Can you tell me,
Is the sky true blue?

Measure the depth
Of my deepest
Fears. Describe all my loves.
Hold up a mirror.

Curse the rain and
Repair my roof.
Belittle the stupid.
Reveal the truth.

Fly me away
To lands unknown,
Where we'll meet with people
Singing Zen koans.

Make my dreams a
Reality,
And make reality
A cup of hot tea.

I can't wait to
Get to know you
Better. I hope you liked
Reading this letter.

I've always liked this poem. I thought it was a pretty good start. Of course, like I've already said, I had no idea what I was doing. But writing the poem gave me a real sense of accomplishment, and I did like that feeling. A little humor, a little whimsy, and just enough honesty to make it worth reading. Was there room for improvement? Of course there was. But isn't there always room for improvement? No matter what you do, and no matter what you write, you could always have done something to make what you've done a little better. But there was one thing I had learned as an architect. Eventually, you have to fish or cut bait. In the end, criticism is pointless because what's done is done.

CHAPTER 8

HARD EIGHT

You might ask, "What did Pamela think of your poetry?" It's a fair question, and I'll try to give you an answer without writing a poem about it.

To understand Pamela's reaction, you have to understand her, and to understand her, you have to understand her upbringing. She was raised by a father who made Rodney Dangerfield look like a college professor and a mother who made Edith Bunker look like Madame Curie. Seriously. I'd never met any people like this in all my life. Pamela loved them, but I thought they were ridiculous.

Pamela's dad's name was Chet, and the mother was Agnes. Chet never finished high school, but according to Pamela, he was a real go-getter. He owned his own used car lot just outside of Portland, and he worked twelve hours a day, seven days a week, where he'd bend over backward to gain an edge on his customers. *A used car salesman?* I thought. *You have to be kidding!* And Agnes? She was the loyal woman behind the man, a kiss in the morning for good luck and a cold beer in hand in the evening. How Pamela ever came from this family, I wasn't sure. She seemed so different.

I remember the first time I met Chet and Agnes. It was spring break, and I drove up from Berkeley to Oregon with Pamela to see them. Pamela and I had been boyfriend and girlfriend for a little over a year, and Pamela thought it was time to meet her parents. Pamela was not ashamed of them, and she thought we would all hit it off. And why not? They had raised her. They were responsible for the way she turned out, and I loved her. I had told her so, and she said she loved me. Marriage was already in our plans for the future, and one day relatively soon, we would all be one big happy family.

"So, you're the artichoke," Chet said to me.

"That's the plan," I said. Artichoke, architect; I wasn't going to argue about it.

I'll tell you what bothered me about Chet. It wasn't that he called me an artichoke. That was actually kind of funny. What annoyed me about the man was his mindset. How can I put this? He belittled and mistrusted all things intellectual. He also had no gray areas; it was all black and white with him. And he considered himself to be well-read because he subscribed to the *National Enquirer*. He believed he was up to date on all things important because he watched reports on scandals, murders, fires, and car accidents on the local six o'clock news. He thought we could've won the Vietnam War, if only we'd dropped an atomic bomb on Ho Chi Minh. He liked to collect guns, and he believed that the more guns people had, the safer our society would be. People would behave themselves better if they knew everyone else was armed. He also thought naming a national holiday after Martin Luther King Jr was a travesty, and he told me, "These blacks ought to be grateful for slavery, because without it, they'd all still be living in Africa. And who in the hell wants to live in Africa?"

I could go on and on. It was amazing how much ignorance Chet was able to spew in just a few hours. I was polite, and I listened to him. And I watched Pamela while the man spoke, and she was smiling. She loved her dad. He had, after all, never even graduated from high school, yet he was able to start his own business selling used cars. And it was a very successful business. They lived in a huge house in a nice neighborhood, and Chet and Agnes both drove brand-new Cadillacs. According to Pamela, she never wanted for anything, and her parents, believe it or not, actually encouraged her to attend college.

"I told her to go ahead and give college a try," Chet said. "I told her we'd pay for it all. Why not? We ought to at least have one egghead in our family, ha, ha. God knows my parents never got much schooling themselves, and you certainly weren't going to find me with my nose in a textbook kissing some professor's backside. No, not me. I graduated from the school of hard knocks. That's where I got my diploma—and look where it got me. I've done fine."

"You should be proud," I said. I didn't know what else to say.

"Anyone want more coffee?" Agnes said.

Good old Agnes. She was Chet's biggest fan, and she was his servant. More coffee? Really? That's all the woman had to say the whole time I was there. Well, that and her opening line, "Nice to meet you, Rick. We've heard so much about you from Pamela."

This was the fertile Oregonian soil from which Pamela grew. This was her home. These were her parents, and it was a little hard for me to believe because she was so smart. But let me tell you something about marriage. There is no more thorough way of getting to know someone other than marrying them, living with them, and raising kids together. You get to know that person better than you know yourself. And here's what I learned about my wife. You could take Pamela away from Chet and Agnes, but you'd only be fooling yourself if you thought you could take the Chet and Agnes out of Pamela. Ha! Every year we lived together, it seemed like I would see more and more of Chet and Agnes manifesting itself in Pamela's words and attitudes. It was uncanny. I thought it would be the opposite, that the greater the distance, the longer the time, the more the separation. But childhoods are most profound, and so are parents.

Which brings me back to the original question—what did Pamela think of my poetry? What did she think of her husband becoming a poet? She certainly *acted* like she was okay with it, and she didn't tell me not to do it. And she didn't poke fun or laugh at me—not to my face, anyway—but I could tell that something about it didn't sit quite right with her and her roots. For openers, she had no interest in reading any of my work. She said poetry wasn't her thing and that she'd be the wrong person to pass judgment on it—or even enjoy it. I'll be honest. This did make me feel a little bad. It hurt my feelings. I mean, it was important to me, and I thought that if it was important to me, it would automatically be important to her. But not so.

Then my mind began to gravitate toward what I perceived as the truth, and what I determined was upsetting. Pamela was disappointed, and I grew resentful. So much so that some days I wouldn't even talk to Pamela. I would ignore her, and I guess you could say I was pouting. I *knew* what she was thinking; she was wondering why a grown man with a wife and children would spend all his free time in a dreamworld, writing poetry? Poetry? Little girls wrote poetry, not grown men. Grown men took up golf with their buddies. Or they worked on their tennis games. Or they worked on cars. Or they drank beer and played poker with their friends. They didn't sit in their home office writing something as superfluous and dainty as poetry.

Rick, the poet.

What was the point? Who would want to read any of it? What in the world did I think I was doing? And perhaps worse than anything, what was Pamela supposed to tell her friends? That her husband was a poet? They'd all roll their eyes and say, "That's a good one, Pamela, but what's he *really* doing?"

The next time I saw Bartholomew, right off the bat, he wanted to talk about Pamela and my poetry. This was a good thing since the subject was fresh in my mind—and since I had yet to come up with a sixth story about myself. It isn't easy coming up with stories about yourself. You'd think it would be easy, but it isn't. You want the stories to be just right. You want them to be representative of your life, yet you find yourself asking, "So what the heck *is* my life? What does it all mean? Anything? Everything? Nothing at all?"

"I have two questions for you," Bartholomew said.

"And they are?" I asked.

"First, whatever gave you the notion that you can read people's minds? And second, what right do you have to expect anyone not to have their own tastes and opinions?"

"When did I ever say I could read minds?"

"You claim to read Pamela's mind."

"Do I?"

"You've attributed opinions to her that you don't even know exist."

"I don't think I'm doing that at all," I said.

"That's *all* you're doing."

"Well," it's not like she keeps any secrets about the way she feels."

"How we feel is always a secret—and it's often a mystery even to the person having the feeling. Feelings change in intensity. They morph from one shape into the other. They're impossible to pin down. A person may feel one way today, and another way tomorrow, or one way this hour, or another way the next. Feelings are not concrete. They are like the clouds in the sky, moving, breaking apart, coming together, and constantly changing shape, depending on their nature and the forces acting upon them. You think you can read the feelings of another? You think you can read Pamela? I say you are either fooling yourself or outright lying. And since you are not by nature much of a liar, I can only conclude that you are fooling yourself."

"But she's made it clear to me. She *told* me that she doesn't like poetry. She *told* me she doesn't have any desire to read what I'm writing."

"So what?"

"So what?"

"So, she doesn't like poetry. That doesn't mean she doesn't love you. That doesn't mean she doesn't respect you. That doesn't mean she wants you to play golf or tennis, work on cars, or waste time playing poker with pals. All it means is that she doesn't like poetry. Not now, anyway. Which brings me to my second question—what right do you have to expect others not to have their own tastes and opinions? Since when is your way the only way? Seriously. There are seven billion people in the world with seven billion different perspectives. They all have their own collections of innate natures, experiences, feelings, opinions, and viewpoints, and not one of them is exactly the same as the other. Pamela has just as much a right to be herself as you have to be you, and she should be able to be herself without you questioning her love or loyalty to you. You do love her, right? Do you love her any less for being herself?"

"Of course not," I said.

"You love *her*?"

"Yes," I said.

"Do you remember when I asked you earlier about distorted thinking?"

"I do," I said.

"Talk to your thoughts," Bartholomew said. "Make the necessary corrections."

I thought about this and then asked, "What does that even mean?"

Bartholomew just laughed.

I finally decided what my sixth story was going to be about. I would tell Bartholomew about our trip to Las Vegas. We don't go there often, but we go there every now and again. I would tell him about our most recent trip, the one where I "won" over thirty thousand dollars playing craps. It was a lot of money, right? Lucky me!

We went there for a show and a dinner. Every so often, Pamela and I would drive to Las Vegas to see one of the shows and have dinner at one of the restaurants. Then we'd come back the next day. On this trip we went to see the Blue Man Group; it was a great show, and we had dinner in the faux Eiffel Tower, at the Paris. It was a great evening, but for me, things were just getting started.

When we returned to our hotel room after dinner, Pamela climbed out of her dress and put on her pajamas. She brushed her hair for a minute and then said, "I'm exhausted. Are you coming to bed—or are you going to watch TV?"

"I think I'm going downstairs," I said.

"Downstairs?"

"I brought a few hundred bucks. I'm going to play some craps."

"I'd rather you just came to bed."

"We're in Las Vegas," I said. "It's what you do in Vegas. You gamble."

"Ugh," Pamela said.

"I won't be that long."

"You always lose."

"I have a feeling tonight's going to be different."

"What a waste of money."

"I didn't bring that much."

"How much did you bring?"

"Five hundred," I said.

"Don't stay out too late," Pamela said, and she climbed in bed while I made my way to the door. "And take your phone with you."

"I have it."

"In case I need to get ahold of you."

"It's in my hand," I said.

"And no drinking."

"No," I said. "I don't plan on drinking."

Pamela rolled to her side and pulled the covers up to her nose while I opened the door to leave.

The hallway smelled like stale cigarette smoke, and the fluorescent lights were humming. I remember that. I walked down the hall and to the elevator, and the next thing I knew, I was in the noisy casino. There were flashing lights as far as the eye could see. Electronic music. Hundreds of people talking, laughing, and yelling. I made my way into the bedlam and went directly to the cashier. A lady about my age wearing too much makeup and a name tag that said "Susan" asked how she could help. Actually, she just said, "Yes?"

"I need chips, please," I said.

"How much?"

I removed a large stack of hundred-dollar bills from my pocket and pushed the money toward her. "Thirty-five thousand in thousand-dollar and hundred-dollar chips."

The amount of money didn't faze her. She did, however, call over a man standing behind her to approve the transaction. I was required to show my driver's license.

The man looked at a few of the bills carefully and then nodded his head. He initialed a piece of paper, and Susan counted out my chips. She pushed the chips toward me. "Good luck," she said.

"Thanks," I replied.

That was easy.

I moved forward to phase 2 of my plan. I stuffed all the chips into my jacket and pants pockets and looked for the casino's craps tables. I found one that was moderately busy, with room for me to step in. There were four other players. A cocktail waitress stepped up to me and asked if I wanted a drink. "No thanks," I said. "I'm here to win."

"If you say so," she said.

The man next to me ordered a rum and coke. He was the shooter, and as the waitress walked away, he picked up the dice from the table. He shook them and blew on them, and then he said, "Baby needs new shoes!" He let the dice fly, and they came up eight.

"Point is eight," the stickman said.

"Hard eight," I said, and I tossed a hundred-dollar chip on the table.

This was how my night started.

CHAPTER 9

COMPUTERS!

I never have been very lucky. Not at anything. How does that old blues song go? "If I didn't have bad luck, I wouldn't have any luck at all." For the most part, that was me in a nutshell. I didn't win contests, and I didn't win lotteries. I didn't win raffles, races, drawings, or even board games or card games. That was just me, the consummate loser, the sucker, the straggler, the also-ran. I'd resolved myself to this sad fact many years ago, and I knew nothing would ever change to improve my luck. It just was what it was. Some people were lucky, and some people weren't.

But this trip to Las Vegas was going to be different. No more hard-luck Rick. No more coming back to the hotel room with empty pockets and a frown. By God, I was going to come back a winner!

I played craps at the same table for about two hours. People came and went from the table. Some people won, and most of them lost. Me? I was making hundred-dollar bets on the pass line and doubling my odds. My stack of chips went up, and then down, and then up, and then down. And then down even more. After my two hours were up, I figured I'd lost about two thousand dollars. Then I walked away. It was time for phase 3 of my plan—the fun part of it all. With my pockets still full of more than thirty thousand dollars of chips, I walked to the elevator and pressed the up button. The doors opened, and I stepped in. Then I went to our floor and walked down the hall. I was laughing. Yes, I was laughing out loud. Pamela was not going to believe her eyes. Lucky me!

When I stepped into the hotel room, I turned on the light. "You're not going to believe this," I said.

Pamela woke up.

"What happened?" she asked.

"Take a look at this!" I exclaimed. I stepped to the bed and began emptying my pockets.

"What the heck—where did you get all those chips?" Pamela asked.

"Playing craps."

"You won them?"

"I'll bet there's over thirty thousand dollars here."

"Good God, Rick."

"All from a five-hundred-dollar stake."

"I can't believe it," Pamela said.

"Believe it," I said.

"What are we going to do with it?"

"Buy that Rolex," I said.

"What are you talking about?"

"We're going to get you that Rolex. The one you saw in the jewelry store over at Caesar's."

"It was too much money."

"You liked it, didn't you?"

"Of course I liked it. But that was just a silly fantasy. I don't really need it."

"But we're getting it."

"Come to bed, and we'll talk about it tomorrow."

I scooped up all the chips and put them in a dresser drawer. Then I undressed and climbed into bed.

Pamela was smiling, facing me.

"I love you," I said.

"I love you too," Pamela said.

The next morning, we went to Caesar's and purchased the Rolex. I insisted, and you know what? Pamela didn't put up much of a fight.

"It's nice to be lucky," I said.

"It is," Pamela agreed.

When I told this story to Bartholomew the next time we met, he leaned back on the sofa and laughed. We were in the family room. It was early afternoon, and Pamela was out running errands.

"Where did you get the money?" Bartholomew asked.

"I took it out of our savings account the day before we left for Vegas," I said.

"And Pamela didn't notice?"

"I handle all the family finances. So long as the bills are being paid, she's fine. I don't think she even knows we have the savings account."

"Ah," Bartholomew said.

"You disapprove?"

"Does it matter what I think?"

"I suppose it doesn't."

"But I'll tell you anyway."

"I figured you would."

"You think you're unlucky?"

I laughed and said, "I *know* I'm unlucky."

"I don't think you even know what good luck is."

"Winning thirty thousand dollars at a Las Vegas craps table is pretty good luck."

"Except you didn't win it."

"My point exactly."

"*Your* point?"

"I was never going to win. I was never going to win anything. But now? I won thirty-thousand dollars, and I could buy something special for Pamela. And how would she see me? As a loser who always lost money, or as a charmed man—her charmed husband. She would call her stupid parents and tell them, "You're not going to believe what Rick did. He played craps for two hours in Las Vegas, and he turned five hundred dollars into thirty thousand. He bought me a new watch, and we're putting what's left over into savings. You guys said Rick would never amount to anything. Well, you were wrong."

Bartholomew laughed and said, "I thought you didn't like Pamela's parents."

"I don't, but I want them to say to themselves, 'Maybe we were wrong about Rick. Thirty grand? Playing craps?' Chet would probably scratch his head and say, 'I'll be a son of a gun. Well, *that's* something.'"

"You're funny," Bartholomew said.

"Can you picture it?"

"Yes, I can picture it, but I don't see why it matters so much to you."

"Well, it doesn't really matter."

"Sure, it does. You mentioned it. If it didn't matter to you, you wouldn't have brought it up."

"Okay, maybe it does matter."

"You think you're unlucky, but you want others to think you're charmed."

"Maybe I do."

"The question is why?"

I thought about this for a moment. I didn't have a good answer for Bartholomew. Why was it so important to me? Why did I care?

"The way I see it, you're a pretty lucky guy to begin with. You're one of the luckiest guys I know."

"Me?" I asked. "You've got to be kidding."

"It's all a matter of how you look at things," Bartholomew said. "It's about how you look at your life and how you think about it. I'm afraid that distortions have become your Achilles' heel.

"My Achilles' heel?"

"Do you remember when you were five, when you broke your father's window with that rock? Lucky kid. You were the luckiest kid on the street that morning. You were lucky that your father wasn't in his den when the rock flew through his window. You would've been caught red-handed, playing in the forbidden rock bed, batting rocks like an idiot, doing exactly what your parents told you not to do. As it turned out, you were able to hightail it to the backyard and blame the broken window on that kid. What was his name?"

"Bobby Richardson."

"Yes, I remember Bobby," Bartholomew said, laughing. "You were just lucky. Your dad would've whipped you for sure."

"He would've," I said.

"And how about when you and Ralph dumped those boxes of yard debris into the Elliots' swimming pool?"

"What about it?" I asked.

"You were lucky then too."

"How so?"

"What if someone had seen you? What if they told Julie about it? And then she told her parents, and then her parents would've called your parents. Can you imagine the trouble you and Ralph would've been in?

Can you imagine how embarrassed you would've been? It was a miracle that no one saw you boys, given all the kids who were at the party. That's all it would've taken. One eyewitness."

"You're probably right," I said.

"And what about your little drunk-driving stunt? When you planned to drive to Mexico? Driving around with an open bottle of scotch in your car, your blood alcohol level way up over the limit. You could've been arrested. You could've been thrown in jail. And even worse, you could've gotten into an accident and maimed or killed some innocent driver. Or yourself. Or a child. You were a disaster waiting to happen. There was no excuse, and you knew there was no excuse. You could've been charged with vehicular manslaughter. You could've had someone's blood on your hands. How long do you think it takes to recover from something like that? But no. Pure luck. That nice man in the tow truck took you home and got you off the streets. I don't see how anyone could've been luckier."

"I guess I've been lucky a few times."

"A few times? You also have your health. How lucky is that? Do you know how many people in the world struggle with health issues, especially at your age? Health is huge. And it's purely the luck of the draw. And your marriage? You have a good marriage, don't you? Do you have any idea how many people experience problems with their marriages? Divorces. Separations. Toxic relationships. People living together who can't stand each other, who are jealous of each other, who cheat, who don't talk. A good marriage is to be treasured. Sure, it takes work, but let's be honest, it's largely a matter of luck. Then there are your finances. You've done well for yourself, and you really have no large financial problems to worry about, not like so many others. You're a fine architect, but you're certainly no financial genius, Rick. For the most part, it's been luck. It's like they say, 'You should count your lucky stars.' There are lots of people in the world who can barely afford to buy groceries. Not everyone can afford to sit around in a nice house, in a nice neighborhood, drinking coffee and writing poetry."

"I'm not exactly rich," I said.

"You're not poor either."

"I could be happier, though."

"You could be, but do you want to be? That is the question, isn't it? What do you want to be? There are hundreds of books on the shelves, but which book are you going to choose to read?"

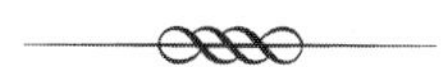

Shortly after this conversation with Bartholomew, I got a call from my son, Zach. Isn't this the way it always happens? Just when you think you're making progress, something comes up to set you ten steps backward? Before I tell you why Zach was calling me, let me tell you a little more about him. He was a good kid, but Jesus! I had no idea.

Zach was twenty-nine and a student at USC. He was studying to get his undergraduate degree in computer science, and he had been going to school for the past year. You might ask why he was nearly thirty and still going to school. In fact, Zach had not originally planned to go to college at all. When he graduated from high school, he had big dreams, and college was not a part of them. Zach wanted to be an artist. Specifically, he wanted to become a sculptor. Pamela and I tried to talk him into studying art in college, but Zach would have no part of it. He said high school was about all he could take of teachers, textbooks, and schooling, and when he was done with high school, he got a part-time job as a laborer with a local construction company to pay the bills, spending his free time working on his art projects.

Was he any good? How would I know? You would think that as an architect, I would have an opinion regarding Zach's work. But it was so different. It was not like anything I'd ever studied in school. I'll tell you the truth—I thought it was *too* different. His sculptures were interesting enough, but they were not the kinds of things that I imagined people would want in their homes. They looked like trash, and that's exactly what they were. Zach would go to the dump and pick out pieces of trash that he thought he could do something with, and he would then wire, and glue, and weld them together into his "visions." That's what he called them. Visions.

Zach spent ten years living the life of a starving artist. I respected him for it, even though I didn't understand his sculptures. More power to him. He knew what he wanted to do, and he found a way to make it happen. Were Pamela and I a little disappointed? Despite that we wanted Zach to pursue his dreams, it's fair to say that we might have been a little happier knowing that he was doing something more … what? More profitable? Dreams are one thing, but living like a pauper is another. And he had no love life. I don't even think he dated. I don't know if he even had any friends. He seemed to be spiraling further and further into a life with no real rewards, isolated, poor, and growing more jaded each year. Then it happened. Like a spark igniting a flame!

Zach came to me and told me he had had enough. "I'm going to do it!" he exclaimed.

"Do what?" I asked.

"Go to college."

"To study art?"

"Forget art," Zach said. "My life is going to take a whole new direction."

"Oh?" I asked.

"I'm going into computers."

"Computers?"

"Anything to do with computers. They are the future of the world. They are the art of the twenty-first century."

"Wow," I said. It was surprising, but it was a very pleasant surprise—and I encouraged Zach. "That sounds like a wonderful idea," I said. "Where do you plan on going to school?"

"I already applied to USC, and I was accepted."

"Really?"

"I just need someone to pay for it."

"We'll pay," I said.

"It's a lot of money."

"It would be worth it."

"I was thinking of asking Grandma."

"Grandma? You mean my mom?"

"She has more money than you," Zach said. "And she told me several years ago that if I ever wanted to go to college, she would pay for it."

"That's crazy," I said. "We can afford it."

"That would be great," Zach said. "I'll pay you back."

"Don't worry about it. Just go forward with your life. It's a great big world out there. I want you to go for it." I thought for a moment and then said, "Are you sure you want to do this? What about your art?"

"Honestly, I've run out of ideas," Zach said. "This past year, I've just been spinning my wheels. Junk is junk. Do you know what I mean?"

"It was your dream."

"Dreams end. We all wake up from them eventually."

"You should tell Mom about this."

"I assumed you would tell her."

"I think it would be best to hear it from you."

"If you think so."

"She'll be so happy."

Chapter 10

Healing the Soul

It was right after Bartholomew lectured me on how lucky I was that I got the phone call from Zach. Here, I thought Zach was finally getting somewhere. A future in computers. A college degree! The call took me completely by surprise—and not in a good way.

"I have to talk to you," Zach said.

"About what?" I asked.

I immediately knew something was wrong. It was in the tone of Zach's voice. It was unsteady, as if searching for the right words to say.

"I don't exactly know how to say this," he said. "It's about school. It's about me."

"Go ahead," I said.

"I've got a problem."

I had no idea what he was talking about. "A problem with what?" I asked.

"I think I'm an addict."

"An addict?" I asked.

"A marijuana addict."

Was there such a thing? I had never heard of marijuana being addictive, but what did I know? I knew next to nothing about it. "Are you sure?" I asked.

"I can't stop."

"Have you tried?"

"It didn't used to be a problem when I was working on my art. In fact, I think I was doing better when I was high. But now with school, it's a different story."

"You think you could do better?"

"I just want to pass."

"Pass?"

"I've been failing all my classes."

"All of them?"

"I'm so far behind. I'm never going to get caught up. I don't know what to do."

"What have you been spending your time doing?"

"Getting high and playing video games."

"Playing video games?" I asked.

"I'm sorry. This whole thing is turning out to be a big waste of time and money. I'm not sure if I'm cut out for this. Or maybe I just need help. Honestly, Dad, I don't know what I need."

"I can help," I said. I don't know why I said this. I was actually very angry and disappointed, and what I really wanted to say was, "You idiot, what in the hell is wrong with you and why are you smoking weed and playing video games when you should be studying? It isn't rocket science. You do the work and get the grades. Then you graduate and get a job."

"They put me on academic probation."

"What does that mean?" I asked.

"I've got to raise my grades."

"Okay," I said.

"But I don't see how I'm going to do it. I've tried quitting weed, but I can't."

"If you want to, you can."

"You don't understand."

What a mess.

Zach was right. I didn't understand. Why would he shoot himself in the foot like this? There was no good reason for it, and he certainly wasn't brought up this way. We didn't have any addicts in our family. So, he was going to be the first? I told Zach to sit tight. I would get back to him. I told him I would find a solution, but that I needed to think about it. I told him in the meantime to work on his schoolwork, and he said he would. But I knew. As soon as we hung up, I knew he'd be getting high, probably playing video games or maybe watching TV. Loser. My son, Zach, the pothead. Zach, the former artist. Zach, the disaster.

Fyodor Dostoevsky wrote, "The soul is healed by being with children." Do you believe this? As you know, Pamela and I have two sons, Zach and Nate. I've told you a little about Zach, but let me now provide a few words about Nate. Then tell me how *my* soul has been healed.

Nate is three years older than Zach. The boys are as different as night and day. Zach was the artist and the rebel, while Nate was the straight arrow. Nate always did well in school, and his teachers liked him. He played a lot of sports, and he was particularly good at baseball. He was a shortstop on the high school baseball team, and he nearly broke the school record for hits in a season. And the girls liked Nate. He always had a girlfriend. Good-looking girls. Girls with pleasant personalities and good families. When he graduated from high school, Nate went to UCLA; he majored in business administration and earned a degree with honors. He also met his wife there, a charming blonde named Emily. Like Pamela and me, they got married during their senior year.

What was Nate's ambition? It was to be an entrepreneur of one kind or the other. He didn't have a craft, a skill, or a passion—he just wanted to start a business and grow it into something everyone could be proud of. He wanted to start with nothing and end up owning a mansion in Newport Beach. He wanted to fund his venture by the skin of his teeth, and ten years later, be making a down payment on a forty-foot yacht. Who was I to argue? His enthusiasm was contagious, and Pamela and I never did anything to hold him back. Was it a little shallow? Maybe it was, but Nate was so sure of himself, and so determined, and so happy, that there seemed no reason to interfere. Our son, the businessman!

Nate's first job out of college was with a man named Harvey Pullman. It was the perfect job. Harvey was an inventor, and he'd had some great success bringing some of his contraptions to market. His specialty? He was known for coming up with totally unnecessary gizmos and then convincing the public that they *had* to buy them. He marketed his products using the infomercials that you see late at night on TV. One of his products was a battery-powered wine bottle opener, and another was a special glass-cutting device that people could use to turn their empty wine bottles into wind chimes. "Think of the money you'll save!" I'd seen some of these infomercials, and while I wasn't tempted to buy any of his products, his enthusiasm was undeniable.

Nate was hired to put together a campaign for Harvey's latest brainstorm: the "Forever Shoelace." Space-age materials. High-tech design. Made to outlast even the longest-lasting athletic shoes. It seemed sort of silly to me, but Nate took the assignment very seriously. He worked his tail off coming up with the perfect infomercial for Harvey's new shoelaces, and I remember staying up late at night to watch it. It was thirty minutes long, and it ran every night on several channels. Nate was thrilled. The orders came pouring in. "Buy one pair—and get a second pair free!" They came in a variety of colors and lengths. "If you love your shoes, you're going to love these shoelaces!"

Success.

Maybe it went to Nate's head. He was put in charge of more and more of Harvey's crazy products, and each of them was a smashing success. And Harvey paid Nate well. But it didn't take Nate long to realize that the *big* money was in being Harvey. The guy was raking it in.

A couple years ago, Nate finally decided to go out on his own and sell his own products to the public. It was around then that he came in contact with a man named Clarence Powell. Clarence had run a small ad in the local paper in the business opportunities section that stated simply, "Inventor looking for investors. Call me now for more info." The ad caught Nate's attention. Who knew? Maybe this guy had the next Forever Shoelaces, the next do-it-yourself wind chimes, or the next battery-powered wine bottle opener. It couldn't hurt to give the guy a call and see what was up his sleeve. Nate called the number in the ad and set up an appointment with Clarence at his home in Costa Mesa.

Clarence brought Nate into his garage where he worked on all his projects and took Nate on a tour of his menagerie of odd inventions.

Nate finally said, "Stop! What is this?" He picked up a pillow from one of the tables. "It looks like an ordinary pillow."

"Ah," Clarence said. "But it's not ordinary at all."

"No?" Nate said.

"That's my Sleep Sound Pillow."

"What does it do?"

"It looks like an ordinary pillow, and it feels like an ordinary pillow. But built into the stuffing is a tiny sound machine and a network of tiny speakers. The controls are on the side of the pillow, right there."

"I see," Nate said.

"It's a sound pillow. Lay your head on it, and it emits a selection of pleasant sounds. Softly. Gently. Quietly, so only you can hear them. You choose the specific sound you want, and you dial in your desired volume."

"What kinds of sounds?"

"Crickets, rainfall, white noise, a gentle breeze through the trees, a babbling brook, a waterfall, classical music—even the sounds of a big city at night, if that's your thing. Imagine the possibilities! Imagine falling asleep with your head surrounded by your favorite sounds."

"Of course, they already sell sound machines."

"But this one is *inside* the pillow. No one hears the sounds but you."

"Yes," Nate said.

"Can you see what I mean?"

"I can," Nate said.

"I applied for a patent. The technology is unique, and I'm sure they'll give me one."

"I think I can sell this," Nate said.

"Of course you can," Clarence said.

"I mean, a lot of them," Nate said.

So, the venture began. At first, Clarence was disappointed to learn that Nate was not actually an investor, but a promoter, but Nate assured Clarence that he could raise the necessary funds to get the pillow on the market. He convinced Clarence that he had the expertise to sell the pillow. He described all the campaigns he had worked on for Harvey Pullman, and he recited the impressive sales figures. Nate was a winner, and the Sleep Sound Pillow would be a winner. "Everyone and their brother will want to buy one of these things!" Nate said to Clarence. "We're going to be rolling in orders."

Nate found several investors, and he promised them the moon—and then some. Everyone was going to get rich. He had thousands of the pillows manufactured, and he created the infomercial. He set up everything. They were ready to start taking orders and shipping product.

That was a few months earlier. I hadn't heard anything from Nate. I just assumed he was busy. But then wouldn't you know it? Just a week after I got the call from Zach about his weed problem and academic probation, I got an equally disturbing call from Nate. He needed money. And he needed a lot of it! His pillow venture had turned out to be an unmitigated disaster, and now he owed money all over the place. People were angry. They were making demands. They were filing lawsuits. They were even claiming fraud. And Nate had a warehouse full of Sleep Sound Pillows that apparently no one was interested in buying. And that was all he had.

"I hate to ask this," Nate said to me.

I wanted to say, "Then don't ask." But instead, I said, "You can ask me anything."

"How much can you loan me?"

"Loan you?"

"I'll pay it back."

"How much do you need?" I asked.

"A lot," Nate said.

"We're not exactly made out of money," I said. "I mean, we have *some* money."

"I'll take whatever you can spare."

"What are you going to use it for?"

"First, I need to stay out of jail."

"Jail?" I asked.

"I probably did some things that I shouldn't have done. I mean, in hindsight, it wasn't too smart. But I honestly thought this pillow thing was going to pay off."

"How many have you sold?"

"Hardly any."

"I saw the infomercial," I said. "I thought it was pretty good."

"It was a flop."

"Wow," I said. I didn't know what else to say.

"Can you loan me anything?"

"Give me a day," I said. "Let me look over my finances. Do you have an attorney? It sounds like you need an attorney."

"I can't afford one."

"I'll call you in a day," I said.

"Thanks, Dad," Nate said.

"I'll help," I said. "We'll talk tomorrow."

That evening, I broke the news to Pamela. The news about *both* of our boys. So far, I had told her nothing about either phone call.

"This is very upsetting," she said.

"It is," I agreed.

"Here I thought everything was fine."

"Everything is not fine at all," I said. "It's all one big disastrous mess."

"Where did we go wrong?"

"I don't know," I said.

"What are we going to do?"

"I don't know that either."

"It's overwhelming," Pamela said. She was staring at me, hoping I would tell her otherwise.

"It *is* overwhelming," I said.

"How is Emily taking all this?"

Emily, Nate's wife. I had forgotten all about her. "I have no idea," I said.

"Does she even know the trouble Nate's in?"

"I don't know."

"It's a good thing they don't have kids."

"Why do you say that?"

"It would just make everything more complicated."

"I guess it would."

"But maybe if they did have kids, Nate wouldn't have taken so many chances."

"That could be true."

"And Zach. He was such a wonderful little boy. So creative—and so full of life. Maybe if he was married, he wouldn't find it necessary to smoke weed."

"That's possible."

"Kids," Pamela scoffed. "They break your heart."

CHAPTER 11

SANDWICHES

I couldn't sleep that night. I was too worried and nervous to even make an attempt at it. I tried writing some poetry in my study, but I couldn't concentrate. I watched a little TV in the family room, but the dialogue went in one ear and out the other. Then I went into the front room to read a book. I pulled one off the shelf, sat down, and opened it to the first page. "This is no good," I said to myself. "I can't read, I can't write, and I can't even watch TV."

"But you can certainly talk to me," a voice said. It was Bartholomew, and he was sitting in the chair by the window. He was a sight for sore eyes. I needed someone to talk to.

"Where have you been?" I asked.

"Here, there. I've been around."

"You were wrong," I said.

"Wrong?"

"You said I was lucky."

"You *are* lucky."

"Everything has all gone wrong," I said. "It's all one ridiculous mess."

Bartholomew laughed.

"You think this is funny?" I asked.

"I think *you're* funny."

It was annoying. I wanted to take the book in my lap and throw it at my so-called friend. But I kept my cool. "I feel like the unluckiest man on earth right now. It's all gone wrong. Horribly wrong."

"Why don't you tell me about it?" Bartholomew asked.

"You don't already know?"

"I want to hear it from you."

"Fine," I said. I took a breath and let it rip. I told him all about Zach and Nate. I was totally honest. I explained every upsetting detail of their predicaments. "Pamela is beside herself," I said. "Neither of us know what to do."

"Whoa there, cowboy," Bartholomew said, laughing again.

"Whoa there what?" I asked. I still had no idea what he thought was so funny.

"You *are* the luckiest man on earth."

"Am I?" I asked.

"The goose has laid the golden egg!"

I glared at Bartholomew. He wasn't taking our problems seriously. Goose? Golden egg? What the hell was he even talking about?

"Good fortune has fallen in your lap," Bartholomew said. "You now have an opportunity to do something truly meaningful with your life. You have an opportunity to help. You have an opportunity to be a father in the truest sense of the word. Your boys need you, and they *want* your help. Now's your chance to do something significant."

"And that makes me lucky?"

"That makes you the luckiest man on earth. You know what your problem is? You see this opportunity as an imposition, as a chore, as a parental nightmare. But it's the opposite, isn't it? It's your chance to shine. And it's your chance to make a difference in the lives of others, namely your sons. Namely Zach and Nate."

"I suppose that's one way of looking at it," I said.

"One way?"

"Yes, one way," I said.

"It's the only way. Again, with the distorted thinking. Poor, pitiful me. Forget that! Look your thoughts right in the eye and talk to them. Argue with them. Set them straight and count your blessings."

I thought about this and then said sarcastically, "Oh, lucky me."

"Yes," Bartholomew said.

"I am more like Sisyphus."

"No," Bartholomew said.

"No?" I asked.

"More distortion. More errant thinking. It's the wrong way of looking at it. It's the wrong way of looking at any boulder placed in your path. You should relish your life's obstacles and difficulties. You should be smiling and pushing on them with all your might. An obstacle or difficulty is a gift from the gods, and taking the initiative required to move them is what gives your life meaning."

"But I—"

It was no use. Bartholomew had vanished, and I was sitting alone on the sofa.

I finally went to bed at about four in the morning.

Pamela woke up as I climbed under the covers. "Are you just now coming to bed?" she asked.

"I wasn't tired," I said.

"Thinking about the boys?"

"Yes, that," I said.

"Me too," Pamela said.

I closed my eyes and quickly fell asleep. I was exhausted. I was tired of thinking about Zach and Nate, tired of thinking about everything. I fell into a dream. I felt like I'd had this dream before, but I still didn't know what was going to happen.

Pamela and I were in the house alone. We were eating lunch at the kitchen table. I was eating a bologna sandwich, and Pamela was eating a salad. The kitchen TV was on, but we weren't watching it. Then the doorbell rang, and I stood up to see who was at the door. "Are you expecting anyone?" I asked Pamela, and she said no.

The doorbell rang again. This time, three times in a row. Whoever was there was anxious for us to open the door. Then they started knocking.

"I'm coming," I said. "Hold your horses."

When I opened the door, there were three men. They were all wearing suits and ties. The man in front was holding something in his hand, and he wanted me to look at it. He held it up higher, and I could see what it was. It was his wallet with his police identification, a badge, and an ID card. "I'm Detective Smith," he said. "Can we come in?"

"Sure," I said, and I stepped aside so that the three men could enter the house. I then closed the door behind them and asked, "What's this all about?"

"You don't know?"

"I don't," I said.

"Is your wife here?"

"She is. We were in the kitchen, eating lunch."

"This concerns you *and* your wife."

"Follow me," I said, and the three men followed me into the kitchen.

When we stepped into the kitchen, Pamela looked up from her salad.

"These men want to talk to us," I said to her. "They're cops."

"Cops?"

"Yes, ma'am," Detective Smith said.

"What do you want with us?" Pamela asked.

"We have some questions."

"Sit down," I said, and I sat down on my chair, picking up my bologna sandwich.

"Can I get you something to eat?" Pamela asked the men.

"No ma'am," the detective said. "I've already had lunch."

"Please sit," I said.

"We'd prefer to stand."

"Okay," I said.

"Do you have two sons?" the detective asked.

"We do," Pamela said.

"Named Zach and Nate?"

"Yes," I said. "Is this about them?"

The men looked at each other. One of them whispered something into the detective's ear.

The detective nodded his head and then looked at me. "Frank here would like a sandwich," he said. "He hasn't had lunch yet. I mean, if it's not too much trouble."

"No trouble at all," Pamela said, and she stood up. She stepped to the refrigerator. "Is bologna okay?" she asked.

The man whispered into the detective's ear again, and the detective said, "He'd prefer liverwurst."

"How about you?" Pamela asked the third man. "Can I make you something too?"

The man shook his head.

"He doesn't eat much," the detective explained.

"A body needs fuel," Pamela said.

"We keep telling him that," the detective said.

"You say you're here about our boys?" I asked.

Pamela was preparing the man's sandwich, and the detective gave me a puzzled look. "You know?" he asked.

"Know what?"

"Here," Pamela said. She handed the sandwich to the detective's hungry sidekick, and then she sat back down.

"Maybe you don't know."

"I don't have the slightest idea what you're talking about," I said.

The man with the sandwich had taken a bite, and he was whispering in the detective's ear again.

The detective asked, "Do you have any mustard?"

"It's in the fridge," Pamela said. "Help yourself."

"It's in the refrigerator," the detective said to the man.

The man opened the refrigerator door, looking for the mustard.

"In the door," Pamela said.

The man found it and added the mustard to his sandwich.

The detective said, "Do you people watch the news?"

"Sometimes," I said.

"You're aware?"

"We have a good idea of what's going on."

"Have you heard of the Clown Bandits?"

"Clown Bandits?" I asked.

"I've heard of them," Pamela said.

"I haven't," I said.

"I see," the detective said. He rubbed his chin. Then he turned and grabbed the liverwurst sandwich from his friend. "Give me that," he said. He took a bite from the sandwich, and then he handed it back to the man. "Fuel," he said.

"We all need fuel," Pamela said.

"But too much mustard."

"What about these Clown Bandits?" I asked.

"They've been terrorizing banks all over Orange and LA Counties for the past couple months."

"And getting away with it?" I asked.

"Unfortunately."

"I see," I said.

"But we're going to catch them. It's just a matter of time. And that's where you come in."

"Me?"

"Both of you."

"You think we can help?"

"Do you know where your boys are right now?"

"At this moment?"

"Yes," the detective said.

"We have no idea."

"You don't keep tabs on them?"

"They're adults," I said. "They're not little boys. They have their own lives."

"Adults," the detective scoffed.

"Are you saying they have something to do with these bank robberies? Do you think they know something about these Clown Bandits?"

"Ha!" the detective laughed, and his two friends laughed with him.

"What are you saying?" I asked.

"Your sons *are* the Clown Bandits."

"That's impossible," I said.

"We're going to catch them—with or without your help. But we'd rather you helped us out. It'll cast you in a better light when this whole thing goes to trial."

"Trial?"

"What kind of parents are you anyway?"

"We're good parents," Pamela said.

"You don't even know where your boys are. They could be anywhere, doing anything."

"You're crazy," I said.

"Crazy like a fox."

"Like a fox?" I asked.

"Foxes aren't crazy," Pamela said.

"I'm going to ask you again—where are your boys?"

"I don't know," I said.

"Harboring fugitives is a serious offense."

"Fugitives?"

"Where'd they get the guns? I suppose you provided them with the guns."

"Guns?" I asked.

"You're only digging yourself down deeper."

"We don't believe in guns," Pamela said.

The man who was eating the sandwich was done with it. He whispered something to the detective again, and the detective asked us, "Frank here wants to know if he can have a glass of milk."

"Help yourself," Pamela said to Frank.

Then, just as Frank was pouring a glass of milk, I could hear the front door open. And I heard voices. It was Zach and Nate! They came to the kitchen, carrying several suitcases.

"Ah," the detective said. "Right on cue."

"Who are these jokers?" Nate asked, looking at the cops in the kitchen.

"They're police officers," I said.

"Cops?"

"The party is over, boys," the detective said.

"The party is over for *you*," Nate said, and he pulled out a revolver, aiming it at the detective.

"Nate!" I said.

"It's all right, Dad. Zach and I will handle this."

"Have you boys eaten lunch?" Pamela asked.

"No," Zach said.

"You need your fuel."

"First things first," Nate said. Then, to the cops, he said, "All of you sit down. Sit in the chairs and put your hands behind your backs. Zach is going to tie you up. Zach, tie these jokers up."

Zach opened one of the suitcases and removed an armful of ropes. He proceeded to tie the officers to the chairs. Also in the suitcase was a large amount of cash. Bundles of hundred-dollar bills. "That ought to hold them," Zach said.

"Now," Nate said to me. "The question is—what do we do with you."

"Do with me?" I asked.

"Now that you know."

"So, you *are* the Clown Bandits?"

"Mom, make us something to eat," Nate said to Pamela, and then he turned to me. "Dad, stay in your chair. Don't make us tie you up too."

"I'm not going anywhere," I said.

"Are bologna sandwiches okay," Pamela asked the boys, and they both nodded their heads. Pamela then stood and stepped to the refrigerator.

"Why?" I asked.

"Why what?" Nate said.

"Why are you doing this?"

"You lied."

"I lied about what?"

"The rock through Grandpa's study window," Nate said.

"He *did* lie," Zach said.

"You blamed us!"

"I blamed Bobby Richardson."

"We are Bobby," Nate said.

"What are you even talking about?"

"I ought to shoot you right here and now. I ought to put a bullet between your eyes."

"Do you boys want mustard?" Pamela asked.

"Mustard is fine," Nate said. Then he stepped closer to me and pressed the nose of his revolver to my forehead. "What's to keep me from pulling the trigger?"

"I can help," I said.

"Sure, you can help."

"He always says he can help," Zach said.

"This is it," Nate said to me. "I'd suggest closing your eyes. On the count of three. One, two, and—"

I woke up.

Pamela was shaking me. "You're having a bad dream," she said. "What were you dreaming about?"

"I wish I could remember," I said, lying. In fact, I could remember all of it. "I'm hungry," I said. "Maybe I'll go to the kitchen and make a sandwich."

"There's bologna and a fresh loaf of bread in the fridge," Pamela said. "But I think we're out of mustard. I'll get some the next time I go to the store."

Chapter 12

When It Rains

Bartholomew was right about one thing. It was nice that my boys had come to me with their problems. True, I would rather that they had no problems at all, but given that they did have them, it was good to know they felt they could turn to me for advice. But this also made me feel guilty. I didn't deserve it. I had my own problems when I was their age, and who did I turn to? My father? No, I didn't turn to anyone. I was selfish and headstrong, keeping my problems to myself, and I never did give my own father the chance to *be* a father. Maybe if I'd been a better son, Dad would've been a happier man.

My affair with Janet Jones comes to mind. What a mess that was. I was in my early thirties and working at an architectural firm in Santa Ana. The name of the firm was the Winchester Group, and I worked there for eight years prior to being hired by John Wiley. Those were exciting times. Nate and Zach were born around then, and it's always exciting to bring new lives into the world. I hadn't yet fallen into the grind of work and parenthood, and everything in my life seemed so new and full of promise. And I was being given more and more responsibility at my job. I was getting somewhere—and being paid well for it. My boss liked me. My fellow workers respected me, and the clients adored me.

The clients weren't the only people who adored me. There was also Janet Jones. She was a new hire, fresh out of college, and she assisted me on many of my projects. In the course of our work together, we became good friends. And then I noticed something. She really did like me. I could tell. She would stand close to me at every opportunity, and she would flirt with me. Small flirtations, but noticeable. She was a very attractive girl, about six inches shorter than me. She had very nice lips and perfect teeth, and her eyes! I swear when she was looking at me, she was looking right into my soul. When I told her jokes, she laughed out loud. When I asked her to do something for me, she never questioned me. And she told me I was smart.

Every man likes to be told he's smart. Clever, handsome and physically fit? They are all fine, but to be told that you're smart is maybe the ultimate compliment. Anyway, for me, it was, and the longer I worked alongside this girl, the more I liked her. I got from her the kind of adulation that I no longer got at home from Pamela. Pamela was obsessed with our boys. Nate and Zach were the world to her, and I was just the guy who happened to be around, the guy who was necessary to get her pregnant, and then? After the boys were brought into the world, I was just a mundane dad. Just a husband. A guy who snored in the bed.

Maybe it's not fair to make these assumptions about how Pamela felt about me, but I can only tell you how I felt. Maybe I was wrong. In fact, I probably *was* wrong, but it didn't seem like I was wrong at the time. And then there was Janet. She paid attention to me. I was special to her. I excited her and stoked the fires in her young heart. The more obvious Janet became about her feelings for me, the more I reciprocated. It's funny. It seemed so okay and right. It also seemed so what? So thrilling? The next thing I knew, she had invited me to her apartment after work. I told Pamela I would be working late that night, and she didn't even question it. The very idea that I was having any kind of a fling with a young girl didn't even cross her mind. "Work as late as you need to," she said. So, I did.

I loved Janet's apartment. It was very girlie. Honestly, it was like a teenager lived there, from the childish posters she tacked on the walls to her apple blossom-scented candles. She had a wicker sofa in the apartment with big floral pattered cushions, and when I sat on it, I felt like I was inside a cloud. And when she sat next to me, it was heaven! She was soft and perfumed, warm like a loaf of bread fresh out of the oven. The first night I came over, all we did was talk, but it was the most fun I'd had with anyone in years. I learned about her, and she learned about me. We talked about our childhoods, and we talked about our high school years. When ten o'clock rolled around, I kissed her goodbye and drove home to Pamela and the boys.

I can't count the number of nights I went to Janet's apartment after that first visit. I went over there a lot, always calling Pamela first and telling her I had to work late again. "Don't stay up for me," I'd say. Pamela, the trusting soul. I don't think she suspected anything, ever. She was just proud that I was working so hard to support our young family. I told her I was getting paid overtime, which was a lie. But like I said earlier, I always handled the finances, so only I knew how much money I was bringing home. Yes, she was proud of me, and she was glad I was her husband. As far as Pamela was concerned, I was doing my duty, and I was responsible. But I was actually going to Janet's apartment and loving every minute of it.

I don't know what I expected to happen. I wasn't really thinking clearly. Some people say men think with their penises, but that wasn't really it. True, we were having sex, and I enjoyed it. And we touched a lot, and we kissed a lot. But more than anything, I just liked being around the girl. She made me feel important, and loved, and special. If you're married and you've had an affair, you probably know exactly what I'm talking about. If you haven't had an affair, you might think I was a little crazy. And maybe I was. Like I said, I wasn't really thinking clearly. Then, out of nowhere it seemed, the storm clouds gathered overhead, and the rain fell, washing me clean. Ugh. Janet was serious!

"We need to talk," Janet said, so we sat down on her overstuffed sofa. She looked me right in the eyes and said, "I need to know where we're going, Rick. I think you know how I feel. I love you. But where are we headed? I need to know when."

"When?" I asked.

"When are you going to tell your wife?"

"Tell her what?" I asked.

"Tell her it's over. Tell her about us."

Well, this was not at all what I expected. I don't know what I expected, but I certainly didn't plan to end my marriage. I liked Janet. I liked her a lot, and I enjoyed being with her. But that was it. Clumsily, I said, "I'm not sure I feel the same way about you as you feel about me."

"You love me, don't you?"

"But I have a family."

"You told me she takes you for granted."

"Did I say that?"

"You did," Janet said.

"I'm not sure what I said."

"You definitely said that."

"I thought we were just having some fun," I said.

"Fun?"

"You know," I said. "Just two people having a good time, having fun with each other."

You should've seen the look on the poor girl's face. You'd think her mom just died. Or her dad. Or her cat. The entire mood in the room changed. At first, she was hurt, and I tried to think of something kind to say. Then, like someone flipped a switch, she turned angry. "You bastard!" she said, and she slapped my face. It was the first time I'd ever been slapped in the face by a woman. It's terribly disconcerting, especially when you're not expecting it. And it stung. She had hit me pretty hard. "Just leave," she said. "Get the hell out of my apartment."

"We should talk," I said.

"I've heard all I want to hear."

"I don't want you to be angry."

"I went out on a limb for you," Janet said.

A limb? I felt like an idiot. What was I supposed to say to her? I didn't want her to hate me, but I also didn't want her to love me. I had a wife, and I had a family. I thought Janet knew that. "I'm sorry," I said.

"Just get out of here."

"Okay," I said.

"Now!" Janet shrieked.

"Okay, okay," I said, and I stood up to leave.

It's clear now. It wasn't at all clear then, but it is clear now. I should've gone to my dad. Not Mom, who would never have got it. I should've told Dad what was going on, and I should've asked him what to do. But I didn't think he'd understand either, and I thought he would judge me. I thought he'd say something like, "What in the hell is wrong with you? Are you an idiot?" No, I don't think we give our parents enough credit for wanting what is best for us, for having experience, for being the most appropriate source of advice when we make mistakes. I gypped my dad. I didn't believe in him the way my boys believed in me. You know, I also never did tell Pamela about Janet. She didn't show up for work the next day—or the day after that. She refused to answer her phone when the office called her. She just quit. She just disappeared. My boss said, "You two seemed fairly close—do you have any idea what happened?"

"No idea," I said.

"Weird, isn't it?"

"It is," I said.

What would my dad have told me to do? Honestly, I have no idea. Most likely, whatever it was, it would've been a vast improvement over the way I did handle things. To this day, I still feel guilty about the whole thing, the fact that I had an affair, the fact that I lied to Pamela, the fact that I hurt Janet, and the fact that I didn't seek help from the one man in the world my honesty and confidence would've meant the most to. My dad.

Like I needed more on my plate, but when it rains, it pours. I got a call from the director of Mom's assisted-living facility, a woman named Shirley Gaines. Shirley was the one who gave us the initial tour, and she was also the one who had us sign all those papers. "We're having a little difficulty with your mom," she said.

"With *my* mom?" I asked. I acted surprised.

"She's been drinking."

"Drinking?"

"We've found her drunk in her room three times now. We've explained the rules to her. Drinking is not allowed on our premises. It's an insurance thing. We can't take on that kind of liability."

"Of course not," I said.

"Did your mom have a problem with alcohol before she moved in with us?"

"Not that I'm aware of."

"You need to have a serious talk with her."

"I will," I said.

"If she continues to drink, we'll be forced to ask her to live somewhere else."

"Okay," I said.

"I know it sounds harsh, but we're responsible for our guests. She could fall and hurt herself. There are any number of bad things that could happen."

"Has she been belligerent?"

"No, she's been cooperative. We find her inebriated and put her to bed. There haven't been any confrontations. We tell her that drinking isn't allowed, and she says she understands. Then the next day, when she doesn't show up for dinner, we go to her room and find her drunk again."

"I'll talk to her," I said.

"Make sure she understands. I'd hate to have to ask her to leave. We like her here."

"I'll make sure she gets it," I said. "But can I ask you a question? How is she getting her hands on the booze?"

"She must be buying it when we take her to the store."

"Can you check her grocery bags?"

"We can, but there are other ways."

"Other ways?"

"She could be getting it from someone else. A friend, perhaps. Or someone who works here. No way of knowing for sure. Keeping alcohol out of our facility is like keeping drugs out of a school or a prison. If someone wants it, they can usually get it. We try our hardest, but the best thing you can do is to talk to your mom and make sure she understands and follows the rules."

When my call with Shirley was over, I immediately drove to the facility to talk to Mom. If they kicked her out of this place, it could be a big problem. *Then* what would we do with her? I had to make sure Mom understood the severity of the situation.

"I understand you've been drinking," I said.

"Who told you that?"

"Shirley, the director."

"Tattletale," Mom scoffed.

"You can't be doing this. I didn't even know that you drank. Since when did you take up drinking?"

"It's something to do," Mom said.

"Something to do?"

"This place is boring. It's still boring when I drink, but when I drink, I don't care if it's boring."

"Don't you have friends here?"

"I've met a few ladies."

"And?"

"They're boring. All they want to talk about is their dead husbands and their successful children. Or they want to gossip. Or they want to complain."

"What have you been doing with your time?"

"I've been watching a lot of TV. Garbage mostly. That's all that seems to be on these days."

"Have you tried reading? You used to like to read, didn't you?"

"My eyes aren't what they used to be."

"How about the activities here?"

"I've tried a few."

"Don't they have organized bus trips?"

"I've already been to the places they go to. At my age, there isn't much in Southern California that I haven't already seen."

"I don't know what to say," I said.

"I'll survive. I don't want you worrying about me."

"But the drinking?"

"I'll stop."

"Do you have any booze in the apartment?" I asked.

Mom thought for a moment. At first, I thought she was going to lie to me, but she said, "I still have half a bottle of vodka."

"Where do you keep it?"

"It's hidden in the cupboards, behind the oatmeal box. On the left."

"I'm going to take it," I said.

I stood up and stepped to the cupboard. Sure enough, I found the bottle. I poured the vodka down the kitchen sink, put the bottle in a plastic trash bag, and pushed it into the kitchen wastebasket. "Promise this is the end of it?"

"I promise," Mom said. But honestly? I didn't know if she was being sincere—or if she was just trying to get me to leave her the hell alone. My mom was a good person. And she was always smart about important things, but she also had a mind of her own.

CHAPTER 13

THE CARPET SALESMAN

I didn't see Bartholomew for several weeks. During this time, I tried to help Nate and Zach with their predicaments, and I was keeping an eye on my mom to be sure she wasn't drinking again. I would make impromptu visits to see Mom in the early evenings. Spot-checking her, if you will. So far, so good. She was sober every time I saw her, and we had some nice talks about the good old days. She did most of the talking. She liked talking about Dad. She really missed him, and I couldn't help but think that if he was still alive, her life would be much different. They were good for each other.

It was on the way home from one of these visits that I did it again. It was dumb. I was certainly old enough to know better. I seemed to do this every six months or so with surprising regularity: me, sitting on the side of the freeway, cars whizzing past me, cursing and waiting for AAA to call me back. Yes, I had run out of gas. I called AAA, and they said they would call back with an ETA for the service truck. Waiting. Cursing. How old would I finally have to be before I learned to keep an eye on my gas gauge?

Finally, my cellphone rang, and when I answered it, the lady told me the service truck would arrive in approximately forty-five minutes. I had no choice but to wait.

"Again?" Bartholomew asked.

I turned to look, and he was sitting in the passenger seat. "I don't know why I do this," I said.

"Cars need gas."

"No kidding," I said.

"How's your mom doing?"

"She seems to be fine," I said. "At least, she seems to have stopped drinking for now. I'm telling you—if it's not one thing, it's another. That's all I seem to be doing these days. Putting out fires."

"Would you have it any other way?"

"Actually, yes," I said.

"Be careful what you wish for."

"So they say."

"What did you tell your boys to do? Were you able to help?"

"I think I was."

"You think?"

"How should I know? I mean, how do I really know? It's not like I'm some kind of omniscient wise man. Often, I feel like I'm bumbling through my life with no more wisdom than the next guy in line. It's not like I'm some sort of paragon of success and great judgment."

Bartholomew laughed and said, "No one is. What did you tell Zach to do?"

"I asked around, and everyone I talked to said he ought to go to rehab. That was the consensus. But I'll tell you the truth. I didn't like this idea much."

"Why not?"

"I think there's a stigma attached to doing this rehab thing. People will talk. People will say, 'Did you know that *he* went to rehab?'"

"And that's a bad thing?"

"It's like telling people you go to a psychiatrist. They wonder what's wrong with you."

"So, what did you tell Zach?"

"I told him he needed to go to rehab. I couldn't come up with anything better. He needs help. He's obviously not able to solve this problem on his own. Pamela and I looked around and found a program that seemed right for him. There's a waiting list to get in, so it'll be a week or so before he can go there. These places cost a fortune, but Zach's health insurance carrier has agreed to pay for part of it. We'll pay the rest."

"And what about school?"

"He'll need to meet with his counselor and tell her what's going on. My guess? He's going to be suspended until he proves he has his life in order. I've asked around about this too, and Zach will probably have to go a community college for a couple years and show he's serious about getting good grades. Then he'll be able to transfer back."

"And Zach is okay with all this?" Bartholomew asked.

"He doesn't have much of a choice."

"Did you ask him how he felt?"

"I didn't," I said. "I just told him what he needed to do."

"And Nate?"

"I told him the first thing we needed to do was keep him out of jail. We talked, and I think he was honest. The only law he seemed to have broken was writing bad checks. We had to make good on the checks. Some of them had already been turned over to the police department. There were about six of them total. They added up to quite a bit of money, but I figured I could tap our retirement savings and pay them off. Of course, Nate would owe me the money. I wasn't just going to get him off the hook without being paid back. I made sure he understood this. He was very apologetic, and he promised he would repay every dime. Then there was the rest of it."

"The rest of it?"

"Nate still owed a ton of money."

"And what was the plan for that?" Bartholomew asked.

"In a word? Bankruptcy. I didn't see any other way out. Nate argued at first, and he said it would ruin him. He said it would destroy his credit and his reputation, but I told him, 'You've already done that. You may as well get off the hook and start over again. If you don't file bankruptcy, you'll be paying these people back until you're fifty or sixty—and none of them will have anything good to say about you whether you pay them back or not.'"

"Wow," Bartholomew said.

"Did I do the right thing?"

"How should I know? I mean, it all sounds logical to me. Tough decisions for tough problems. How does Pamela feel about it?"

"She doesn't understand what happened."

"She's upset?" Bartholomew asked.

"Of course she's upset. Who wouldn't be? It's not like either of these boys came from a bad home. It's not like we didn't do our best as parents. What are we supposed to tell people when they ask how our kids are doing? The truth? 'Oh, one got kicked out of college and is in rehab, and the other is bankrupt and was nearly thrown in jail.' You say I'm lucky that they came to me for help, but I don't feel it. I feel like you're just rationalizing. I feel like I've been playing a long game of poker, dealt nothing but shitty hands. Lucky? You've got to be kidding. And then there's my poor mom, wasting away in an assisted-living facility that she hates. What's next?"

"You're throwing the baby out with the bathwater."

"Pardon me?" I said.

"That's what you're doing."

"You know," I said. "I've never really understood what that expression means."

"Then it's time you learned."

I looked in the review mirror, and I saw the AAA truck pull up behind us. "The gas is here," I said, but when I turned my head toward the passenger seat, I saw that Bartholomew was gone.

The next thing I knew, the AAA guy was knocking on my window. "Rick?" he asked.

"That would be me."

"I come with gas."

"You're a lifesaver," I said.

"I only brought a gallon, so you'll need to get to the closest gas station to get filled."

"I feel like such an idiot," I said.

"Listen," the man said. "Without people like you, I'd be out of business."

When I was thirty-seven, I took up tennis. I'd never played the sport before, and I had no idea what I was doing. I bought a racquet and some tennis clothes, and I joined a club in Newport Beach. I signed up for lessons twice a week with a kid who was in his twenties. He said he'd been playing tennis since he was eight years old, so I figured he knew what he was doing. After about two months of lessons, the kid said I was ready to start playing others. The club would set up matches for the members, pairing players of similar skills.

My first match was with a man named Jimmy Hubble. Jimmy was probably in his early fifties, about fifteen years older than me. The first thing I noticed about him was the braces he was wearing; there was a brace on each knee and one on his elbow. He didn't look like much of an opponent, and I thought, *This ought to be relatively easy.* But the guy surprised me. I mean, he was terrible, but at least he was trying. I stuck with it and won almost all of the games, and when we were done, we shook hands.

"How long have you been playing?" he asked me.

"A little over two months," I said.

"Stick with it. You're a natural. I've been playing for ten years. You're going to be good."

"Thank you," I said. It was funny. A two-year-old probably could've beaten this guy. He hobbled off the court, grabbed his bag, and headed for the gate. He talked the entire time he was walking, but not to me. He was talking to himself about our match and all his shortcomings. Then as I followed him through the gate, he turned to me. "Each match is a learning experience," he said.

"Yes," I said.

"You take away what you put in."

"Sure," I said.

"Stick with it, Rick. That is your name, right? Didn't you say your name was Rick? Your backhand is a little weak, but you're going to get better. You're a good player."

"Thanks," I said.

Weird.

Jimmy was a nice enough guy, but he was kind of out there. I wondered what it would be like to be his age, to have played for ten years, and still be so inept. I felt for the guy, talking to himself, shaking my hand, carrying his tennis bag back to his beat-up car in the parking lot. I saw the car, and I wondered what this poor guy did for a living. A janitor? A maintenance man? A security guard? Half his paycheck probably went toward his tennis club dues. I should've let him win. It would've made his day.

My next opponent at the club was better. This time, I played a man in his sixties named Burt Bright. He was older than me, yes, but he was a pretty good player. He wore no knee or elbow braces, and he was in good physical shape for a man his age. Beating him was tougher than beating Jimmy, but I had still yet to be paired with someone who was much of a challenge for me. And I thought, *Maybe I am pretty good. Maybe I'm better at this than I thought!* I asked the girl at the front desk to put me up with tougher competition.

Well, the competition did get tougher, but I was improving with every match. I really was enjoying myself—even when I lost. It was a challenge. I'd never had a sport before, and I was learning just how much fun it could be. Slowly but surely, I was establishing myself as a pretty good player, and I found myself up against some formidable opponents. At my level, anyway. Then they moved me up a level at the front desk, and I found myself playing even tougher opponents. But I was still doing pretty well. And I was getting better, making some new friends and winning matches. Then along came Jonathan Birch. He would change everything.

I noticed him watching a few of my matches. When we made eye contact, he smiled. He seemed like a nice guy. Then, finally, the front desk paired me up with him, and we played against each other. He was good. Then they paired us up again, and then again. I would win, then he would win, and then I would win. He complimented me on my abilities, and I complimented him on his. I felt like we were becoming friends, and I liked him.

One day, he said, "Let's make this more interesting."

"How?" I asked.

"Let's play for a little money."

"Money?"

"We'll each put up a bet on ourselves to win—winner take all."

"Like betting on a pool game?"

"Something like that," Jonathan said.

"Like how much?"

"How does five hundred sound?"

"Five hundred?"

"To make it interesting. It's got to hurt a little to make it interesting."

"I don't know," I said.

"You can't afford to lose five hundred?"

"I can afford it," I said. I didn't want the guy to think I couldn't handle a five-hundred-dollar bet.

"Well then?" Jonathan was smiling, and his smile made everything about this seem okay. A friend. A friendly bet. A tennis match for a little cash.

"You're on," I said.

We shook hands, and Jonathan arranged the match with the front desk. We were to play the next day in the afternoon. When the time came to play, we were not alone at the court. Jonathan had invited a group of his friends to watch. It hadn't even occurred to me to invite my own friends since I thought this was just between Jonathan and me.

I served first, but Jonathan won the first game easily. Then more people came to the court, and they too were watching. Suddenly, there was quite a crowd. It seemed like everyone at the club was interested in this five-hundred-dollar match. I didn't even know who most of the people were.

Long story short, Jonathan proceeded to beat the pants off me. It wasn't even close. And every time Jonathan won a point, the crowd would cheer for him. It was humiliating. And worst of all, I had to write Jonathan a check for five hundred dollars when the match was over. He took it from me, folded it in half, and stuffed it into his pocket.

"Beer?" he asked.

"Beer what?" I said.

"I'll buy you a beer at the clubhouse."

I was confused, and I didn't know what to say. I said, "Why not?"

I followed Jonathan up to the second-floor clubhouse, and we sat at a table near the windows. The waitress came, and Jonathan ordered us a couple of beers. "You put up a good fight," he said. "I guess I was on my game."

"Right," I said.

"What do you do for a living?" Jonathan asked.

"I'm an architect."

"Ah, do you work in Orange County?"

"Our office is in Orange County, but we have projects all over Southern California."

"Commercial or residential?"

"I do a lot of custom homes."

"Do you like it?"

"I enjoy it," I said. Then I changed the subject and asked, "Where did you learn to play tennis?"

"I've been playing off and on since I was a kid."

"You're good."

"Thanks," Jonathan said.

"What do you do for a living?" I asked.

"I'm a carpet salesman. You know, to large corporations with large facilities. It's boring as all get-out. I'm looking to change jobs soon."

CHAPTER 14

THE RED JACKET

I told Bartholomew about my stint as a tennis player. It was my seventh story, and he listened patiently as he always did, never interrupting. It was early in the morning, and we were in my den.

When I was done telling him the tale, he asked, "So that was *it*?"

"That was my tennis career," I said. "Game, set, match. I haven't played since."

"Not at all?"

"Not even a little," I said.

"Because Jonathan Birch beat you?"

"I guess so," I said. "I really thought I had a chance, but I didn't even come close. It was no contest. He made a total fool of me. And who did I think I was? I was an easy mark for a carpet-selling tennis hustler. It wasn't so much the amount of money I lost because losing five hundred bucks wasn't such a big deal, and I could afford it. But the fact that I *thought* I could win, and the fact that I *was* such an easy mark—it was humiliating. And then there the guy was, pretending to be my friend, buying me a beer. A carpet salesman."

Bartholomew laughed and said, "He had you pegged from the start."

"He did," I said.

"He even brought along an audience," Bartholomew said, laughing.

"It was awful. I was such an idiot, and everyone at the club would know about it. News about these kinds of things travels fast. They'd all be talking about it, how I was dumb and cocky enough to bet Jonathan Birch that I could beat him, and how I got my clock cleaned and had to write a check for five hundred dollars. They'd say, 'Ha, ha, I guess Jonathan taught *that* dope a lesson.'"

"Do you think you might've been overreacting?" Bartholomew asked.

"No," I said.

"Do you remember President Kennedy?"

"As best as can be expected. He was killed when I was in the third grade. I was only nine years old."

"But you do remember him?"

"I do," I said.

"Do you remember what he said about putting men on the moon?"

"Kind of," I said.

"On May 25, 1961, before a special joint session of Congress, Kennedy made the announcement. He said the United States would land a man on the moon before the end of the decade. It was a huge promise. Back then, sending a man to the moon was the stuff of wild science fiction novels. Kennedy was assassinated in 1963, but his promise lived on. In July of 1969, Neil Armstrong set foot on the moon, making Kennedy's promise a reality. It was as if Kennedy was superhuman, willing the event to occur even after his death, from his grave, from the afterlife."

"And?" I asked.

"*He* made a bet, and he won it."

"And I didn't?"

"Kennedy's promise was the stuff of legends. And legends are what? A reality? I hardly think so."

"I don't know what you mean by that," I said.

"The truth is that more often than not, we do not live up to our expectations and promises. The truth is that failures are an everyday occurrence. The truth is that most promises are not worth the paper they are printed on. In the long run, do you know who makes the most money when bets are placed? It's the people handling the bets. Because once and a while you'll win, but the fact is that most of us are just plain old human beings: fallible, faulted, crooked, inept, imperfect, and clumsy. Failure, and not success, rules the roost. How we deal with our failures is what will define us—not whether or not we succeed."

"Okay," I said.

"Do you believe me?"

"I guess I do."

"Can I point something else out to you?"

"Sure," I said.

"You are also way too concerned with what other people are thinking."

"Am I?"

"I think you are. So, you lost a tennis match to a hustler and lost five hundred dollars? So, he wiped the court with you? And maybe some people did talk about it, but who cares? What do you care what they're thinking? Odds are that to most people, the event meant nothing, that it was just a passing curiosity. You made it important *in your mind*. You are just not that critical. It's not like you're the president of the United States making promises to the public. You are just another man. You are Rick Harper, the architect. And you are not Frank Lloyd Wright, Christopher Wren, or Philip Johnson. You are a guy who designs custom houses for a living for a decent wage at a run-of-the-mill architectural firm in Orange County, California. You have a wife and a mortgage. You have two imperfect sons. You have a habit of running out of gas—and a mom in an assisted-living facility."

"That sounds so depressing," I said.

"Depressing?"

"You make me sound so insignificant."

"More distorted thinking."

"You keep bringing that up. What exactly are you talking about?"

"You are significant, just not in the way you want to be. Do you remember Zach's red jacket?"

"Red jacket?"

"The leather one. The shiny red jacket."

"Yes," I said. "I remember it."

"He *had* to have it."

"We were shopping for a winter jacket. He was growing so fast, and his old jacket was too small. We went to the store, and there it was."

"A shiny red leather jacket."

"It was pretty loud and showy. But Zach was drawn to it like a honeybee to a flower. He was all over it. 'I want it,' he said. I asked if he was sure. He said he was positive, and then he tried it on. He walked around in it, and he looked at himself in the mirror. He really looked ridiculous, but he was in love with it."

"So, you bought it?"

"It cost a fortune."

"But you bought it anyway?"

"I did," I said.

"And he wore it to school the next day?"

"He couldn't wait. I thought it was funny how a jacket could be so important to a boy."

"And then?"

"I picked him up when school was out. He climbed into my car, and I asked him how his day went. His lips pouted, and he started crying. I asked him what was wrong, and at first, he didn't want to tell me. Then he spilled it. He said the other kids in school ridiculed his jacket. 'They called me a fag,' he said. 'They said I was wearing a fag jacket.' He was really hurt. I wanted to laugh, but I didn't. The poor kid had spent all day wearing a jacket that he now wished he'd never put on. And I think he felt especially bad about the price of the jacket. I had made a big deal about the price when we bought it, and now there was no way he'd ever be caught dead in this thing again, anywhere."

"What did you do?"

"I told him not to worry about it."

"And?"

"I told him the other kids were probably just jealous. I said we'd go back to the store that night and find a more appropriate coat."

"You didn't lecture him about wasting money?"

"No," I said. "He felt bad enough as it was."

"You were a good father."

"I tried to be," I said.

"You were significant."

I thought about this and said, "Maybe I was at that. I just tried to do the right thing."

"Sometimes that's all it takes to be significant. Chalk one up for you." Bartholomew clapped his hands. He applauded for me, and then he disappeared.

When it came time for Zach to go to rehab, Pamela and I picked him up and drove him there. You know, I didn't tell my mom about it. I didn't see any reason to upset her at the time, although I knew she'd eventually find out. Or maybe I was just ashamed that Zach had made such a mess of things, ashamed that I hadn't done a better job as a father.

The rehab facility was called the Pines, and it was located in San Diego County. It was out in the middle of nowhere, over an hour's drive from our house in Irvine. It was billed as "rustic," which I decided upon actually seeing the place was a euphemism for "this place is a dump." Seriously, you couldn't get me to stay a month at this place if it was the last option left on earth. But Zach liked it right away. "I thought it was going to be like a hospital," he said. "It's more like a camp." Maybe he was right, and maybe I was being too critical.

We checked Zach in at the front office and met a man named Dewey Chambers. Dewey was a cheerful man who exuded optimism, which we appreciated. He went through all the rules and schedules, giving us an idea of what Zach was in for. Zach listened quietly. I'm not sure what he was thinking. Then we were introduced to Zach's counselor, a muscular man in his thirties with a tight T-shirt and tattoos up and down his arms. His name was Glen. I was surprised when we shook hands. He had a soft and gentle handshake. "Your boy is in good hands," Dewey said. "Glen has been with us for five years now. He got sober here when he was a teenager, and now he's a counselor. He knows the ropes."

"That's good to know," I said.

Pamela was quiet. I knew that Pamela was not fond of tattoos, and I could only imagine what was going through her mind.

Are you aware of the statistics? I looked them up while I was looking for a place to send Zach, and I was surprised to discover that about 90 percent of addicts who go through treatment programs go back to their same old drugs a year after being released. So, what exactly were we doing? Were we making a bet against all the odds? We were hoping for something that had very little chance of being successful. Were we setting ourselves up for heartache and disappointment? Zach was our son. We had to give him a fighting chance. I told myself it was worth it, but what was the truth? Was I just serving the ball to Jonathan Birch again?

Damn.

I wrote a poem about Zach. It was a poem I would never share with him. In fact, I would never share it with Pamela or anyone else, but it expressed my feelings at the time. It was personal. I was talking to myself, alone with my memories and morose eddies of thought. I titled the poem "An Apology," and it went as follows:

An Apology

Wish I had a crystal ball
For the days ahead. Where
Will you be five years from now?
Who'll be sleeping in your bed?

Will you get married someday?
Will you take a wife? They
Say you've a 10 percent chance
Of having a decent life.

Tell me how it came to this.
Where did I go wrong? What
Sharp pencil could I have used
To compose a better song?

What instrument did I play?
What words did I sing? No,
You trusted me, and I have
Made a mess of everything.

Every young boy depends on
His father to lead. What
Was I doing? Where was I
During all your times of need?

Do you remember those years?
I recall them clear. There
Were toys and stuffed animals;
Your favorite was a blue deer.

You didn't like the monkey.
Talked to you at night. Your
Second favorite was the
Old toucan, fuzzy and bright.

I recall your ball and bat.
Gramps got them for you. That
Was before you could walk.
Then your mantel clock struck two.

Mom and I bought you a trike.
You adored that thing. You
Were riding on the sidewalk
When you got your first beesting.

First grade, second grade, and third.
You grew like a weed. And
Time stood still for none of us,
And you followed our lead.

Eighth grade, ninth grade, and tenth.
A mind of your own. Girls,
Cars, sports, and a desire
To be free and left alone.

And somehow just as quickly
As the world spins, you
Grew into a man—screws and
Nails, needles and pins.

You opted for your sculpture,
And I let it be. How
You want to move on, but you
Are now anything but free.

Locked up in rehab, learning
How to function true. Like
I said, the odds are against
It. It breaks my heart in two.

I let you down. I'm sorry.
I should've known.

Listen, I know that I'm not a great poet. In fact, you might not like my poetry at all. But please give me credit for one thing. It comes from the heart, and dropping Zach off at the Pines was one of the hardest things I've had to do in my life. Rustic? Hell, the place was wretched. I had come to the equally wretched realization that it was very likely that Zach would never stop smoking weed, that he would be unable to ever get back into USC, that at the age of thirty, he was doomed to a life of what? Getting high and playing video games? Watching TV? Eating potato chips and brownies? Living in that hovel he's called home for the past ten years? He wanted a better life for himself. He had said so. There was a spark, a glimmer of hope, a door opened. But would it be enough?

CHAPTER 15

EVERYTHING'S GREAT

Meanwhile, I had Nate to contend with. I had paid off all his bad checks, which totaled about twice what he had originally told me. I then put him in touch with a bankruptcy attorney, who immediately notified all Nate's creditors of the bankruptcy. A hearing date was set, and they were all allowed the opportunity to plead their cases. I didn't go to the hearing with Nate. He said he wanted to handle it on his own. "Don't worry, Dad," he said to me. "I'll be wearing a bulletproof vest and a helmet." He was kidding of course.

But I was worried about Nate. That go-getter spirit of his had been beaten senseless by his business failure. He used to be so upbeat and optimistic. It was getting bad. His wife, Emily, was now supporting the two of them. She worked for a pharmaceutical company, talking doctors into prescribing their drugs to patients. She made a decent living at it, so she and Nate did have an income. But Nate was going nowhere. He was hanging around the house while Emily worked. I'm not sure what he was doing with his time. He did the house chores. He worked in the yard. He watched a lot of TV.

Do you remember *The Little Engine That Could*? I thought of this story when I was thinking about Nate. It was what Nate needed. Belief in oneself. Optimism. That *I can do it* attitude. Pamela and I read this book to our boys when they were little—where did the lesson go? "I think I can, I think I can, I think I can!" Chug, chug, chug. Up and over the hill we go.

I talked to Pamela about Nate's funk, and we agreed that we needed to talk to him. He needed a pep talk. He didn't need to be lectured; he just needed to be lifted up a little and pointed in the right direction.

Pamela said, "Maybe you should do it. You're his father, and he'll listen to you. I think it's a father-son conversation."

So, I talked to Nate, but here's what's funny. In talking to him, I was also talking to myself. I didn't realize what I was doing at first, but Bartholomew pointed it out when he visited me the morning after my talk with Nate. It was early again, and I was on my first cup of coffee, starting a new poem.

"Another poem?" Bartholomew asked.

"I just started it," I said.

"What's this one about?"

"The talk I had yesterday with Nate."

"How's the kid doing?"

"Hard to tell," I said.

"You went to cheer him up?"

"I went to give him a pep talk," I said. "So, yes, I guess I went to cheer him up."

"To get him going?"

"Yes," I said.

"What did you say to him?"

"I told him a story. He didn't know anything about it, so it was news to him. It embarrassed me, and I never exactly made the story public knowledge. But it was true. It happened to me, and I survived it."

"I'm interested," Bartholomew said. "Can you tell *me* the story?"

"It's about my brief stint as a real estate investor."

"And?"

I went on to tell Bartholomew the story. This was right before the Great Recession hit, when people were making money hand over fist in the real estate market. Seriously, these people were making a killing, buying houses and selling them a year later at ridiculously higher prices. A friend of mine in the office was doing it. Next thing I knew, he traded in his Ford Taurus for a brand-new Maserati. "How is it done?" I asked him. He told me there was nothing to it; all I had to do was buy some houses and hold on to them for a year. He said the economy would do the rest. He said the real estate market was unstoppable, and I figured it made sense. I had seen prices going up and up, and what was the worst that could happen? Maybe the prices would reach a peak, but I'd still have assets left that I could sell to get my money back. Real estate, what could be safer?

So, I bought four houses in Mission Viejo. They were occupied by tenants who were paying good rent. The bank barely required anything from me; it was like they were loaning pretend money. I could've bought more if I'd wanted to. It was great. Who knew that an everyday artichoke on a fixed salary could so easily become a real estate tycoon! I kept my eye on the market as the months went by, and sure enough, the houses were appreciating. And then it happened. It was like someone flipped a switch, and everything changed. The Great Recession hit, and the real estate market went upside down. Before I knew what was going on, my four houses were worth about half what I'd paid for them.

To make things even worse, three of the four tenants moved out, breaking their leases and leaving me with nothing to pay the mortgages. All three of them left me with a mess. The carpets were ruined, and all the rooms needed paint, and there were broken doors and leaking faucets. It was going to cost me a fortune to get the houses back on the rental market, and meanwhile, rents plummeted. There were too many empty houses and not enough tenants. My venture into the real estate business had turned into a very real nightmare. I never did calculate how much damage this recession had done to my retirement accounts; I didn't want to know. It made me sick to my stomach. It took me years to recover, and I learned some very valuable lessons; the first lesson was if it seems too good to be true, it probably is.

Bartholomew laughed and asked, "Did Pamela know about all of this?"

"Of course," I said. "But we kept it to ourselves. No one wants to broadcast to the world that they are a failure."

"No," Bartholomew said, smiling. "You've got to keep up appearances."

"I guess," I said.

"But you did tell Nate."

"I did," I said. "I wanted him to understand that we all make mistakes at one time or the other, and sometimes, they are *big* mistakes. The question isn't whether you've made a mistake. The question is what will you learn from it, and how will you move on with your life?"

"Or will you feel guilty?" Bartholomew said.

"Yes," I said.

"And will you get down on yourself?"

"That too."

"Precisely what I've been trying to teach *you*."

I thought about this for a moment and then said, "I guess you're right. But it's interesting, isn't it? It's so easy to see how others are wrong or misguided, but it's so difficult to see the same errors in your own behavior."

"Ah," Bartholomew said.

"Ah, what?"

"Ah, but we're just getting started."

I mentioned Jeff Anderson earlier, but you probably don't remember him. Jeff is a friend I've known since high school. We were good friends back then, and we've kept in touch over the years. It's nice to have a friend you've known so long. Jeff married his high school sweetheart, a girl named Arlene Jacoby, and they stayed married until three years ago when they finally divorced. They had a daughter named Janice who is Nate's age. Jeff remarried, hooking up with a girl named Vicky who is just a few years older than Janice. It seemed kind of weird to me, but who knows? It must work for them; otherwise, they wouldn't have done it. I met Vicky once, and she seemed nice enough. And I'm glad she makes Jeff happy.

Pamela and I had just finished eating dinner when Jeff called. His timing was great; his call got me out of doing the dishes. I took my phone to my study, sat down in my chair, and put my feet up on the desk. "So, what's new with you?" I asked.

"Just touching base," Jeff said.

"How's Vicky doing?"

"She's a fireball, Rick. She's doing great. Marrying her was the best thing I ever did for myself. I can't imagine what my life would be without her. She always has us doing something or going somewhere. Before I met her, I had no idea what it was like to have such a thirst for life. Did I tell you she got promoted? Her boss is head over heels in love with her work, and he promoted her to senior account executive. Now she's in charge of her own accounts at the agency. She has four people working under her, and she's getting paid twice as much. Their clients love her. Her boss loves her. Everyone there loves her to death."

"That's good to hear," I said.

"She's also been lecturing."

"Lecturing?"

"She's been a guest speaker at several local colleges. Her boss got her the gig, and she's made quite a reputation for herself."

"That's great," I said. "And how is Janice doing?"

"I'm so proud of her, Rick."

"Is she still working as a commercial artist?"

"She is."

"And her love life?"

"Ah, I thought you'd never ask. She's been going with a man she met at a Starbucks. Can you believe that? At a Starbucks? It turns out this guy is some hotshot real estate developer, and the guy is worth a fortune. Maybe you've heard of him? His name is Clayton McKenzie. He builds subdivisions in San Diego County, and his developments have won all kinds of awards. Ever since the recession ended, Clayton has been going gangbusters. Janice thinks he's going to ask her to marry him soon. He bought a new car for her. A brand-new Mercedes. Can you believe it? He wouldn't have bought a car if he wasn't serious, right? I should hook you up with him. You guys could talk about houses. I think you'd get a kick out of meeting him."

"No doubt," I said. "How are your mom and dad doing?"

"They're getting old, to be sure, but Dad told me they've never been happier their whole life. Their age has slowed them down a little, but I've got to tell you—you'd never guess they were both in their late eighties. You know what they've been into lately? They've suddenly discovered music. No pop music, or rock 'n' roll, or country, but classical music, as in Bach, Brahms, and Mozart. Dad took up the piano, and Mom plays the cello. You should hear them. They're really quite good. Me? I never cared much for classical music, but I love listening to Mom and Dad play. It's inspiring, and I'm glad they've found something that they both love and enjoy doing. I swear, they're going to live forever."

"And your sister?"

"She still chief of oncology over at Mercy. She took off a couple months with her husband to travel Europe. She got back last month. She still has pictures to show me. What a life, right? Taking a couple months off? Traipsing around Europe without a care in the world. Like kids. I should've been so lucky when I was working. Of course, now I can do anything I want. I love being retired. Life is good. But how are you doing? Enough about me. How are the kids?"

"They're doing great," I said, and I asked myself, *Why am I lying?*

"Is Zach still making those sculptures?"

"Actually, Zach is moving on. He wants to do something with computers. He's very excited about it, and he's going back to college to get a degree in computer science."

"That sounds promising," Jeff said.

"We're so proud of him," I said. "He's a smart kid, and he's doing well in school. He always was smart. It's not that his art venture was a waste of time. He was selling sculptures and making a name for himself, but I guess he just decided that it was time for a change. More power to him. Life is so full of opportunities, and I'm glad to see Zach reaching out to take advantage of them."

"What school is he going to go to?" Jeff asked.

"He got into USC, but he's decided to do a couple years at a community college. To save us some money, you know. Then he'll transfer to USC."

"And Nate?"

"Nate the entrepreneur," I said.

"Wasn't he working for that guy who does all the infomercials? For those inventions?"

"He was," I said.

"What's he doing now?"

"He's on his own. He's doing the same thing, but now he has his own ventures."

"Ah," Jeff said.

"He's hooked up with an inventor who has all kinds of great ideas. I think the two of them are going to go far. It's been a little rough going at first, but Nate's a trouper. You know Nate. There's no keeping him down. The kid is a bottomless pit of energy and optimism."

"I always knew Nate would make it big."

"Same here," I said.

"And Pamela?"

"Pamela is doing fine. She keeps busy. She's always got a hundred projects going. But you know, I think she finds great satisfaction in seeing our boys do so well. You always wonder when you're a parent. Am I doing the right thing? Am I raising my kids right? Is there something I'm missing?"

"Tell me about it," Jeff said.

"Then you do know what I mean?"

"I do," Jeff said. "And how's your mom doing? It's been years since I've seen her."

"We just moved Mom into an assisted-living facility. She didn't want to move at first, but she needed to. She's getting too old to take care of herself alone. We asked her if she wanted to move in with us. Pamela and I were all for it, but Mom said no, that we didn't need some needy old lady living with us. So, I found a great facility for her. And do you know what? She loves it there. She's making all kinds of new friends and taking part in the activities. They always have things for her to do. And they keep her mind agile and her body in good shape. And the food there is great. Every other Saturday, Pamela and I have dinner with her in the cafeteria. We've met some of her new friends. Great people. And the staff there is great too."

Chapter 16

Balancing Act

I had an interesting visit with my mom. I went over to her place at about seven. She had eaten dinner, and she hadn't been drinking. Good thing. The drinking seemed to have stopped for now, and it was a relief to see her behaving herself.

When I arrived, Mom was watching *Wheel of Fortune*, and she was dressed in her bathrobe. "Still checking up on me?" she asked.

"Just being a good son," I said. "How are things going?"

"They're going."

"Did you go to your exercise class this morning?"

"I did," Mom said.

"It's important for you to keep active."

"Did you know tomorrow is your father's birthday?

"I knew that," I said.

"He would've been ninety-six."

"Wow," I said.

"He was a wonderful man, Rick. I know he was strict with you boys, but he loved both of you. He only wanted what was best for you. He tried so hard."

"That's good to know."

"Do you know what he told me right before he died?"

"No," I said.

"He said he loved me. And then he said, 'Do you know what life is? It's a balancing act between doing your best and accepting that you are only human.'"

"He said that?"

"He was more human than he wanted to let on. I guess that was his way of telling me he was sorry."

"Sorry for what?"

"Do you remember Jennifer Comeau?"

"Vaguely," I said.

"We had her over at the house several times. A couple times for dinner. She was an administrative assistant at work who your father took a liking to. She was fifteen years younger than your dad and very attractive. Nice personality. I guess I can't blame him. She nearly ruined our marriage."

"What did she do?"

"I don't think she did it intentionally. She seemed like a nice person. Moral. Intelligent. She knew right from wrong, but your father, God rest his soul, fell head over heels in love with the woman. It wasn't that he didn't love me, but the two of them were drawn to each other. The situation seemed innocent enough at first, and I could understand the workplace friendship. And what was I supposed to do? Pretend that your father would never be attracted to another woman for the rest of his life? So, I put up with it. Your dad would talk about her, and I would listen. Your dad would work late in the office just to be around her, and I kept myself busy while he was gone. I was hoping it would pass, like a temporary fever. I kept telling myself that things would cool down and get back to normal. But, no, it got even worse."

"Worse how?" I asked.

"Your father had an affair with Jennifer."

"An affair? *My* dad?" I laughed at the absurdity of it, and then I realized my laughter was inappropriate.

"It was awful," Mom said.

"How old was I?"

"You were eleven, and Ralph was fourteen."

"Wow," I said. "I had no idea."

"It was kept from you. You had no way of knowing."

"So, what happened?"

"I finally confronted your dad about Jennifer. I told him I knew everything. Of course, I didn't know *everything*. But by telling him that, well, it was like hitting him over the head with a sack of bricks. He had thought it was his secret, and now the cat was out of the bag."

"What'd he say?" I asked.

"At first, he denied it and said I was imagining things, but I wouldn't let him off the hook. I told him that either we both had to be honest—or I would be asking him to pack his things and leave. He was floored. He'd been living in a fantasy world, and now he was suddenly being forced to face facts. I wasn't the one who had to make a decision. I didn't have to do anything. I was the victim. 'You love her, don't you?' I said. He wouldn't answer my question. I knew he had told her, but he didn't have the nerve to tell me."

"And?" I asked.

"He opted for me."

"Just like that?"

"It took a few days. I gave him time to think it over. Honestly, I don't think he ever deliberately meant to hurt me. I felt for him because he was a victim too. He was a victim of his own heart. Poor, rational man."

"So, he dumped Jennifer?"

"He put an end to their romance. I wouldn't say he dumped her. I'm sure he was very gentle with her. I wasn't there when he gave her the news, and I promised him I wouldn't interfere. But he did it. He told her. She quit her job a week later, and that was the last I ever heard of her."

Of course, I thought about Janet Jones, my own indiscretion. Do you remember Janet? Who was I to pass judgment on my father? Were we cut from the same cloth? Was I more like my dad than I realized? It was weird. I'd never thought of my dad being capable of losing control, of being anything less than responsible, of carrying on with a younger woman and being caught by his wife. Not *my* dad. "Why are you telling me all this now?" I asked.

"I don't know," she said.

"There must be a reason."

"Maybe as you're older, you let down your guard."

"What does that mean?"

"All these years, Rick. It seems like for all these years I've been trying so hard to pretend. I've never really been honest. I've always wanted to believe I was above the fray. But you know what? I think I'm tired of it. It requires too much energy, and at my age, energy isn't easy to come by. And what is the point? No one is perfect. Who am I trying to kid? Myself? I know better. It's all okay, every misguided thread in the cloth. Every stray bullet. Every missed opportunity. Your father had it right when he passed away. Life *is* a balancing act. It's a lesson I learned way too late in life. It's something you need to know, that often it's okay just to be human."

"Your mom and dad were wise people," Bartholomew said. We were in the car, on our way home from Mom's place. Bartholomew was sitting in the passenger seat, fiddling with the automatic window button, making the window move up and down. "They didn't have these when we were kids," he said.

"They had them on Cadillacs," I said. "They might have had them on Lincolns."

"But now practically every car has them."

"It's the forward arrow of technology."

Bartholomew laughed and looked out the windows. "Look at all the people. Driving their cars and walking down the sidewalks. Coming in and out of buildings with shopping bags and briefcases. Even flying overhead in jetliners, eating little pretzels and drinking Diet Cokes. They are everywhere you look."

"Yes," I said.

"Have you ever stopped to think about it?"

"About what?" I asked.

"So many languages. So many fashions. So many perfumes—and so many hairstyles."

"Okay," I said. I didn't really see where Bartholomew was going with this.

"Pick a card, any card."

"A card?" I asked.

"A card, a life, a philosophy, a religion."

"You're not making any sense."

"Oh, but I am," Bartholomew said. "It's amazing is what it is. No, it's more than amazing. It's stupendous. It's the greatest show on earth! It is at once as intimate as an atom and as large as an entire galaxy. A poem only scratches the surface. A full-length novel barely contains it. A canvas can't do it justice, and a symphony orchestra only squeezes out a few notes of it. Nearly eight billion people, Rick. Eight billion swirling combinations of dreams, loves, aspirations, foibles, strengths, weaknesses, fears, misunderstandings, insights, habits, addictions, and aversions. And here you are, a sixty-four-year-old guy named Rick Harper, driving home in your car after checking up on your mother. Rick, the son. Rick, the husband and father. Rick, the *you*."

Bartholomew had finally stopped playing with the automatic window. He had his hands folded in his lap, and he was looking straight forward. The car ahead of us stopped for a red light, and I stopped behind it. "A lot of traffic this evening," I said.

"There is," Bartholomew said.

"I should've told Mom about the boys," I said.

"I thought you didn't want to."

"I didn't."

"But now you're changing you mind?"

"I'm conflicted. On one hand, I don't want to upset her. But on the other, I don't like holding back. It isn't fair to her. She should know that Zach's in rehab, and she should know about Nate. They're her grandchildren. I think she has a right to know what's going on in their lives."

"You're not being honest," Bartholomew said, and this took me a little by surprise. He wasn't usually so blunt.

"You don't think I'm being honest?" I asked.

"You might not want her to worry. That might be a part of it, but the *real* reason you've been keeping the truth from her is that you think she'll see their problems as a result of your shortcomings as a father. You think she'll judge you. You're worried about what she'll think."

I thought about this and then said, "In a way, maybe you're right."

"In a way?" Bartholomew said, laughing.

"You think I spend all of my time worrying about what other people think of me?"

"I do," Bartholomew said.

"I don't think that's entirely accurate."

"You have a very high opinion of yourself, thus a very low opinion."

"What does that even mean?"

"You imagine that you're perfect, or that you should be perfect, and then you topple backward when you find out you aren't. You do a lot of toppling."

"I know I'll never be perfect."

"Do you?" Bartholomew asked.

"Of course I do."

"Then why do you get so upset at the prospect of other people noticing and recognizing your shortcomings? Why does it bother you so much?"

"I don't know that it does."

"You're not being honest with yourself."

"No?" I asked.

"Take tonight. Your mom just got done telling you about your father's affair with his young administrative assistant. She revealed a part of her life to you. Maybe for the first time in her life, she was truly honest with you. It couldn't have been easy. She said she was just letting her guard down, but there was more to it than that, wasn't there? She was sharing an embarrassing weakness in her life with you that you previously knew nothing about. Did she care what you thought? Of course she did. But she took a chance that you would be understanding and see your father and her as human beings rather than as make-believe role models. And how did you respond?"

"I listened."

"Did you tell her you were glad she told you?"

"I don't think I did."

"Did you thank her?"

"No," I said.

"Did you tell her about Janet Jones? Did you share your own embarrassing foray into infidelity?"

"I didn't," I said.

"It's not like you didn't have the perfect opportunity. The door was wide-open. All you had to do was swallow your false pride and walk into the room. Surely, you're not going to say you were trying to protect her?"

"No," I said.

"All these people," Bartholomew said.

"Pardon me?" I asked.

"Eight billion people on this planet. Just think of it. It's a little hard to believe. Continents, countries, counties, and cities. Houses and office buildings. Shopping centers and hospitals. All these *people*! All of them going about their business, earning money to buy groceries, to pay the rent, to pick out clothes to wear. Making friends and enemies. Making appointments with doctors. Strolling through parks and watching baseball games. Watching TV. Reading books. Sleeping in beds and snoring at the end of the day. What makes you think you're so special? Where did you ever get the idea that you had to be the one unique person in the world who had to be perfect? Is that really what you think people expect from you? Do you really think your world would collapse if others saw you for what you are?"

"I suppose not," I said.

"Food for thought," Bartholomew said.

I looked to my right, and Bartholomew was gone. The passenger seat was empty.

When it came time to pick Zach up from rehab, Pamela and I drove there together. It was kind of weird. We were excited to be getting our son, but we also had no idea what to expect. Would he act different? Look different? Talk different? Who knew what kind of effect rehab would have had on him? Maybe he would thank us, maybe he would resent us, or maybe he would be no different at all.

"What do you think he'll be like?" I asked Pamela as I drove.

"I don't know," she said.

"Do you think he'll be any different?"

"I don't know what to expect."

"I'd like to think he got something positive out of this experience."

"Of course he did," Pamela said.

"You're optimistic."

"I am," Pamela said. "Zach's a good kid."

"Doesn't it feel like it's been longer than a month?"

"It does."

"I hope Zach isn't angry."

"It was for his own good."

"He came to me with the problem, right? He was looking for a solution. I asked around."

"He's not going to resent us," Pamela said

I thought for a moment and then said, "Do you think he should be living with us for a while? So we can keep an eye on him?"

"That would be nice."

"I don't think it's a great idea for him to go back to his house in Costa Mesa. Too many triggers. Too many negative memories."

"You'll have to ask him."

"I will," I said.

"And maybe you should ask his counselor. You know, to get a professional opinion."

"That's a good idea," I said.

CHAPTER 17

FAITH

We arrived at the Pines at five-thirty. I parked the car in the gravel parking lot, and we walked to the main office. Sure enough, Zach was there in the lobby with his packed suitcase. He was sitting on one of the threadbare sofas. He stood up, grabbed his suitcase, and smiled. "You made it."

"Of course we did," I said.

"You look like you've lost weight," Pamela said.

"Maybe a few pounds."

"Are you ready to go?"

"I'm chomping at the bit," Zach said.

"Let's do it," I said, and the three of us began to walk out of the lobby. Just as I pushed open the door, Zach's counselor appeared from one of the offices. He had even more tattoos than I remembered, and his hair was slicked back like he'd just gotten out of the shower. He looked like a convict, like someone out of a TV show.

"Good luck, Zach," he said.

"Thanks," Zach said.

"He's a good kid," the counselor said to us. "We liked having him here."

"That's good," I said.

"Thanks for all your help," Pamela said.

"Yes, ma'am."

"Do you need anything else from us?" I asked.

"No," the counselor said. "He's all checked out."

"One day at a time," Zach said to the man.

"That's it," the counselor said.

Then we were out in the parking lot. We stepped to the car, and I opened the trunk for Zach. He dropped in his suitcase and slammed the lid shut. We all climbed into the car, and Pamela let Zach sit up front. I started the engine, and off we went.

"Your counselor seems like a nice guy," I said.

"He was good," Zach said.

"It's good to have you out."

"It feels good to be out."

"Have you had any dinner?"

"No," Zach said. "They eat at six."

"What do you feel like?"

"There's a McDonald's near the freeway. I remember it from when you dropped me off."

"McDonald's?"

"I'm dying for a Big Mac and fries," Zach said.

"Then McDonald's it is."

"Was the food there any good?" Pamela asked.

"It wasn't anything to write home about," Zach said. "I don't mean that it was bad. It was definitely edible, but they served the same old stuff over and over. And I like eating when I want to eat. Breakfast was every morning at seven, and lunch was at twelve. And dinner was at six. It was hard being on such a strict clock-ruled schedule. If I was hungry, I'd have to wait, and if I wasn't hungry, I had to eat. It could become pretty annoying."

"I think they were trying to create some structure in your life."

"I know what they were trying to do, but that didn't make it any less annoying. I like to eat when I want to eat."

"Did you make any friends?" Pamela asked.

"Oh, yeah," Zach said. "I made some friends."

"Was your counselor helpful?" I asked.

"He was a good guy."

We were all quiet for a while, and we finally reached the McDonald's by the freeway. I parked, and we all walked into the restaurant. It was busy, and we had to wait in a long line. Finally, we ordered. There were plenty of chairs and tables, and Pamela and Zach picked one out while I waited for our food. When it was ready, I took the bags and drinks to the table. "This must be their busiest time of day," I said.

"It's amazing how many people come to these places," Pamela said. She was not a fan of fast food.

"Nothing like a Big Mac and fries," Zach said, opening his bag and removing his food.

"Mom and I have been talking," I said.

"And?" Zach asked.

"We've been thinking that you might not want to move back into your old house. You know, with so many memories. With so many triggers. It might be too easy for you to fall back into bad habits."

"It's a thought," Zach said.

"You can stay at our house tonight."

"And not go home?"

"You can stay with us and think about it. Until you decide what you want to do."

"What am I going to do with my old place?"

"How long is your lease for?"

"It's month to month."

"So, you can move out whenever you want?"

"I can," Zach said.

"I mean, living with us is one option. You could also find a nice place somewhere else."

"What am I going to do with all my stuff?" Zach asked. And by stuff, he meant all his junk artworks. There were rooms full of the stuff, and the yard was also full. And the garage was overflowing.

"What do you *want* to do with it?" I asked.

"I don't know," Zach said.

"I could keep paying the rent on the house until you decide what to do with everything. I mean, not like forever, but for a while. Until you decide."

"In the meantime, you could live with us," Pamela said. "We just don't think it's wise for you to move back into that house right after getting out of rehab."

"Then there's the question of school," Zach said. "I called the community college, and the next semester doesn't start for a couple months. What am I going to do for two months to keep busy? I guess I could see if my old boss still has work for me, but I don't know. Working construction for him might also be a trigger."

"You could work for us," Pamela said.

"Doing what?" Zach asked.

"We've been meaning to redo the landscaping in the front yard for several years," Pamela said. "And the garage is a disaster. Someone needs to clean and organize the garage. And some of the rooms in the house need to be painted. I don't know when the last time was that we painted."

"It would only be temporary," I said.

"Until you get your footing," Pamela said.

"We're not telling you to do this. We just want you to know it's an option."

"I appreciate that," Zach said.

"We just want to help," Pamela said.

By the time we were done eating dinner at McDonald's, Zach had decided to take us up on our offer. He told us he was serious about quitting weed for good, and he wanted to do everything possible to make it a reality. Moving back into the Costa Mesa house was not a good idea. Ten years of bad habits. And all that artwork. Zach didn't say this, but I think all his art projects symbolized the Zach-the-artist lifestyle he so much wanted to put behind him. Junk? I didn't dare call it that, but that's what it was. And I think Zach was realizing this too, although it was hard. I said to Zach, "When I was a child, I spoke and thought and reasoned as a child. But when I grew up, I put away childish things."

"Who said that?" Zach asked.

"It's from the Bible," I said.

"But who said it?"

"I haven't got the slightest idea," I said. "Some biblical dude with a robe and a beard."

Zach laughed.

That night, we brought Zach to our house, and he took his suitcase into his old bedroom. We all watched a little TV before going to bed.

"I'm glad Zach is here with us," Pamela said to me in bed.

"Yes," I agreed.

Do you know what I missed most with the new Zach? I liked that he had some goals, and I liked the fact that he wasn't wasting his time smoking weed. But he lacked something that he used to have. The best way I can put it is to say that he lacked self-confidence. He no longer had a hot fire burning in the chambers of his heart; it had been doused.

Actually, I noticed this with both of my boys. Just a couple years ago, you couldn't get either of them to shut up about their lives. They were going somewhere. They were excited about everything. Opportunity was practically breaking the door down. But now they were both at phases in their lives where the world had more or less kicked the crap out of them. Was this normal? I couldn't remember having the same problem when I was their age.

"Do you know what your problem is?" Bartholomew asked.

"My problem?" I asked.

"You overestimate your importance, and you discount your influence."

"What does that even mean?"

Bartholomew laughed. We were in my den, early in the morning. As usual, I had been working on a poem. Bartholomew didn't show any interest in reading what I had written, but he was interested in me. He was always interested in me.

"You look at your boys, and the first question you ask is, 'Where did I go wrong?' You survey the past, and you survey the present. Surely, if you were a better father, your boys would be doing better. They'd be successful. They'd be happy. That fire you noticed? It would be roaring in their hearts. They'd be breaking records and astonishing their peers. They'd be the darlings of their superiors and the pride of their communities. What do you have instead? You have one boy who's terrified of what life will be like without his drug of choice and another boy who's bankrupt and defeated."

"So, what did I do wrong?" I asked.

"You're asking the wrong question."

"How can I know what the right thing to do is if I don't know where I went wrong in the first place?"

"Who says you went wrong at all?" Bartholomew asked.

"Clearly, things did not go well for either of my boys."

"Because of you?"

"In part, I guess. I'm their father."

"Some of the happiest and most successful people in the world come from the worst parents. Some of the most miserable people come from very good parents. It's a fact of life. Yes, it matters what kind of parent you are, but it has far less influence on your children than anyone would like to admit. There are so many factors. There are friends, relatives, teachers, bullies, teammates, brothers, sisters, celebrities, athletes, newscasters, bosses, fellow employees, students, authors, television stars, scriptwriters, pastors, cartoon characters, neighbors, customers, clients, doctors, lawyers, judges, nurses, barbers, store clerks, and hundreds of other people who will—no doubt about it—affect your child's life and mold his attitudes, emotions, opinions, goals, and enthusiasm. You may be a parent, but honestly? You are just a drop in the bucket."

"Wow," I said.

"And that's just the beginning."

"The beginning?"

"Pick a son, any son. First and foremost, there is his brain. It is unique. It is all his own. It is one of a kind out of eight billion functioning brains on the planet. And it's a crapshoot. Who knows what you're getting when you bring a child into the world? It's not like you were able to order the thing from a catalog or off a menu, and yet if you're honest about it, it *is* your child. Do you know much about psychiatry? Have you heard of the *DSM*? It's a book they put together describing mental illnesses in an attempt to get a handle on them all. More than a thousand pages—and those are just the hiccups they've been able to put into words! Yes, the human brain. A hundred billion neurons. Each neuron with thousands of connections to other neurons. And each of us with our own version of the apparatus, thinking, feeling, deciding, running, jumping, planning, scheming, and desiring. You want to take responsibility for it? You want to blame yourself when things go wrong? In the scope of things, you are a grain of sand on a mile-long beach. You are an asteroid in a galaxy of stars. Certainly, you are much less than you think you are."

"I've never thought of it quite that way."

"I know," Bartholomew said. "Not many parents do."

"This makes me feel so—"

"Helpless?"

"And hopeless," I said.

Bartholomew stared at me for a moment, and then he said, "But there is love."

"Love?" I asked.

"Do you love your boys?"

"Of course I do."

"And do they love you?" Bartholomew asked.

"I think they do."

"You're their father, for crying out loud. Of course they love you."

"Okay," I said.

"Love is life-giving. It is the air in your lungs. It is the blood pulsing through your veins and arteries, the messages traveling through your nervous system. It's the water running through rivers and streams, the fish in the sea, the corn in the fields, and the sun that burns in the sky. It's the cloud that drops rain, the wind that spreads seeds, and the bees that pollinate the flowers. In your case, love is the bond that makes your words and actions significant to your children. They see you. They hear you. True, you are but just one in a million, or a billion, or a trillion voices, but love makes it possible for you to break through the noise and confusion. Never underestimate the power of words spoken by a parent to a child. Never underestimate the light. Never underestimate the influence of a parent's actions. You should never sell love short—not ever."

"Then I *do* influence them?" I asked.

"If you act out of love."

I thought about this and asked, "But how do I know if I'm doing or saying the right things?"

"You have to have faith."

"Faith in God?"

"No, no, not faith in the supernatural. I'm talking about faith in yourself. Faith in life. Faith in good outcomes. You have to have faith that there is more to the world than we know and faith that the world—despite all of its evils and weird aberrations—is a place where men and women *can* find happiness. You have to have faith. If you don't have it tucked safely in your pocket, then there isn't any point to anything, and given the miracle of life—life being what it is—a faithless world would make no sense at all. Things *have* to make sense. Nothing this extraordinarily rich, complex, and prodigious could possibly exist without a force of good behind it. We can imagine it; therefore, it must be. We can see it, so it exists. We can feel it, and we feel it because it is real. Have faith, Rick. You will not be let down."

Chapter 18

A Good Excuse

Bartholomew was good at giving pep talks. But the thing about pep talks is that they can get you all riled up and enthusiastic for about an hour, or maybe for day, or maybe for a week, but sooner or later, the weight of reality is upon you, pressing on your shoulders and spirit. For me, the effect of the talk was only temporary. It was like drinking a glass or two of wine and feeling all warm and fuzzy, only an hour or so later feeling empty and lethargic. Yes, Bartholomew told me to have faith, and I wanted to have it. I wanted it in the worst way, but my life was not cooperating. It was saying, "You've got to be kidding!"

Listen, it was only a couple weeks before Zach started smoking weed again. A couple of weeks. All that time and money for a mere couple of weeks. He didn't flaunt it; in fact, he tried to hide it at first. I don't know where he got the stuff or where he found the money to buy it. I thought we were keeping a pretty good eye on him, and I knew he didn't have much cash. But addicts are devious. I first noticed the odor of marijuana in Zach's bathroom. He'd smoke it in the shower stall and blow the smoke into the running water. Then I noticed it in his bedroom where he tried to blow the smoke out the window. I didn't want to believe it, and I told myself I was imagining things. You know, like I imagined Bartholomew. But then Pamela noticed it too, and I had to ask Zach. "Have you been smoking weed? Mom and I think we can smell it."

"Just a little," Zach said.

"A little?"

"Not like I used to."

"I thought the idea was to stop completely."

"I don't want to do that."

"You don't want to do it? I thought you did."

"I was just going along with the program because I didn't know any better. But, honestly, I can't picture myself giving up weed completely. Forever is an awful long time, and there's nothing wrong with smoking a little now and again—as long as I don't let it get out of hand like before. As long as I'm aware of what I'm doing."

"And if it interferes with your life again?"

"Then I'll stop."

"And I suppose you'll need to go to rehab again?"

"No, no, once in rehab was enough. Don't worry about it, Dad. You worry too much. Mom worries too much. Let me find my own way through this. There's no need to overreact to what is otherwise not much of a problem. Kids my age smoke weed all the time. I met kids in college who smoked weed every day, and they were pulling down all As and Bs. I can do it. Let me prove to you that I can."

This was not what I wanted to hear. I told Zach that I would have to think about it. But what was I going to do if I couldn't accept Zach's plan? Kick him out of the house? Make him move back to Costa Mesa, which would even be worse. Let him smoke weed every day and fail at school again? Let him throw away his life? I had options, but I didn't like any of them. And I'll tell you the truth—I was angry at Zach for putting me in this position.

When I told Pamela that Zach *was* smoking weed again, she was terribly upset. Her baby! Her marijuana-smoking baby! "Surely there is something you can say," Pamela said to me. "Surely there is something you can do. You're his father. He's your son."

Meanwhile, things at work were taking a turn for the worse. Do you remember Ned and Sylvia Waterhouse? They were the couple with the laundry room. I had fixed the problem, and the project was moving forward. The engineers were busy doing their thing with my design, and I was adding in all the details and notes for the contractors. Then, out of the blue, John Wiley got a letter from Ned. It was sent certified mail, and John had to sign for it. The Waterhouses' attorney was copied on the letter, and so was I. Apparently, Ned and Sylvia had taken my design drawings to a third party, an architect in Laguna Beach to whom Ned was referred to by a friend. The name of this architect was Chad Peterson. I wasn't familiar with Chad, but Ned assured us in his letter that Chad was an expert when it came to the design of upscale homes. Ned said he had asked Chad to take a look at my design and make comments and provide relevant suggestions. Well, hell. This clown proceeded to write a twenty-two-page letter on the subject.

Chad's letter was included with the letter Ned sent to John, and in so many rather angry words, Ned was insisting that all the problems Chad noticed be addressed and rectified. Not just addressed and rectified, but addressed and rectified free of any additional charge. "These are all aspects of the design that Rick should've been aware of. Either his head was someplace else when he was working on our project, or he is just incompetent. Which is it? It doesn't matter to us. We are not looking to file a lawsuit, but we do demand that the necessary corrections be made to our plans before your drawings are submitted to the city for a permit—and before the job goes out to bid."

I had lost them. Sometimes everything goes great, and you have your clients in the palms of your hands. And sometimes you lose them. They turn on you, and they no longer trust you. You'd think that at the age of sixty-four, I'd have developed enough self-confidence not to let something like this bother me. You win some, you lose some. Not every client is going to think you walk on water, and not every client is going to like you. I think it all started with that stupid laundry room and Sylvia's friend who said I'd made a mistake. That was the seed. Then it grew in Ned and Sylvia's heads—how many other mistakes did this joker make on our project? Then along comes some up-and-coming architect named Chad Peterson, trying to make a name for himself. At my expense.

I folded up Ned's letter and stuffed it into my top desk drawer. It was about three in the afternoon. I went to John and told him I needed to take the rest of the day off.

John had Ned's letter on his desk. "We'll address this tomorrow?" he asked, tapping the letter with his finger.

"I'll be in first thing tomorrow morning."

"It was the laundry room," John said, shaking his head.

"Yes," I agreed.

"You think you have everything under control, and then it comes out of nowhere."

"So it seems," I said. I didn't really want to talk about it. I just wanted to go home.

"What time will you be in tomorrow?"

"I'll be here at eight," I said.

"We'll go over this then."

"Okay," I said.

"I'm sorry this happened."

"So am I."

"Maybe I should hand this project off to someone else in the office."

"We'll talk tomorrow," I said.

"Take care of yourself."

Take care of myself? John had no idea. I had a client who now hated me and a son at home who couldn't make it two weeks after rehab before going back to his weed. I had a wife who expected me to solve Zach's problem and a mother who was wasting away in a prison for old people. And Nate? That was another story, a story that would explode just a few hours later.

At a little after eight, my phone rang. Pamela and I were watching TV. It was a very confusing night. I don't even remember what show we were watching. When I took the call, I figured it was probably a telemarketer, and I was prepared to hang up on them. I get a lot of spam calls, but it wasn't a spam call. It was Nate's wife, Emily, and she was very upset. I could immediately sense the stress in her voice.

"You have to come over here," she said.

"What's up?" I asked.

"Nate's gone off the deep end."

"How so?" I asked.

"He's locked himself in the bathroom. He has a gun, and he says he's going to shoot himself!"

"Jesus," I said.

"I called 911."

"You called the police?"

"I didn't know what to do. Now I don't know if I did the right thing. But someone has to talk some sense into Nate. He's very upset. Oh God!"

"What?" I asked.

"The police are at the front door."

"We'll be right over," I said. I could hear Emily walking to the front door and letting the cops in. Then I ended the call and told Pamela, "Let's go!"

"What's going on?" Pamela asked.

"Nate's threatening to kill himself. That was Emily. He's locked himself in the bathroom. Emily called the police."

"The police?"

"Emily didn't know what to do. She called 911."

When we arrived at Nate and Emily's house, there were several police cars and an ambulance. We rushed in through the front door and found the interior of the house filled with first responders.

"Who are you?" one of the cops asked me, and I told him we were the parents. "He's still in the bathroom," the man said.

Then Emily appeared from the hallway, her face wet with tears. "They're trying to get him out," she said.

"And?" I asked.

"He won't put down the gun. Oh, God, I don't know what to do. I didn't see this coming. I have no idea what to do. He won't even talk to me!"

There were four cops in the bedroom, and one of them was near the bathroom door. I guessed he was the negotiator, and I assumed he knew what he was doing. He held his hand up to keep Pamela and me at bay. Then he whispered, "We're making progress."

"They've been at this for half an hour," Emily said.

"Try to keep quiet," the cop whispered. Then I heard Nate's voice. He seemed rational, but obviously he wasn't. But his voice *was* calm, and I took this as a good sign.

"I'm in too deep now," Nate said.

"You made a mistake," the cop said. "We all make mistakes. I make mistakes all the time. Problems come, and problems go. Don't solve a temporary problem with a permanent solution. I don't think you really want to do that."

"How do you know what I want to do?"

"Give us a chance, Nate."

"A chance to do what?"

"A chance to help you," the cop said. "Give your wife a chance. Give your parents a chance. Your mom and dad are here now."

"My parents are here?"

"They just got here."

"What the fuck? I thought this was a free country. Can't a guy put a bullet through his head without attracting an audience from all over town?"

"They're here because they love you."

"Too late."

"No!" I shouted.

The cop put his finger over his lips, telling me to keep quiet. Then, to Nate, he said, "I know you don't really want to do this. Let's just call it off for now. Put the gun on the floor."

"Jesus," Nate said, and he began to sob.

"Is the gun on the floor?" the cop asked.

"It is," Nate said, still sobbing.

"Can you unlock the door for me?"

There was a pause. Then the door unlatched, and the cop carefully pushed it open. There was Nate. He was standing in the middle of the bathroom with the gun at his feet and tears rolling down his cheeks. Two of the cops rushed in and put him in handcuffs. He was so pathetic. He had been defeated. For now, the mayhem of the emergency was over, but all I felt besides a big sense of relief was my concern wondering, *What comes next?*

Nate would be taken to a local mental hospital for a seventy-two-hour observation period. My son, the pillow entrepreneur. My son, the mental patient.

The cops and paramedics finally left the house, and the driveway was empty again.

Pamela and I stayed with Emily for a couple hours, trying to console her, trying to make her understand that none of this was her fault.

"I just never saw it coming," she kept saying.

I told her that none of us did. I told her not to blame herself. "These things happen," I said. "It doesn't do anyone any good to point fingers." I felt like I was reciting lines from a corny TV screenplay, saying what was expected of me. *Of course these things don't just happen,* I thought. *Suicide? And where the hell did Nate get the gun?*

When Pamela and I drove back home that night, we barely said a word to each other. I think it's fair to say we were in shock. It's hard to explain how something like this makes you feel as a parent. It's like someone has just let all the air out of your tires. You feel flat, spent, and like you've been run through an emotional wringer. A gun? The police? And poor Emily. The girl was really beside herself. I believed her when she said she didn't see anything like this coming. I mean, I knew that Nate was upset, and a little down, but I certainly didn't see anything like this happening. It wasn't like Nate to give up, to call it quits.

When Pamela and I got home, it was after our bedtime. Pamela went straight to the bedroom, and I watched a little TV to get my mind off things. I don't remember what I watched, but I wasn't paying attention anyway. The dialogue went in one ear and out the other, and all I could think of was seeing my son standing in his bathroom with the gun on the floor and tears streaming down his cheeks. And then there was the mad scramble to handcuff him and drag him out of the house. "Be careful with him," Pamela said. "Don't hurt him."

I poured myself a scotch and water. It was mostly scotch with a dab of water. I drank the concoction rather quickly, and then I poured another one. I was not the sort of person who drank every time he had a problem, but this night, I felt like I deserved it. I owed it to myself to get good and drunk. I would let the alcohol erase my tapes and cleanse my soul. Then I would drift off to sleep. A forgetful sleep. A deep and groveling sleep. And this is exactly what I did. After my fourth drink, I was seeing double. I had no idea what was happening on the TV. It was some stupid story. Some crime show. Good guys against the bad guys, police sirens, and cops chasing suspects down fire escapes. And then *boom*, I was asleep. I was out like a light.

Pamela was up at seven, but she didn't wake me up. She let me sleep. I did not wake up until a little after nine, and I sat up on the sofa, rubbing my groggy eyes. Reality slowly made its way into my consciousness, and I looked at my glass on the coffee table, wondering how much I drank. And I had a headache! Not a bad one, but a headache nonetheless brought on by my previous night's drinking.

"You were drinking last night," Pamela said.

"I was," I replied.

"I don't blame you. If I hadn't been so exhausted, I would've joined you."

"I've got a headache."

"How much did you drink?"

"I don't remember exactly."

"Take a shower and some Tylenol," Pamela said. "You'll feel better."

"Jesus," I said.

"Your phone was ringing. I put it in the kitchen so it wouldn't wake you."

"My phone?"

"John Wiley has called several times."

"I was supposed to meet him this morning at eight," I said. "He was expecting me."

"It's not like you don't have a good excuse for missing the meeting."

"Yes," I said. "A good excuse."

Chapter 19

Progress

I explained missing the meeting with John by telling him I had some personal issues that kept me up late at night. I didn't tell him anything about Nate's suicide fiasco. I just said that something important came up and that I had to address it. John didn't press for details. I think he knew that if I wanted to talk about it, I would've been more forthcoming. He was letting me have my space, which I appreciated. But John also said he went ahead and handed Ned and Sylvia's project over to another designer at the firm. I told him I thought I could've handled it, but John said, "It's just better this way. I'd rather have you being productive."

He was right, of course. Nothing good could come out of me working any further with Ned and Sylvia. At first, I felt a little insulted, and then I felt relieved.

In the meantime, Nate's evaluation proceeded at the mental hospital. The time went by quickly. Then next thing we knew, they were releasing Nate back into the real world, back to his life with Emily. They wanted him to hook up with a psychiatrist, someone who could help Nate continue to work through his issues. It was a good idea, but it also made me feel like an outsider. You would think I could help him, but it was decided that a third-party psychiatrist was the best route to take, and the doctor at the mental hospital gave Nate three names to call. He told Nate to meet with each of them and choose whichever shrink he felt the most comfortable with. "This is all for your benefit, and you should be in the driver's seat. If you don't like any of them, keep looking further. It's important that you find someone you can trust."

Nate picked the first name on the list and told us, "I like this guy."

"Didn't the doctor tell you to check them all out?"

"I don't need to look any further."

Either Nate simply didn't want to keep looking—or he genuinely liked the doctor. His name was Dr. West, and he had an office in Tustin.

"Can I meet him?" I asked.

"I'll ask," Nate said.

"I don't mean to interfere," I said. "But I would like to meet him."

"I don't think he'll object."

And he didn't. Nate told Dr. West that I would like to come to one of the sessions, to get to know the doctor. Nate told me that the doctor said, "Your dad's probably as curious about me as I am about him."

I asked Pamela if she wanted to come, but she declined. "I think it's better if just you went. You are his father. I'm just a mom."

"Maybe later," I said.

"Yes," Pamela said. "Maybe later."

Don't you think it's sort of weird how Pamela was taking a back seat in all this? Maybe she would get more involved later, but she was letting me take charge for now. Maybe she thought it wasn't her place. Maybe she thought mental problems were a father-son thing. Pamela was smart and insightful, and her opinions would certainly not have been discounted. Anyway, whatever the reason, I would be the first to meet with Dr. West. The appointment date was set after Nate had been seeing the doctor for a little more than a month. When I showed up at the doctor's office, the two were already talking.

"You must be Rick," Dr. West said, standing up from his desk.

"I am," I said.

"Nice to finally meet you."

"Likewise," I said.

"You probably have some questions."

"Not specifically," I said. "I just wanted to meet the man who's in charge of helping my son."

Dr. West laughed. "Nate and I have had some good conversations. I've been trying to get to know him. He's a good kid."

"He is," I said. "Do you have any children?"

"No," the doctor said. "Never got married."

"Ah," I said.

"Married to my work, you know. Typical workaholic. But that's another story."

"Sure," I said.

"I think I can help you guys out."

"He's been helpful already," Nate said.

"That's good to hear."

"I understand you have another son."

"We do," I said. "His name is Zach, and he's three years younger than Nate. He's living at home now."

"At home?"

"He had some difficulties with marijuana."

"Ah," the doctor said.

"He went to rehab for a month. He's doing great now. He should be back on his own soon."

"Liar," Bartholomew said, laughing. "You just want this guy to think you're a good dad."

Bartholomew? I looked to my right, and sure enough, Bartholomew was sitting in one of the chairs across the room. What was he doing there? What did he want?

"What are you doing here?" I asked Bartholomew.

Bartholomew laughed again and said, "No one can see or hear me but you."

"Pardon me?" the doctor asked. "What am I doing here?" Oblivious to Bartholomew, he thought my question was directed at him.

"Never mind," I said.

"We're all here for the same reason," the doctor said.

"Of course," I said. My face was a little warm. I felt slightly embarrassed.

"Just pretend I'm not here," Bartholomew said.

I tried not to look at him. I certainly didn't want to make the mistake of speaking to him again. I certainly didn't want the doctor to know I was seeing and hearing things that weren't actually there.

Well, the rest of my conversation with Dr. West went fairly well. Bartholomew didn't interrupt, and the doctor seemed like a straight shooter. He told me he planned to do a lot of digging into Nate's past in an effort to find the roots of his difficulties. "Somewhere in your son's life history, he has developed the idea in his head that a failure in one venture equates to a total failure of his life. It isn't rational, and it obviously isn't healthy. We're going to do everything we can to identify the source of the problem and take the steps that are necessary to deal with it. Since you are his father, your input could be invaluable. I'd also like to get your wife to attend a few sessions. Her input could be just as helpful. And I'd like to meet Nate's brother."

"Okay," I said.

"There won't be any finger-pointing. My goal is not to blame anyone for Nate's difficulties. My goal is only to help him understand why he feels the way he does. If we can explain the whys, we will be able to tackle the crux of the problem. But you can't know what to do about a problem until you know why the problem exists."

"I guess that makes sense," I said.

What did I know? I didn't know squat about psychiatry or therapy. I never took a psychiatry class in college, and I didn't have any friends who were psychiatrists or psychologists. And I'd certainly never been to see one myself. But what the doctor said did make some sense. Describe the problem, and you were 90 percent there solving it. I had learned that in college. Define the problem, and you have your answer. I was taught that in one of my architecture classes.

"Do you have any questions for me?" Dr. West asked.

I thought for a moment, and then I said, "Not really."

"You're okay with all this?"

"I think so," I said.

And that concluded our meeting. The doctor said, "It's always good to have family members involved. You'd be surprised at how uncooperative some families are."

"I just want to help."

"I can see that." The doctor smiled, stood up, and reached for a handshake.

I shook his hand and said, "I guess you two want to continue talking."

"Thanks, Dad," Nate said.

"I'll leave you men at it," I said.

I stepped out of the office and closed the door behind me. How did I feel? To be honest, I wasn't sure. It all *seemed* okay, and the doctor was a nice enough guy. And Nate seemed to be comfortable with the man. But? There was always a but, wasn't there?

I expected to see Bartholomew appear in the passenger seat of my car on the way home, but he didn't. I was alone, navigating my car though traffic and recounting my conversation with the doctor.

A week after I met with Dr. West, Zach received a call from an art dealer named Ernest Patterson. Since I have never been a big follower of the art scene, the name didn't mean much to me. But it meant a lot to Zach. Ernest had several galleries in Los Angeles where he featured up-and-coming artists from Southern California. Ernest was known for making stars out of otherwise struggling artists. He called Zach to see if he'd be interested in a three-month exhibit featuring his works at his gallery in the Beverly Center. Honestly? I'd never seen Zach so pumped up about anything. Forget about school. Forget computers. Forget this pesky sobriety thing. *Now* Zach was getting somewhere!

"I'd be crazy to say no," Zach told me. "It's the break I've been waiting for."

I was torn. I should've been happy for my son, but that's not exactly how I felt. I mean, yes, I was happy that someone like Ernest was taking an interest in Zach's work, and I could see what Zach saw, a confirmation that the past ten years of his life were not a waste of time. "That's great," I said. I wanted to say, "Just when you were finally going somewhere with your life, here comes Ernest Patterson. An art dealer. A con man, making you think that all that junk you've been assembling is worth money to a horde of pretentious art collectors who wouldn't know art if it jumped up and bit them on the nose. Here today—and gone tomorrow. Fads. The latest thing. Getting your hopes up." But I didn't say any of that. I thought I should've, but I didn't.

So, you tell me, was I a good dad or a bad dad? No doubt Dr. West would have something to say about it. I was supportive of my sons, no matter what they did and where they wanted to go with their lives, but did I provide any guidance, wisdom, or basic living skills? Junk sculptures? Sound pillows? My dad must've been turning in his grave. My dad was so proud of me and my goal to become an artichoke. Someone who would be respected and be successful in the more traditional sense of the word. I would have a steady job, a wife, children, a mortgage, and car payments.

I would live in a nice house. We would go on vacations. Every weekend, I would mow and edge the lawn.

Zach jumped at the art exhibit opportunity. He met with Ernest at his Costa Mesa house, and they picked out the sculptures that Ernest thought would be best for the exhibit. Zach was on cloud nine, and Nate was improving too. His sessions with Dr. West were beginning to light a fire under him. And me? I had nothing to do with any of it. I was just an observer. A bystander. Bartholomew had told me that *this* was my chance to do something, to be a good father, to make a difference in my sons' lives. He said I was lucky that life had given me such a grand opportunity. That is what he said, isn't it?

The next time I talked to Bartholomew, I told him how I felt. We were in my den, early in the morning. Bartholomew laughed and said, "Sometimes, by doing nothing, we do everything. Sometimes a zero equals a thousand. Sometimes the best way to help a plant grow is to just give it water and watch the thing take off at its own pace."

"I don't even know what any of that means," I said.

"Distorted thinking again."

"You keep saying that," I said.

"Have you come up with an eighth story for me? You were supposed to tell me ten stories. By my count, you have only told me seven."

"I haven't thought of another one."

"Heard any good jokes?"

"Not recently," I said.

"Let me ask you a question," Bartholomew said.

"Fine," I said.

"You like to write poetry, am I right?"

"I do," I said.

"So, tell me, who is of the most importance to a poem? The writer or the reader?"

"The writer of course."

"Not the reader?"

"Well, certainly the reader is important," I said.

"What is the goal of a poem? To keep the writer busy with syllables and rhymes—or to touch the heart and imagination of the reader?"

"I would say the goal is to stir something up in the reader."

"Then the reader is more important?" Bartholomew asked.

"Maybe the reader is of equal importance."

"Do you think the reader ought to be responsible for making revisions to a poem as he or she sees fit?"

"No," I said.

"Why not?"

"Because that's the poet's job."

"Well, now we're getting somewhere," Bartholomew said, laughing.

"I don't get it," I said.

"You should be proud of yourself."

"Proud?"

"You were helpful," Bartholomew said.

"I feel like I've done nothing."

"You showed your support. Do you remember the story you told me about your school talent contest, how you hit those bad notes in your recital? What did you try to play? It was Beethoven's *Sonatina in G Major?* Imagine this. What if your parents had listened to the performance and said afterward, 'That was really spectacular! Good job, son. Not an easy piece to play in front of a hundred people. You've been getting better and better.' Do you think you would've gone on to take more lessons? You enjoyed the piano, didn't you? It wasn't that you weren't good enough; rather, it was the expectation that you had to be perfect. Do you know how many people in the world give up on things because they're not perfect? And who is perfect?"

"I see," I said. "So, it was my parents' fault that I gave up on the piano?"

"It was no one's fault," Bartholomew said. "We all do it. Parents do it to children. Husbands do it to wives. Friends do it to each other. Your parents did it to you, and you've done it to your sons. But I will say this with confidence—you are making progress."

CHAPTER 20

SHE'S THERE

Bartholomew's definition of progress must've been different from mine. I'd have considered myself to have made progress if the world were becoming clearer to me. If it were coming into focus, if all the fuzzy edges were sharpening. But I felt like the more I talked with Bartholomew, the looser things were getting and the less likely it was that I would be able to pin him down on anything.

Socrates said, "To know is to know that you know nothing. That is the meaning of true knowledge." Maybe Bartholomew *was* teaching me, and maybe Socrates was right.

I made my decision. I now knew what I was going to tell Bartholomew for my eighth story. It was not something embarrassing. Or self-deprecating. Or overtly self-critical. Rather, I would tell Bartholomew about a time where *I* was wronged by someone else. A time when *I* was the victim—and when someone else should've felt guilt. After all, there was plenty of guilt to go around for all of us, and there was no good reason for me to carry it all on my shoulders.

This incident occurred when I was in college. I was taking an architectural drawing class. I was good at drawing. It was one of the reasons I wanted to become an architect. These were the days prior to CAD systems where your skill with a pen or pencil in hand was essential. I miss those times. Every drawing was a reflection of its author and had its own personality, and drawing was such a personal thing. One person, one pen or pencil, one sheet of drafting paper—a labor of love, wit, and skill. Drawings for buildings were works of art themselves.

Anyway, drawing skills were essential to being a good architect, and I took my drawing class seriously. We were assigned all kinds of challenging projects. Over the semester, we would keep our drawings in a personal chipboard portfolio, and at the end of the semester, we would turn the portfolio over to our professor to be graded. It would take a week or so for the grading, and our grades would then be made available. As was done every semester, the best of the best drawings from the portfolios would be posted in display cases on the first floor of our building. I got an A in this class, which was not much of a surprise. Like I said, I was good at drawing. But when the drawings were posted in the display cases, I saw one of my drawings up with my name erased from the bottom—and replaced by another student's name. The name of the kid was Ben Flowers. I had received an A in the class, so I guess it didn't really matter, but I was furious. Who was this kid?

It turned out that Ben must've been in a different drawing class that had many of the same projects we did. He must've rifled through the portfolios that were turned in and nabbed my drawing, erasing my name, adding his, and sticking it into *his* portfolio. Like I said, I was furious. The nerve of this idiot, stealing my drawing and taking credit for it. I would have never known the difference had the professor not picked this particular drawing out to be displayed. Obviously, I had recognized it. It was mine!

So, what to do? I went back to my dorm room that afternoon, and I told my roommate about the drawing. He asked me what grade I got in the class, and I told him I got an A. "Then what are you so worried about?" he asked. "You got your A, and you probably helped some poor slob from failing the class."

"But the drawing is on display," I said.

"It must've been good."

"It was," I said. "And I should be getting credit for it. My name should be at the bottom."

"No one cares," my roommate said.

"*I* care," I said.

My roommate just laughed.

I got different reactions from different people when I told them about the stolen drawing. For example, a girl I was dating at the time told me I should tell the professor about it. "What kind of creep steals someone else's drawing and tries to take credit for it? Turn the creep in and let them lower the boom on him. Teach him a lesson—and put your name back on the bottom of the drawing."

Another friend said I should find Ben Flowers and confront him without getting the professor involved. "Tell him you know what he did. He's probably not going to come clean with the professor, but at least you'll be able to guilt the guy. He should know that you know. Maybe he'll think twice before doing it again."

It was interesting.

You know, I could really have caused problems for Ben Flowers. Cheating was probably grounds for suspension. Or maybe expulsion—if this wasn't his first time. Seriously, what kind of person would do something like this? Someone who was desperate. Someone who was worried about passing his classes. Maybe just someone who had made a dumb mistake. I got my A, right? I got what I needed out of the class, and what's that they say in sports—no harm, no foul? It could've been that, or maybe I was just afraid of a confrontation? Whatever it was, I never did go to the professor, and my drawing hung in the display case with Ben's name on it for more than a month. I didn't run into Ben at school. I had no idea who he was. Maybe he transferred out, flunked out, or changed majors, but I was glad I never met him. It would've been awkward. Not sure what I would've said to him other than, "You owe me a thank you."

As someone who was raised in fear of his dad's leather belt, I've just never been a big fan of holding people strictly accountable for their mistakes. Is this a flaw or an attribute? The answer to this question has never been clear to me. Not that I've thought about it much, but sometimes I do.

When I told this story to Bartholomew, he scratched his head and said, "Interesting story."

"You like it?" I asked.

"I do," he said. "You displayed compassion, empathy, and forgiveness—all good things."

"Do you think I let Ben Flowers walk all over me?"

"In a way, you did. But it's okay."

"I know my dad would disagree with you."

"And your mom?"

"Not sure," I said.

"And Pamela? Does she know about this?"

"I don't think so," I said. "I don't think I ever told her about it."

"How do you feel now? I mean, now that decades have passed, now that you're older and wiser."

"Honestly?"

"Yes," Bartholomew said.

"I don't feel older and wiser. I think I felt older and wiser when I was younger, much more so than I do today."

Bartholomew laughed.

"Does that make sense to you?" I asked.

"It makes perfect sense," Bartholomew said.

"You know, I don't get any great pleasure in holding people accountable for their mistakes. Some people love it. Some people love pointing fingers, but I've never gleaned much joy from it."

"Do you think it's because you're weak?"

"Weak?" I asked.

"Afraid of confrontations? Afraid to take the bull by the horns? Afraid to call a spade a spade?"

"Maybe it is," I said.

"Or maybe you're just a good person."

"Good?"

"Understanding and forgiving?"

"I'd certainly like to think that I'm those things."

"But you're not sure."

"No, I'm not."

It occurs to me that I haven't really told you much about Pamela. I've told you a few things, but there is more to say. In a world that was complicated, confounding, frustrating, and infuriating, she was the lone island with the calm weather. She was a white sand beach. She was the ripe coconuts falling from the trees. She was the person you'd want to take a vacation with. In fact, she was the vacation. She was the day after a storm.

Everything in your life could seem to be going wrong, but a word from Pamela, and the sun would come beaming through. Was she pretty? God yes. In my eyes, she was the prettiest thing I'd ever seen. Everything about her, the perfect size and location. Everything, the perfect shape. Even as she grew older, her age did not diminish her looks; she only looked more beautiful, wiser, and more compassionate as each year went by. You might ask, "So what did she do besides look so good?" She was always there, and she was there for me and for our sons. She was there for her parents—and for my parents. If our lives were to be described as a building, she was the foundation that kept all the beams, posts, trusses, and girders from being swallowed up by the earth. She was never fickle. She was never devious or selfish, and family meant everything to her.

So, how did she ever come to fall in love with someone like me? You know what? I've never really understood it. Except maybe that's the way things were meant to be. They sometimes say that opposites attract, and maybe they're right. And I have thought about it. What would she do without someone like me to contend with, to constantly glue back together, to work on and support? In a weird and unfair way, I have given her life meaning. And our boys? And our crazy parents? They were just the icing on the cake.

What did she do with her time? She helped out family members when a helping hand was needed. She cooked our dinners, washed the laundry, and kept the house clean. She kept our flower beds weeded and filled with flowers. She worked part-time as an assistant and legal secretary for a local attorney named Chip Olson. Sometimes he kept her pretty busy, and sometimes he didn't. It depended on his caseload. Pamela wasn't breaking any glass ceilings or proving that a woman was the best man for the job. I don't think she cared about any of that. She just wanted to be useful to others, and what's wrong with that? There was no greed, subterfuge, or guile running amok; she was just someone who wanted to help.

I've written poems about Pamela. Quite a few of them, actually. I've never had her read any of them; in fact, I've never shared them with anyone. Maybe it was because I thought they were too corny, too enthusiastic, a little over-the-top? And maybe they were, but they were heartfelt. One of them was titled "She's There," and it went as follows:

She's There

It rains buckets, days and nights;
Thunder cracks and lightning strikes.
Trees and plants are sopping wet;
The streets are soaked. Ceilings get

Dark from dripping membrane leaks.
It seems like it has been weeks
Since the sun shone and the sky
Was blue. I can only sigh

And wait patiently for her
To blow the storm away. We're
Stronger together than we
Are apart. Then I can see

She's there,
Sunlight in her golden hair.
She loves me,
And I love her.

When I am consumed with fear,
And look into my mirror
Seeing it at my shoulder,
Much uglier and bolder.

Vacant eyes and gnashing teeth,
Its sharp knife out of its sheath.
Since forever, and eyes so old
They will make your blood run cold.

I wait terrified, for her
To chase the ghoul away. We're
Stronger together than we
Are apart. Then I can see

She's there,
Sunlight in her golden hair.
She loves me,
And I love her.

Someone wrongs me, and I'll boil.
I'll cook them in boiling oil.
I'll gouge out their evil eyes;
I'll feed their corpse to the flies.

I'll torture their pets and blow
Down their house by the hairs of
Their porcine chinny chin chins.
But hold on, it's me again,

On my knees, praying for her
To chase away the hate. We're
Stronger together than we
Are apart. Then I can see

She's there,
Sunlight in her golden hair.
She loves me,
And I love her.
There's nothing worse than the ache
Of being alone. I'll take
The first warm body that comes
My direction, and then some.

Anyone to fill the hole.
I am a burrowing mole,
Pushing dirt with my feet,
Looking for something to eat.

God knows how much I need her
To chase away the pain. We're

Stronger together than we
Are apart. Then I can see

She's there,
Sunlight in her golden hair.
She loves me,
And I love her.

Sometimes I imagine the end
End of the world, all red
With blood and smoldering ash.
Doctors on crutches who ask,

"Where does it hurt?" Looters run
From building to building, some
Laughing, and some are crying,
And everyone is dying.

I relax when I see her
Appear from the rubble. We're
Stronger together than we
Are apart. Then I can see

She's there,
Sunlight in her golden hair.
She loves me,
And I love her.

And for that moment in time,
It'll all be okay.

If you understand this poem, you probably have a good understanding of how I feel about Pamela being in my life. Sure, sometimes I don't show my appreciation for her, and sure, I often forget she's even there. I'll tell you something interesting. Do you know how fast the earth is spinning around the sun? We are traveling around the sun at sixty-seven thousand miles per hour. Hard to believe, right? Wouldn't you think everything would just blow right off its surface? Yet here we all sit, stand, and lie down like it is nothing of note. Sometimes the most amazing and outrageous circumstances feel like nothing. We forget. We move on. We live our lives.

CHAPTER 21

THE TOILET

It was depressing. I hated being depressed about anything, but the more I thought about it, the more it bothered me. Mom, living in that assisted-living facility with all the underpaid South-of-the-Border help and gossiping inmates. And the food. "We have hot dogs on Fridays," Mom said to me—as if it was something to look forward to. "They have good hot dogs here. All beef, and I like the buns they use."

She was fading.

It broke my heart, but there was no better word for it. The crisp lines were disintegrating, and the color was waning. There was now something in her voice that was telling me, "I am turning back into nothing, Rick, and everything is about today. Dreams? Those are for people who have a future. Sure, I dream, but when I dream, I dream about the past. You, Ralph, and Dad in the old house with the big yard and the swimming pool. The cars. The garage full of junk. Our Boston terriers and the plans we made."

Now it was hot dogs on Fridays. *Wheel of Fortune* on the TV. A stack of magazines and brochures on the coffee table. People kept sending them in the mail, like she actually took the time to read them. She looked at the pictures. She didn't dare throw away any of them.

It isn't easy seeing your parents grow old. You want to do something, but what can you do? I asked Bartholomew about this, and as usual, he laughed. "What's so funny?" I asked.

"You are," he said.

"I am?"

"Always lamenting over all the things you cannot change, while letting the things you can change pass you by."

"Meaning?"

"Meaning, yes, your mom is growing old, but today? Today she is still quite alive. Maybe she isn't the mom you remember from your youth, but she is no less alive. These visits you pay her to check up on her are exactly that. They are visits to check up on her, to make sure she isn't drinking again, to make sure she's behaving herself. She knows what you're doing. She's old, yes, but she isn't dumb."

"And what would *you* do?" I asked.

"I would include her in my life. I would make her feel like she was a part of my world—and not just some feeble old woman who needs to be tended to in her final days. Bring her back into the fold. She deserves at least that. She's your mom."

I thought about this, and then I asked, "Are you saying I should be honest with her?"

"That's exactly what I'm saying," Bartholomew said. "To an extent."

"But she could die any day. I don't want her to leave us thinking that everything is a mess."

"Bah," Bartholomew said.

"Bah, what?"

"Everything is not a mess."

"No?" I asked.

"Everything is just everything. Everything is how it's always been—and how it always will be."

"Whatever that means."

"Life is life," Bartholomew said. "Up, down, sideways, and inside out—there's always something. Things are always happening. Hearts are always being broken. Dreams are always being shattered, and runners are always crossing the finish lines. Old stars die, and new stars are born. Inventors come up with new ideas, and scientists make discoveries. Butterflies crawl out of chrysalides, and the sun flies across the sky, over and over. Who are you to deny your mother a part in it? Bring a handful of the real world to her—and watch her eyes light up!"

About two months after Nate's suicide threat, he started talking to his grandpa. Not my dad, since my dad was dead. He was talking to Pamela's dad, Chet. The old guy still lived up in Oregon with Pamela's mom, and they talked on the phone. I don't know how much Nate told him about recent events. Maybe he told him everything.

Nate suddenly got it in his head that he was going to become a car salesman. He told me so. He was very enthusiastic. "Grandpa said they can bring in six figures a year. Grandpa knows the owner of a Ford dealership in Riverside. He says he can get me a job there."

"You want to sell cars?" I asked.

"Not forever. But it will keep me busy in the meantime, and I'll be bringing in money."

"In the meantime of what?" I asked.

"Until I come up with a new idea."

"What do you know about cars?"

"They have four wheels and an engine."

"You're going to have to do better than that," I said, laughing.

"Of course I'll study up."

"Have you told your mom about this?

"I may have mentioned it."

"What did she say?"

"She said she'd stand behind me, no matter what I decided to do."

The next thing I knew, Nate was meeting with Chet's friend about the job. And no surprise. He was hired on the spot, thanks to his grandfather's recommendation.

"Chet says you're a fireball," Blake said. Blake was Chet's friend. They went way back. "That's just what this place needs. A fireball. Someone who can get the dealership hopping."

Nate was thrilled.

Nate was back in the mix. Meanwhile, what about me? That's what I wanted to know. I felt a little out of breath. So much had happened over the past several months. The waves had been knocking me around the rocks long enough. I was dizzy, sore, and bleeding at the knees, and I needed a break. Dry land was what I needed. I needed to towel myself off and soak up some sun. I needed to close my eyes. I needed to drift off into the soft sounds of a day at the beach. Maybe a squawking seagull. Maybe the lonely horn of a distant buoy. Maybe some children laughing and playing—at that age when life hasn't grabbed them by the throats yet. Playing catch with a Frisbee. Making sandcastles. Playing tag. Skimboarding on the glassy shoreline. Or maybe just the sound of a plane flying high overhead, pulling a banner or taking its passengers—who knew where?

"I need a vacation," I said to Pamela.

"So do I," Pamela said.

"We need to get out of here."

"For a week," Pamela said.

"That would be nice."

"Where do you want to go?" Pamela asked.

"Not far, but a week at the beach would be nice."

"The weather has been good."

"Maybe up north," I said.

"Like where?"

"Like Santa Cruz. I've always liked that area. I have good memories of it. Remember our trip there?"

"When the boys were young," Pamela said.

"Good times," I said.

"That was a good trip."

"Just you and me. Santa Cruz, Aptos, or wherever. Just away from here. For a week."

"Do you want me to find a place?" Pamela asked.

"I'll find it."

"We could see if that same cottage is available."

"No," I said. "Something new."

And for the next three days, I searched the internet for vacation cottages near the beach. Finally, I found the perfect place. It wasn't cheap, but it looked very nice, and it was just a block from the ocean.

I told John Wiley that I would be gone for a week, and he didn't have a problem with it. I had no pressing projects in the office. Then we told everyone else, and they all told us to have a good time. "You promise you won't drink while we're gone?" I asked my mom, and she raised her hand like a five-year-old and recited her promise.

"You and Pamela deserve some time to yourselves," Mom said.

Did we ever.

We packed up the car. I locked the house, and I left the TV and several lights on so that it would look like someone was there. Pamela had our neighbor set up to bring in the mail, and we boarded our two cats at the vet. I never did tell you. We had two cats. We got them when they were kittens shortly after the boys left the house. The cats were well-behaved for the most part, and we had very little trouble with them. No wonder so many people had pets rather than children. The worst they ever did was claw at the rugs once in a while. They were indoor-outdoor cats, and a couple times, they caught mice and left the bloody heads on our front porch doormat. This kind of freaked Pamela out, but I explained that this was what cats did.

When we arrived at the cottage in Santa Cruz, it wasn't exactly what we expected. True, it was on its own private street, but the street hadn't been tended to for years, and it was full of potholes and edged with weeds. I guessed this was what they meant on the website by "nestled in natural surroundings." Weeds, potholes, and a few scraggly trees. Then we saw it. It was almost a joke. In front of our cottage, across the potholed street, was an old toilet. I kid you not, sitting out in the open—one filthy old toilet sitting in the weeds. "That's kind of gross," Pamela said, and I agreed with her. What would it have really taken to get rid of the toilet—and what was it even doing there?

We went inside the cottage, and it was nice. It looked just like the pictures. No complaints there. But I did get on the phone to call the rental agency. A very friendly girl answered the phone, and I identified myself.

"How is everything?" she asked. "Can I do anything for you?"

"It's all great," I said.

"You're in one of my favorite properties."

"Just one complaint," I said.

"Yes?" the girl asked.

"There's an old toilet in the front yard. Well, actually it's across the street."

"Oh, that," the girl said.

"We'd prefer not to see a toilet every time we stepped out of the house."

"I can see it from the kitchen window," Pamela said. She was standing in the kitchen. She had opened the blinds and was looking out the window.

"Can't you get rid of it?" I asked.

"It doesn't belong to us," the girl said.

"No?" I asked.

"It belongs to the owner of the duplex across the street from you. He was remodeling. It came from their old bathroom."

"And?" I asked.

"We've asked him to remove it. He says he's been trying to sell it."

"Sell it?"

"We can't very well just go in there and take his property."

"How long has it been there?"

"A couple of months. It'll probably be gone soon."

"Are they going to pick it up?" Pamela asked me. She was now in the family room.

"It doesn't belong to them," I said.

"I'll call the owner of the duplex for you," the girl said. "But I can't make any promises."

"I'd appreciate it," I said.

"Anything else I can help with?"

"That was it."

"We hope you enjoy your stay."

"Thanks," I said, and I ended the call.

Have you ever had something that stuck in your thoughts, something that rubbed you the wrong way, something that you just couldn't ignore no matter how hard you tried? For me, it was this confounded toilet. Every morning, when Pamela and I took off for a day at the beach, there it was. The toilet. A filthy, old, disgusting depository for bowel movements and urine, in the weeds, the first thing we saw each morning. And why? Because the idiot who owned the duplex across the street was too cheap to throw the thing away—and because the guy obviously had no class. Who in the hell leaves an old toilet in his front yard?

On our third day, I called the rental agency again and asked if they'd been able to reach the owner of the property across the street. It was the same girl on the phone, and she said she'd called, but that the man had yet to call her back. "I hate to sound picky," I said. "But this toilet has really got to go. It's not what we paid for. We paid for a vacation rental—not a cottage in the middle of a junkyard."

"I understand," the girl said.

"And?" I asked.

"I'll call him again. But I think he might be out of town. Usually he calls right back, but like I said, he could be out of town."

"Can't you just buy the damn thing from him and take it to the dump?" I asked. "How much does he want for it?"

"I don't know the price."

"Hell, *I'll* pay to have it removed," I said.

"We'll need to talk to him first."

"You can't just have it picked up?"

"It's not our property," the girl said.

Rules. I have a question. Why do people believe so fervently in rules when they have nothing at stake? As long as the situation isn't interfering with their lives, they behave themselves. What's that people like to say? "You can't see it from *my* house, ha, ha." To heck with everyone else. And what leverage did I have? I had paid the entire rental fee up front, a week before we'd even arrived. That was one of the requirements—payment in full, in advance. And no wonder! If I'd known I was going to have to look at a disgusting old toilet every day I stepped outside, I probably would've never rented the place.

I made several more calls to the rental agency about the toilet, each of them a little angrier on my part, but I got nowhere. I spoke to the same girl, and I spoke to her superior. I even went across the street and knocked on the doors of the duplex, but no one was living there. You know who I needed? I needed Bartholomew. Not because he could've told me how to get rid of the toilet by some clever maneuver, but because he could've set me straight.

CHAPTER 22

CIRCUS CLOWN

I finally told Mom the truth. About Nate, anyway. I had told her all about his Sleep Sound Pillow plans, and she had seen the infomercials a few months ago on TV. She asked me how things had gone. I didn't say, "Great! Nate made a killing—we're all very proud of him." That's what I would've said several weeks ago. Instead, I followed Bartholomew's advice and told her the truth. I told her that the pillow venture was an unmitigated disaster. I didn't tell her about Nate's bad checks or suicide threat, but I said, "The sales just weren't there, and Nate had to file bankruptcy. He really took it hard."

"Is he okay?" Mom asked.

"He seems to be doing better."

"You should've had him talk to your brother."

"Ralph?" I asked. "What would Ralph have to say?"

"He could've been helpful."

"How?" I asked.

"His experience."

"His experience with what?"

"Ralph went through the same thing his first time around starting up a business. You know, when he had to file bankruptcy."

"Ralph filed bankruptcy?"

"For his first car repair shop. I thought you knew. Maybe no one ever told you. You weren't very close to your brother back then, so maybe the two of you never talked about it."

"This is all news to me," I said.

"Don't you remember his first shop? It was called Street Wise Auto Repair?"

"It went bankrupt?" I asked.

"It was a mess. Your dad and I had to cover thousands of dollars of bad checks he wrote. Everyone wanted to sue him. He had to file bankruptcy. Your brother took it very hard. He was so down on himself. Dad spent months calming him down and talking him off the ledge."

"Jeez," I said.

"Bankruptcy is a very personal thing. It's not just a business failure. It's a personal failure. You've given your word to trusting people. You've made promises to them. Then, suddenly, you're telling them that your word was no good, that they're not getting paid, and there's nothing they can do about it. It's personal, Rick. It's *very* personal."

"I can't believe I didn't know anything about this," I said.

"Like I said, you and your brother were not very close at the time."

"So, what did Ralph do?"

"He was terribly upset."

"I can imagine," I said.

"But your dad worked on him until he finally got it through Ralph's head."

"Got what through his head?"

"That failure was a part of life. That failure, in one form or the other, is inevitable."

"Dad did that?"

"The whole thing was a learning experience for your father. And for me as well. You know, we tried to be good parents. We really did. If we could only go back in time." Mom paused for a moment and looked up at the ceiling. "Do you remember when you entered that talent contest in school, when you played Beethoven on the piano?"

"Of course I do," I said.

"Your dad and I were wrong."

"Wrong?"

"You hit a few errant notes. We should've encouraged you. We should've explained to you that *people hit wrong notes*. It happens all the time. We are only human beings, and human beings make mistakes because that's what being human is all about."

"Yes," I said.

"I'm tired," Mom suddenly said.

"Have you been sleeping okay?" I asked. "Maybe you're not getting enough sleep."

"I'm sleeping okay, but I still get tired in the afternoons. I think it's an age thing." Mom smiled, and then she closed her eyes. She had placed a pillow behind her head. The next thing I knew, she was sound asleep on her sofa. Her hands were folded in her lap, and the TV was still on.

I turned off the TV and covered Mom's legs and lap with a blanket.

And that's when Bartholomew appeared. He was sitting in the chair near to the patio door. "Out like a light," he said.

"She is," I agreed.

"It's funny, isn't it?"

"What?" I asked.

"How little we really know about each other. How little we actually talk. I mean, we talk all the time, but we don't say much of importance. Did you have *any* idea that Ralph had filed for bankruptcy?"

"I knew nothing about it," I said.

"All these years, and not a word."

"No," I said.

"And now here you are. You offered up a little truth, and you got a little truth in return."

"Seems to be," I said.

"Why are people so adverse to the truth?"

"I don't know," I said.

"Things are what they are. There's no getting around it, yet people are constantly going out of their way to convince each other that opposites are true. If it wasn't so painful to watch, it'd be hilarious. Yet I can't help but think of all the dread and guilt this lying causes. Will my wife find out if I had an affair? Will my teacher find out that I cheated on the last exam? Will my dentist learn that I don't really brush my teeth after every meal? Will my boss find out that I lied on the resume he used to hire me? Will my kids find out that, deep down, I'm a coward and have been ever since I was their age? Will the IRS notice that I didn't report any income from that side job I took? Will they find out that the car I've been deducting isn't really used for business? Will my neighbor find out that I'm behind in all of my bills? Will my mortgage company discover that I inflated my monthly income in order to qualify for the loan? There's no end to it. I could go on and on forever. Big lies—and little lies. Lies to others—and lies to ourselves."

I think I was genuinely happy back when I was in college, all four years of it. Comfortable with my classes. Getting along with my peers. Living away from home. My life was just beginning, and I had so many wondrous things to look forward to. And I didn't have to lie. No, I wasn't a liar, and I was too naïve to know if people were lying to me. Life was what it was, and it *was* good.

And I smoked. I was smoking a pack of cigarettes a day and enjoying it. Cigarettes made me feel good. Funny how the mind and memory work, isn't it? I was now a sixty-four-year-old man, wiser, presumably, and equating the carefree joy and excitement of my youth with the act of smoking cigarettes. That feeling of anticipation I got when I lit the end of my cigarette, that satisfaction I felt as I inhaled the first drag of smoke into my lungs. Ah, if you have never smoked, you probably don't know what I mean, but if you have smoked, surely you know exactly what I'm talking about.

It made perfect sense to me. Happiness equaled smoking cigarettes. Inhale, exhale. Gray smoke. Smoke rings. A pack of cigarettes was like a wallet full of cash. Two weeks after we returned from Santa Cruz, I pulled into our local gas station to fill my car. I knew exactly what I was doing. I wasn't just there for the gas. I stuck the nozzle into the side of my car and went into the convenience store. A small bag of potato chips and a sugar-free energy drink, and then I stepped to the counter. "Will that be all?" the lady asked, and I could hear the words leaving my mouth. Quickly, as if I was embarrassed, I asked her for a pack of Marlboros. And a lighter. I would need a lighter. She told me the total, and I poked my credit card in to charge the sale. She put everything in a plastic bag, and I took the bag back to my car. I replaced the gas nozzle, and I drove off with my booty.

I can't tell you how weird it felt, lighting up that first cigarette. It was a thrill. It made me feel happy. Ah, happy at last! Just me alone in the car with my chips, drink, and cigarettes, driving home with the window rolled halfway down to let out the smoke. The good old days, before marriage, before children, before jobs, before all the work traffic—just me and an endless blue sky full of promise and a horizon that had no end in sight.

Well, this smoking resurgence went over like a lead balloon with Pamela. When she discovered I was smoking again, the first thing she said was, "Are you kidding?" Then when she saw I was serious, she asked, "Is there something wrong?"

"Wrong?" I asked.

"Something making you want to smoke again after all these years? Your mom? The boys? Maybe me?"

"There's nothing wrong with you."

"What then?"

"I just want to smoke."

Pamela stared at me. She looked at me like she'd just discovered that I was an alien from another galaxy. "I don't get it," she said.

"Give me my space."

"Your space?"

It seemed like a reasonable thing to ask for. "How much do I really ask for?" I asked. "I do my share of the chores. I don't mess around with other women. I come home each night, and I write poetry in the mornings. I don't have any vices or bad habits. I'm in good health. All I'm asking for is to enjoy a cigarette now and again."

I wound up getting my way. Although to be honest, there wasn't a lot Pamela could do about it. I know she was just concerned for my welfare, and I couldn't exactly blame her for that. But I wanted to smoke. I didn't smoke in the house, and I seldom smoked in front of Pamela. And I never smoked in front of the boys or in front of my mom. I set up a chair and an end table with an ashtray in the backyard where I would smoke my cigarettes in peace. One after the other. Inhaling and exhaling, feeling pleased with myself and happy that I had stood my ground for *something*.

Two stories to go, numbers nine and ten. It was kind of surprising, that I had already told Bartholomew eight stories. I was having trouble even remembering what they were or why I had told them. What were they? There was the first story about running over that duck. What an awful story to tell. Then there were the stories about Zach and his rare steak, the failed trip to Mexico, and the muffed talent contest. I also told Bartholomew about the yard debris Ralph, Abe, and I dumped into the Elliots' swimming pool. Then there was the Las Vegas craps game story and the story about losing to that tennis hustler. And there was the story about my stolen drawing. Am I missing one or two? Maybe. It's hard to remember them all. But you know what? Stories are just stories.

Or are they?

Maybe there was a method to Bartholomew's madness. Was I beginning to see the light? Bartholomew called it "distorted thinking." I think that was the term he kept using.

He said I was making progress. So, was I? I think Bartholomew was right. My ninth story about myself would be different from the others. Okay, so maybe I wouldn't be a hero. But do heroes really exist? I mean, aside from the rare real-life exceptions and characters in the comic books, there are no *real* heroes. The truth is that we are all just human beings, with flaws aplenty. But we *can* be good, and we *are* capable of doing good things, setting good examples, even leading others to do the same. In other words, we're not *all* bad, and our redeeming qualities should be spotlighted and celebrated now and again rather than shaded by all the ugly and crappy things in our lives.

I'm not looking to be another Pollyanna, but I am looking to improve my outlook on life. And what is wrong with that? I know it can be done. I've seen it done. Not everyone in the world laments the way I do, and surely there are a lot of people in the world whose lives have been a lot worse than mine.

After about a month of smoking, I burned my last cigarette. I did not go to the gas station to buy more. I dropped my dirty ashtray into the garbage can with the rest of our refuse. What had I even been thinking—that smoking cigarettes would make me a happier man? It was laughable. I was a circus clown. I was the guy who got hit in the head ten times with the big rubber hammer. Ha, ha, poor pitiful me. Everyone laughed, not because I was funny, but because I was pathetic.

CHAPTER 23

WE NAMED HIM MAX

I was sitting in the family room, watching another old episode of *Star Trek* on TV. Pamela was at work that evening, working late with her boss on a case that was going to trial soon. They were defending a guy who supposedly had broken into an appliance store and made off with a ton of big-screen TVs. The DA thought he had a good case against him, but Pamela's boss thought otherwise.

"For sure, he's guilty," Pamela told me. "But I guess everyone deserves a defense."

Ah, our legal system.

In the meantime, Bartholomew showed up about halfway through the *Star Trek* episode. I put the show on pause, and Bartholomew took a seat on the chair near the china cabinet. "You still owe me some stories," he said.

"I'm ready," I said.

"Which story are we on?"

"Number nine, number nine, number nine."

"Turn me on, dead man," Bartholomew said, laughing.

"Yes," I said.

"By the way, I'm glad to see you gave up on the smoking."

"It was a dumb idea," I said.

"You were reaching, but you were reaching for the wrong thing," Bartholomew said. "But it's water under the bridge. Let's hear your ninth story."

So, I told my story. It started on a Saturday. It was a Saturday like any other Saturday. Pamela and I were driving home from a visit to my parents' house, and we had both boys with us. Zach was about eight, and Nate was eleven. We pulled onto the freeway, and it was clear sailing for a few miles until the traffic began to slow down a little. I didn't think much of it, until I saw the reason for the slowdown. There was a dog loose on the freeway, walking from lane to lane. The people were driving around it, careful not to hit it, but no one stopped. Meanwhile, the confused dog continued to meander about.

"Someone should do something," Pamela said.

"It looks lost," Zach said.

"Someone's going to hit it," Nate said.

"Jesus," I said. I knew what I had to do. There was no way I was just going to drive on and leave the poor dog roaming around lost on the freeway. I pulled over to the shoulder, and I got out of the car. Then I got down on my knees and said, "Here, boy!" I kept saying it until I got the dog's attention. I don't really know if the dog was smart enough to know that I was trying to save its life. But it did look at me, and it eventually came my way. "Come on," I said. "Come on before you get hit."

"He's coming," Nate had rolled down his window, and he was watching the dog. "Come on boy!" Nate said to the dog. "Just a few more steps."

Finally, the dog was at my knees. It was a friendly dog. His tail was wagging, and he seemed pleased to see me. I don't know why because I never was much of a dog person. "Let's see if you have a name." I checked the dog's neck for a collar and tag, but there was nothing.

"What are we going to do with him?" Nate asked.

"I guess we'll take him to the pound," I said.

"The pound?" Nate asked.

"If the owner is looking for him, he'll find him there. That's the first place he'll be looking."

"Can't we just take him home?"

"We don't know anything about this animal," I said.

"Aw," Nate said.

"Open the door. He can ride in back with you and Zach. We'll take him home, and I'll look on the internet for the closest animal shelter."

"Maybe he's hungry," Nate said.

"We don't have anything to feed him."

"We have some hamburger in the fridge," Pamela said. "Don't dogs like hamburger?"

"I guess," I said.

"Maybe we should stop at the store on the way home and buy some dog food," Zach said.

"The sooner we get him to the animal shelter, the better," I said. "His owner's probably worried sick about him."

"It wouldn't hurt to pick up some dog food," Pamela said.

"I guess we can do that," I said. "But I don't want you guys to get any big ideas. This dog belongs to someone else. You can't just take someone's dog."

I got back in the car, and I pulled into traffic. I looked in my rearview mirror and saw the dog in the back seat with my boys. He was panting and slobbering, and the boys were patting him on the head. The dog was so happy. You'd think he just won the lottery. I stopped at the grocery store, and Pamela went in to buy some dog food. She came back with a whole plastic sack of it. "I wasn't sure which one to get," she said. "So, I got one can of each. I also got him some food and water bowls. And I got him a toy."

"A toy?" I asked.

"A rubber ball with a bell in it."

We didn't even own this dog, and he was already costing us money. When we got home, the boys took the dog to the backyard while I looked up animal shelters. The main shelter was a place in Santa Ana. It wasn't exactly close by, but it seemed to be where everyone went. I went to the backyard to get the dog, to take him to the shelter. The boys were playing fetch with him and his new ball.

"He plays fetch," Zach said.

"Watch." Nate tossed the ball clear across the yard so that the dog could retrieve it.

"That's great," I said. "But it's time to go."

"Come on, Max," Nate said.

"Max?" I asked.

"We named him Max," Zach said.

"It's time for Max to go," I said.

"Can we come with you?" Nate asked.

"I don't see why not."

We all piled into the car with the dog, and off we went. Even Pamela came. I'm not sure what everyone was expecting. Have you ever been to an animal shelter? It was probably one of the most depressing experiences of my life: all those dogs in steel and concrete cages, hoping someone would pick them out, hoping someone would rescue them and take them home. The barking was unbearable, and so was the stench. Aggressive dogs. Shivering, cowering dogs. All kinds of pathetic no-one-loves-me animals, rows and rows of them. Angry eyes. Sad eyes. Rheumy eyes. Matted fur and limps.

"We're really going to leave Max here?" Nate asked.

"It's the best way of reuniting him with his owner," I said.

"This place makes me sick," Zach said.

I found an employee to help us, a pimply kid in jeans and a T-shirt. "We found him on the freeway," I said.

"What's going to happen to him?" Pamela said.

"We keep them for seven days," the kid said.

"And then?"

"If no one claims the animal, we … you know."

"What?" Pamela asked.

"We put it to sleep."

"You mean you'll *kill* Max?" Nate asked. He was obviously horrified.

"We have more dogs here than we know what to do with," the kid said.

"That's so sad," Pamela said.

"Did you hear that?" Nate asked me. "They're going to kill Max if we leave him here."

"His owner will pick him up," I said.

"He was loose on the freeway," Nate said. "Do you really think his owner cares about him?"

"You'd be surprised," I said.

Well, Pamela and the boys were relentless. I hate to say it, but they sort of ganged up on me. I mean, I'm not a coldhearted guy, but did we really want this dog becoming a part of our family? Sure, Max was a fine-looking animal. A German shepherd. I'd guess he was about three or four years old. Maybe five. And he certainly had a good disposition, but what was he doing on the freeway? Did he have a problem being fenced in? Was he a troublemaker in disguise? Was he one of *those* kinds of dogs? "If no one comes in here and picks him up in six days, can you call us?" I asked the kid. "We might take him home with us if no one claims him. We don't want to see him get the needle."

"We can try to do that," the kid said.

"Try?" I asked.

"There's a lot of dogs here to keep track of. Just between you and me, you'd be better off coming in here to check in person."

"Can we?" Zach asked.

"We can do that," I said.

"*Then* we can take him home?" Nate asked.

I didn't say yes, and I didn't say no. I just wanted to get out of that place as quickly as possible. The whole thing was very depressing. The fact that I had now promised to return in six days didn't excite me at all. But the boys were thrilled, and their enthusiasm waxed as each day went by. They marked the days on the wall calendar in the pantry. As each day passed, they drew an X on it. When the day finally came, I took the boys back to the animal shelter while Pamela stayed home. The boys were sure Max would still be there.

Well, wouldn't you know it? We walked the rows of cages full of forlorn dogs, and just as we were about done, there was Max, sitting by himself, next to an empty food dish.

"There he is!" Nate exclaimed.

The sound of Nate's voice immediately got the dog's attention. As Nate and Zach approached the cage, Max jumped up to greet them.

Did he really remember them? It was kind of hard to believe, but what did I know about dogs? Maybe Max was a lot smarter than I'd thought. In a way, it was very sad, and in a way, it was also heartwarming. I couldn't decide which, but the joy in this dog's eyes and his wagging tail were undeniable. Dogs. Only a total ogre could discount their emotions and burning desire to be loved.

So, Max became a part of our family. Pamela went to the store and bought a ton of dog food, a couple dog beds, and enough toys to keep Max busy for weeks. It turned out Max was already housebroken, which was a big relief. I installed a dog door to the backyard, which Max used all the time. We took photos of him. We vacuumed up dog hair from the floors and furniture, constantly played fetch with him, and scolded him when he barked at the neighbor's cat. At night, he would watch TV with us. Well, he didn't actually watch the TV, but he'd sit with us while we watched. He'd usually lay at my feet as if he remembered that I was the one who had rescued him from the freeway, as if he knew that I was the one who drove him home from the pound. He liked the boys, and he liked Pamela, but he was primarily attached to me. I was the boss.

Those were good years. It was fun watching the boys grow up, and Max was always there with them. I got the impression that Max also liked watching the boys grow, although I was probably being anthropomorphic. Or was I? There was something I had learned about dogs during the years Max lived with us. They are very in tune with their human families. True, they are just dogs, but they are also so much more than that. Funny thing about Max. He enjoyed playing fetch right up until his final days on earth. He couldn't get enough of it. Throw a ball or a toy or a stick, and you would make his day. He'd bring it back to you, wagging his tail. "Throw it again," he'd say with his eyes. "Throw it again and again."

This was our life with Max. Were we better off for it? Of course we were. I wouldn't trade the years that Max was in our lives for anything. God, how I loved that dumb animal. When the boys were both teenagers, their interest in Max waned. It was sad to see, and it was sad to see Max approaching the end of his life. He began to have a great deal of difficulty walking, which our vet said is not unusual for German shepherds. It was brutal.

When I asked the vet for a diagnosis, he said Max was suffering from advanced hip dysplasia and degenerative joint disease. "There is nothing that can be done at this point. It's up to you. Max is suffering. You have to ask yourself how long you're going to let him suffer."

Up to me? Why was everything always up to me? Maybe it was premature, and maybe I had waited too long. Who knew? I talked to Pamela about it, and we finally decided it was time to put Max to sleep. Pamela was strong, but I wasn't. I couldn't stop crying. It was like some vital part of me was being yanked from my heart, but I finally did it. I took Max back to the vet, and that was the end of that. It seemed like it was only yesterday that Max was sitting in the back seat of my car after having been rescued from the freeway, panting, slobbering, the boys patting him on the head. Now he was gone forever.

When I told this story to Bartholomew, I got a little teary-eyed. It still hurt. It would probably always hurt. Then I composed myself and said to Bartholomew, "That is the story of Max."

"I'm glad you told this story," Bartholomew said.

"He was a good dog."

"Sounds like it."

"I miss him."

"All your life, you've been looking for perfection, and there it was, right beneath your nose. Perfection. Real, clean, and unadulterated perfection, as cool and crystal clear as mountain spring water. Well, at least as close as you're ever going to get to it. As comforting as the sunlight on a spring day. As pure soft and white as a mountain of summer clouds. As free and unfettered as a bird on wing. It'll never be an accurate description of your behavior or the behavior of others. It'll never be defined by your environment, circumstances, or achievements. But it is! Love, Rick—in love, you will find all the perfection you have ever sought. Heartwarming, pure, and in the end, dreadfully painful. You should relish the discomfort, the dark void remaining, the proof that you have, for a time, experienced it."

Before I had a chance to ask Bartholomew anything, my phone rang. Bartholomew watched me answer it. He was smiling. "Hello?" I said, answering the call.

Then Bartholomew vanished. I hated when he did that, but apparently, he thought the call was more important than anything else he could offer.

It was my mom on the phone. "I need you to come over here," she said.

"What's the problem?" I asked.

"There's no problem."

"Then what do you need?"

"I need to get out of here. Not for good. Just for tonight. Can you take me for a drive?"

"A drive?"

"Please?" Mom asked.

"I'll be right over," I said.

"You're a good boy."

I ended the call with my mom, and then I called Pamela. She was still busy at the office, but she took my call. I told her I was going to Mom's, and Pamela said that was fine, that she still had several more hours of work to do. "Is your mom okay?" she asked.

"She wants to go for a drive," I said.

"A drive?"

"I think she's getting cabin fever."

"No harm in taking her for a drive," Pamela said. "I can't blame her for wanting to get out of that place."

"Me either," I said.

"I'll see you when I get home."

We ended the call, and I put on my shoes and a jacket. I turned off the TV and left the house, and it took me about twenty minutes to get to Mom's place. When I arrived, she was dressed and ready to go. We checked her out at the front desk, and then we climbed into my car. "Where do you want to go?" I asked.

"Anywhere," Mom said. "Drive toward LA."

"LA?"

"Get on the freeway," Mom said. "I'll tell you which exit to take."

"Got it," I said, and off we went. I found the San Diego Freeway and headed north.

"It feels good to be out," Mom said. "Roll down all the windows. I want to feel the air."

"Okay." I rolled down the windows, and the night air blew into the car and all over us. "Windy," I said.

"It feels good."

"And noisy," I said.

"When you and Ralph were little, your dad used to have a convertible. This reminds me of his convertible, his Chevy Bel Air. He adored that car. The four of us would get into the car, and we'd drive all over Southern California. You and Ralph would sit on the back seat. No seatbelts. No child seats. Funny how things change, isn't it? I suppose life is better now, but it seemed a lot more fun back then. Fewer rules, fewer fears, and a lot more fun."

"Where'd we go?"

"Your dad liked taking us to Bob's Big Boy for hamburgers and hot fudge sundaes. They used to have comic books for the kids. You and Ralph loved the comic books. And the ice cream. And especially the hot fudge."

"I think I remember that."

"Sometimes we'd go to the drive-in. We'd put the top down and watch the movies. They had a playground for the kids, and they'd show cartoons. You and Ralph got a big kick out of that place. It was a lot of fun. You and Ralph would always fall asleep halfway through the movies, and Dad and I always brought you pillows and blankets. Sometimes you boys would get stomachaches from eating so much popcorn and candy and drinking so much Coke. Your dad always bought too much. I kept telling him your eyes were bigger than your stomachs, but he'd always say, 'Jeez Louise, you're only a kid once.'"

Chapter 24

Jump In

"Take this exit," Mom said.

"Are you sure?" I asked.

"Please," Mom said.

"Where are we going?"

"Bob's," Mom said.

"Bob's Big Boy?"

"We used to live close to here, back when you and Ralph were kids."

"I know," I said.

"There's a Bob's about half a mile from here. Go east. It'll be on the left-hand side."

"Okay," I said.

"We can get hot fudge sundaes." I looked over at Mom, and she was looking out the window. "So much has changed," she said.

"All of Southern California has changed," I said.

"There used to be a bowling alley over there to the right. And a supermarket. Now it's a Best Buy. What do they even sell in those places?"

"TVs and computers," I said. "That's where I got your new TV."

"You got it here?"

"No, at the Best Buy in Irvine."

"Ah," Mom said.

I drove on.

Mom continued to look at the scenery, all the buildings, the streetlights, and the trucks and automobiles. We passed a mailbox on a corner, and Mom told me she used to mail letters there. "It was painted different colors back then. Red and blue—remember those? In fact, it was probably a different mailbox. But that's where it was."

"Interesting," I said.

Then, there it was. Bob's Big Boy was on the left. I made a turn into the parking lot and pulled the car into a vacant space.

We walked into the brightly lit restaurant.

The hostess sat us next to a window that looked out toward the boulevard, and Mom looked toward all the traffic. "There are so many people these days," she said. "With so many places to go."

"Yes," I said.

When the waitress showed up with our menus, Mom told her we didn't need menus. "We'll each have a hot fudge sundae," she said. "That's all."

"Nothing to drink?"

"Water is fine," Mom said. When the waitress left, Mom said, "I'm buying."

"If you insist," I said, smiling.

"Your father loved this place. I never quite got it, but I loved it because he loved it. And you and Ralph loved it. You boys loved the ice cream and comic books."

"I remember that," I said.

"Do you miss your father?"

"Of course I do."

"So do I," Mom said. "Did you know your dad was an artist?"

"An artist?"

"He liked to draw and paint."

"I had no idea."

"Late every night, he'd work at it in his study. Sometimes I wouldn't see him for hours. He was very self-conscious about it, and he seldom shared his work with me. He kept all his paintings and drawings locked in the study closet, and when he finished his pieces, he'd keep them for a few days, and then he would destroy them. God knows how many paintings and drawings he completed. I don't have any of them. He destroyed all of them. Wouldn't get them framed or show them off. He'd just work on them for hours, and then—*poof*—they were gone. He was never satisfied."

"That's a shame," I said.

"He had me pose for a couple of portraits."

"Did you keep those?"

"I never even saw them. He wouldn't let me look at them. He said they were terrible."

"I wish I'd known," I said.

"To what end?"

"I would like to have seen what he was doing."

"He wouldn't have shared them with you. Like I said, he was very self-conscious about it. Do you want to know who he admired most in our family?"

"Who?" I asked.

"He admired Zach."

"Zach?" I asked.

"Zach and his sculptures."

"I never would have guessed."

"He was so proud of that boy. Having the courage to let others in on his creations. Having the courage to pursue his passion. You have no idea how much your father looked up to that boy. He never came right out and said it, but I could tell. A wife knows these things. A good wife understands her husband. It was a shame your father was so self-conscious about his art. Just think of what he could've passed down to us. Think of what he could've shared."

The waitress brought us our hot fudge sundaes—vanilla ice cream and hot chocolate fudge. Just like old times. Mom dug in with her tall spoon, and so did I. I liked it. It was actually pretty good.

The next morning, I wrote a poem about my father. It was a strange feeling. I felt as if I knew him better now after he was dead than I did when he was alive. Time, combined with a little honesty from my mother. Actually, I only just started the poem the next morning because it took me an entire week to write the thing. I shared the poem with Bartholomew, and after he read it, he smiled. "Now we're getting somewhere," he said. "You're finally catching on." The poem was a letter from me to Dad, and it went as follows:

> Dear Dad,
>
> Once upon a time
> You were somebody's baby,

Head full of black hair,
Ten fingers and ten small toes,
Red cheeks and a button nose.

Once upon a time
You were wrapped in a blanket,
Held in Grandma's arms.
Inky pink and eyes of blue,
Couldn't take her eyes off you.

Flesh and blood, blood and
Flesh—you were their trick to the
Future, their little
Magician who would turn strife
Into a much better life.

They would teach you and
Mold you and shape you into
Someone who knew the
Difference between right and wrong,
Who knew a short word from long,

Who knew this from that,
Who knew when to be honest,
And when to stretch the
Truth. A man's man. A man
Who came, saw, and said, "I can!"

All parents want what's
Best for their children. And you
Would never let them
Down. Reach for that distant star
And you would always go far.

The devil isn't
In the details. The devil
Resides and does his

Deeds in mediocrity,
As deep as the deepest sea,

High as a mountain
Peak. You discover its strength
Is the strength of the
Earth itself, the muscle of
All that is cherished and loved.

Perfection is what
You were taught. Mistakes were to
Be avoided at
All costs. Can't do the math?
Travel down a different path

And seek another
Star. Maybe a little to
The left, or to the
Right, or up or down, or here
Or there. Grab the wheel and steer.

Once upon a time,
I was brought into the world,
And you taught me what
Your father taught you. Here I
Am, reflection in your eye

As miserable
As you, a handful of gold
That was mine for the
Taking, avoiding the fights,
Those that exceeded my might.

File my name under
Men who errantly thought that
Dreams were for losers.

I've had a wife; I've had two
Sons and parents and pets who

Love me.
And that should be enough
To fill the cup of
Any man.

"Do you think your dad was an unhappy man?" Bartholomew asked.

"I do," I said.

"Why?"

"For the same reasons I am struggling today," I said. "Life can be very disappointing. Life is disappointing. People are disappointing. *I* am disappointing."

"You can't see the forest for the trees."

"Something like that."

"What do you think would've made your father happy?"

"Maybe if he'd been the CEO of a more glamorous company. Maybe if he'd been in the news. Maybe if he'd written a best-selling book about his life. Maybe if he was interesting. But it was like he'd come to the highest step he dared to take, and why? It was because my dad was terrified of failure. Somehow, in his upbringing, he was taught that failures were to be avoided at all costs and that failures were a revelation of weakness, something to be sorely ashamed of. When Ralph failed at his first business, my dad told him that failure was just a part of life, but did he mean it? I don't think he did. Honestly? I think Dad felt as bad about Ralph's failure as Ralph did, and his words of consolation and optimism were spoken more out of pity and necessity than out of conviction."

"You think your father lied?"

"I think he said what he knew he had to say, being that he was a father."

"Interesting," Bartholomew said.

"And I'm really no different."

"No?" Bartholomew asked.

"Zach and Nate's failures hurt me. But why did they hurt me? At the end of the day, it's really more because of the embarrassment I felt than anything else. What did I do wrong as a father? What mistakes did *I* make?

What could I have done differently? Whatever made me think I could be a good father to them?"

"And yet?" Bartholomew said, laughing.

"And yet what?" I asked.

"Neither of your boys is a failure."

"No?" I asked.

"Each of them has chosen a path for his life, and each of them has followed that path. Sure, there are stretches in the paths have been washed out, there are fallen trees to be stepped over, there are steep parts to the paths that sometimes seem *too* steep. No path is perfect. There are times when they will question the paths they took, and there are also times when will enjoy every step of their journey. Embarrassed? That's the last thing you should be. You should be proud, fascinated, and always there to lend a helping hand when the trek is rough and the odds against them are formidable. Out of love, Rick. Love is what matters."

"And what about my life?" I asked.

"What about it?"

"Like my father, I have chosen the path of least resistance. Am I doomed? I guess the apple doesn't fall far from the tree."

"Your life is hardly over."

"I'm sixty-four years old."

"So?"

"Where do I go from here?" I asked.

"As I see it, you've already made a choice."

"Have I?"

"Poetry," Bartholomew said.

"Mental masturbation."

"Hardly," Bartholomew said. "Not if you write about things that matter. Not if you write about things you've learned. And certainly not if you share your poetry with others. Do you plan on sharing your poetry with others?"

"I don't know," I said.

"Jesus, Rick. This is your chance. Maybe it's come time in your life to end this silly quest for perfection and let the chips fall where they may. Hold your nose and jump in the water. Trick-or-treating is now over with—take off your Halloween mask and let people see who you really are.

Put a hold on the expectations and accept the world as it is. So, you go to Santa Cruz and there's a toilet in the yard across the street? So what? So, you've done a few things you're not proud of? Who cares? The world keeps orbiting the sun at sixty-seven thousand miles per hour. Spring, summer, autumn, and winter. The time on your wristwatch keeps advancing. And you? Well, you're not getting any younger."

"Is this supposed to be a pep talk?" I asked.

"Take it as you wish."

I thought for a moment, and then I said, "It just makes me feel old."

"Old, young, it's all up to you."

Up to me.

Again.

Chapter 25

Famous Last Words

We decided to go out to dinner together. Somewhere nice. Someplace that could seat us all. We picked the Doryman Bistro in Newport Beach. I reserved a window seat looking out over the bay, and the sun would be setting down into Catalina Island around the time we placed our orders. The place was a little pricey, but they had good food and service. There was Pamela and me. There were Zach and his latest girlfriend, Mary Ann. There were Nate with his wife, Emily, and of course my mom would be there. Also at the table were Ralph with his wife, Suzy. Ralph and Suzy's kids lived in Phoenix, so they weren't there. Altogether, there were nine of us. The dinner was Pamela's idea, but everyone agreed that it sounded like fun.

We all placed our orders with the waitress, a tall blonde girl with a nice personality. Zach's girlfriend was new to the group, but it didn't keep her from talking. Mary Ann was a loquacious little thing with bright pink pigtails and a nose ring. Lose the nose ring, and she'd be a pretty good-looking girl. I never was much one for facial piercings, especially in noses. But, hey, to each their own. Who was I to make judgments?

"I love family gatherings," Mary Ann said.

"We don't do it often enough," Pamela said.

"We've always been a close family," Ralph said.

"Just the opposite of my family," Mary Ann said.

"You don't eat together?" Pamela asked.

"We don't eat together. We don't talk to each other. We're all like strangers. Strangers with the same last name. Well, except for my sister. She got married last year and changed her last name."

"What is your last name?" I asked.

"Cobbledick."

It was quiet for a moment, and then I said, "No wonder your sister got married."

Everyone laughed, including Mary Ann.

"You wouldn't believe the crap I took in high school."

"I can imagine," I said.

I thought it was funny. Here was this rather naïve girl tagging along with Zach, impressed with our family. She said her family all treated each other like strangers, and it's true, that was kind of sad. But what were we?

"I heard you got a showing in Los Angeles," Ralph said to Zach.

"At the Beverly Center," Pamela said.

"It's not a big deal," Zach said humbly.

"It's a *very* big deal," Pamela said.

"How many pieces have you sold to date?" I asked Zach.

"Seven or eight."

"That sounds like a big deal to me," Pamela said.

"It's encouraging," Zach said.

"You should see how much they're asking," Pamela said. "It's a lot of money."

"It's more than I planned on," Zach said.

"No accounting for taste," Nate said, grinning. "You should title your exhibit *Junk from a Dump*. All those pretentious Beverly Hills doctors and lawyers won't be able to open their checkbooks fast enough."

"You should be proud of your little brother."

We were all was quiet for a moment. "I think it's good that you guys are honest with each other," Mary Ann finally said.

The waitress brought a couple baskets of bread to the table, and everyone reached for a roll.

Honest with each other? Poor misguided Mary Ann. Poor little Mary Ann Cobbledick with the pink pigtails and the ring in her nose. *Honest* was the last word I'd use to describe *my* family. On the surface, yes. But it was all on the surface. Heck, you could go back far into my childhood. Remember when I broke my dad's study window batting rocks in the front yard? I never did tell my parents it was me who broke the window, and I blamed it on Bobby Richardson, as if he didn't already have enough to contend with. Only Bartholomew knew about this, and it was Bartholomew's advice that prevented me from getting whipped. Bartholomew, who lately has been encouraging me to be more honest.

Then there was the trash we dumped into the Elliots' swimming pool. Only Ralph, Abe, and I knew about this one. Not even Pamela knew the story. Another secret. Another lie. And there was the affair I had with Janet Jones. No one knew about it. Only Janet, and I can't even imagine the problems it would've caused if Pamela ever found out. Honest? How about my thirty-thousand-dollar heyday at the Las Vegas craps tables? Ha! Lucky me, pulling the wool over Pamela's eyes again. Or how about my little attempt to escape to Mexico? I told Pamela about this one, but no one else in the family knew what I fool I had made of myself. Drinking and driving? Mexico? What was I even thinking? I could go on and on. The truth was that my family knew as much about me as they did about Zach's silly girlfriend. And what about the rest of our "honest" family?

My mom knew nothing about Nate's suicide night. In fact, no one but Pamela, Emily, and I knew about it. It was hush, hush. And Zach's stint in rehab for his marijuana addiction. Only Zach, Pamela, and I knew anything about this one. And what about Ralph's bankruptcy. I mean, jeez, I had just found out. And Dad's artwork? It was kept secret for years, and as far as I knew, only Mom and I were even now aware of it. And so many of the poems I had written? For my eyes only. My secrets. My secret poems. It's not like I was in the front yard with a bullhorn, yelling, "Hey everybody, come over here. Read my poems. Learn about my deepest feelings and most personal fears. Laugh if you like—but get to know *me*!"

Bartholomew would laugh, wouldn't he? The Harper family and their little pink-pigtailed guest, all present and accounted for, pretending that life is exactly the way it ought to be, all with their preconceived notions of a good life which, by hook or by crook, would not elude them. I ordered the crab cakes, and you know what? No matter how they were prepared, and no matter what I actually thought of them, I would say they were delicious because that's the way I wanted them to be. And when the waitress brought out my order, I stuffed a forkful of the food into my mouth and chewed.

"How are your crab cakes?" Pamela asked.

"Great," I said. "How's your halibut?"

"It's perfect."

"This chicken is so tender," Mary Ann said.

"I don't think there's a bad dish on the menu," Ralph said.

"My steak is a tiny bit tough," Mom said. "But it's very flavorful."

"What do you do for a living?" Pamela asked Mary Ann.

"I'm still a student."

"Where are you going to school?"

"At USC," Mary Ann said. "That's where I met Zach."

"We were in an English class together," Zach said.

"I thought he was into computers then, just taking English to fill his general ed requirements. I had no idea he was an artist. I'm an art major. It's like we were drawn to each other by fate. You know, kismet."

"Ah," I said.

"Rick and I met in college," Pamela said.

"In a classical literature class," I said.

"I thought it was a history class."

"No, it was classical literature."

"Classical literature, history, what's the difference? It was boring."

"I asked Pamela out for coffee."

"Next thing you knew, we were married."

"I'm a long way away from marrying anyone," Zach said with his mouth full.

"Same here," Mary Ann said.

I suspected she was a little disappointed to hear Zach say that.

"It creeps up on you," Nate said. "One minute, you're going out to a movie, and the next thing you know, you're wearing a tux and agreeing to vows."

"*You're* the one who wanted to get married right away," Emily said.

"Is that true?" Zach asked.

"I guess it is, but I didn't exactly hear Emily complaining about it."

Everyone laughed.

"Do you guys have any kids?" Mary Ann asked.

"Not yet," Emily said.

"What do you guys do?"

"Emily sells pharmaceuticals to doctors for a drug company. I'm an entrepreneur."

"An entrepreneur?"

"I'm kind of in between projects."

"He's selling Fords," Zach said.

"It's just temporary," Nate said. "You know, a way to pay the bills. I work at a dealership in Riverside."

"If you know of anyone looking for a car, send them Nate's way," Pamela said. "He can get them a good deal. New or used. You sell used cars too, right, Nate?"

"We have a used car inventory."

"My dad sold cars for a living," Pamela said. "Up in Oregon. He did very well for himself. Selling cars is nothing to be ashamed of."

But it wasn't what Nate wanted to talk about, and he changed the subject. "What do your parents do?" he asked Mary Ann.

"My dad is an engineer at Rockwell, and Mom works as an administrative assistant at the Taco Bell headquarters in Irvine. They both hate their jobs. They never come right out and say it, but I can tell. You know about them when you live with them for twenty-one years. It becomes obvious."

"You still live with your parents?" I asked.

"I do," Mary Ann said. "When I graduate from college, I'm going to get my own place. Mom says she can get me a job at Taco Bell. Not like I would want to work there forever, but it will pay the bills."

"What about your art?" Pamela asked.

"I'll do it in my spare time.

"She's quite good," Zach said.

"Of course, that's the goal—to make a living selling my art. Just like Zach. You know what they say. Do something you love for a living, and you'll never have to work a day in your life."

"So true," Pamela said.

"What do you guys do?" Mary Ann asked Pamela and me.

"I'm an artichoke," I said.

"An artichoke?"

"It's an inside joke," I said laughing. "That's what my father-in-law calls me. Actually, I'm an architect, and Pamela is a legal assistant. I design houses for rich people, and Pamela helps her boss keep their guilty clients out of jail."

"Not every one of our clients is guilty," Pamela said.

"Enough of them."

"Do you guys like your jobs?" Mary Ann asked.

"My job has its moments," I said.

"I like going to work," Pamela said.

"I thought of going into architecture," Mary Ann said. "It is an art, but it's also a little too nuts-and-bolts for me. I'm not really a nuts-and-bolts kind of girl. My art is more whimsical than it is nuts-and-bolts."

"Do you do sculptures like Zach?" Pamela asked.

"Oh, no. No sculpting. I work primarily in pen, ink, and watercolors. I've been doing it since I was a little girl."

"Interesting," I said.

You know, the odds of this girl ever making it financially doing pen, ink, and watercolors was about a million to one. Of course, I'd never seen any of her work, but most of this kind of work was, well, a dime a dozen. Heh, since she was a little girl? Rainbows and unicorns. It was a good thing her mom could get her a job at Taco Bell. But she was a nice girl, and I didn't want to rain on her parade. "Keep at it," I said. "You never know *what* might happen. You could be the next Beatrix Potter."

"I love her work," Mary Ann said.

So, our conversation went on. Everyone liked dinner, and everyone was gregarious and polite. When we got the bill, I was going to pay for it, but Ralph insisted on paying for half. We used my credit card, and Ralph paid me with cash. For not making much money, it was amazing how much cash he always carried around in his wallet. Maybe having a wallet full of cash made him feel wealthier. Who knew?

Everything seemed great.

Who had any idea what would happen next? Certainly not me, and certainly not Pamela. Nate seemed to be in good spirits, and Emily didn't act like anything was wrong. We all left the restaurant and went our separate ways. Ralph wanted to take Mom back to her apartment. We hadn't ordered any dessert at the restaurant, and Pamela wanted something sweet to eat. So, we stopped at the grocery store, and Pamela bought a pint of Ben & Jerry's. Me? I never was much one for dessert, but I tagged along. "I'm not going to eat the whole thing," Pamela said. "You can have some if you want."

"Thanks," I said.

Then we got in line at the checkout stand. I paid for the ice cream with a credit card, and we walked back to the car. "Everyone seemed to be in good spirits tonight."

"They did," I agreed.

"What did you think of Zach's girlfriend?"

"She seemed nice enough."

"Without the nose ring and the pink hair, she could be a real looker."

I laughed. "Kids," I said.

"I suppose we looked just as ridiculous to our parents as our kids now look to us. I remember your long hair. You usually kept it in a ponytail. When my dad first met you, I thought he was going to have a heart attack."

"Your dad," I said.

"First time anyone ever called you an artichoke?"

"It was. And no one since."

"My dad likes you."

"He does?" I asked.

"He still thinks you're kind of an egghead, but he does like you. If he didn't like you, you would know it."

"I suppose that's true," I said.

"Our family is in a good place right now."

Famous last words.

When we got home, I parked the car in the garage. We put on our comfortable clothes, and I turned on the TV. Pamela dished herself a bowl of ice cream. I don't know why she bothered to put it into a bowl, when she knew good and well that she was going to eat the entire pint. She may as well just have eaten it out of the carton. Fewer dishes to clean, but that was Pamela. Everything had to go in either a bowl or on a plate. She'd been that way for as long as I could remember.

I turned on a show, and we got comfortable on the couch. I don't recall what we watched. I certainly do remember when my cell phone rang. The phone was on the coffee table, and I picked it up to answer. My heart sank. It was Emily, calling from their house, and she was sobbing.

"Try to stop crying," I said.

"It's Nate," she said.

"What about him?"

"He did it again. He tried to kill himself. This time, he cut his wrists in the bathtub. I called 911. I'm on my way to the hospital."

"We'll be there," I said.

Emily ended the call, and I set my phone back on the coffee table.

"What happened?" Pamela asked.

"It's Nate," I stammered. I barely got the words out of my throat.

CHAPTER 26

LIFE DOESN'T PAUSE

We got in the car. I started the engine, and the first thing I did was turn off the radio. I wasn't in the mood for music, and I was sure Pamela wasn't either. What to say? We were quiet the whole way there except when Pamela said, "He seemed to be doing so much better."

"He did," I said.

"You'd think we would've noticed *something*."

Wow.

The thoughts that go through your head at a time like this. The hindsight. The second-guessing. The search for clues. How could we have been so wrong about something so serious? The silence wasn't helping, and my mind wandered. Nate in high school, Nate in college, Nate when he married Emily, and Nate when he was working for Harvey Pullman. The infomercials and the two-for-one deals. You know, everyone always thought Zach was the sensitive one. The artist. The emotional one. The one who shunned the marching orders of college to chase after his dreams, the one with his head in the clouds, but Nate was sensitive too—maybe even more so than Zach. Maybe he was more emotional and sensitive than any of us realized.

When we arrived at the hospital, we found Emily. She was in the emergency waiting area, and she had yet to see Nate. "He lost a lot of blood," she said. "But now they say he's going to be okay."

"What happened?" Pamela asked.

Emily told us what had happened. She and Nate had come home from the dinner, and they were going to watch some TV. Emily said Nate was very quiet the whole way home, and he said he wanted to take a bath before watching TV to unwind. This seemed a little odd to Emily since Nate was not one to take baths often. He usually showered. But she thought, *Oh, well, let him take a bath if that's what he wants.* Emily put on her pajamas and went to the family room to turn on the TV. She had made a cup of tea. She waited for Nate to show up, but he didn't. After finishing her tea and waiting about twenty minutes, she went to the master bathroom to see when Nate was going to be done taking his bath. She knocked on the master bathroom door, and at first there was no answer. Then she knocked again. "Go away," Nate finally said. "Leave me alone."

"What are you doing in there?" Emily asked.

"I just want to be left alone," Nate said.

"Are you okay?" Emily asked.

"Just leave," Nate said.

Emily knew right away that something was wrong. Call it a sixth sense. Call it intuition. She knew how to open a locked bathroom door. All she needed was a toothpick to stick in the little hole in the door handle, so she went to the kitchen to get a toothpick. Then she came back to the bedroom and poked the toothpick into the hole until—*click!*—the door was unlocked. "It was awful," Emily said. "Nate was in the bathtub, but the bathtub water was all red. He had cut his wrist with a razor, and the blood was flowing from the open wound. He wasn't even naked. He was wearing his boxer shorts. I guess he didn't want to be found naked. He left a suicide note on the bathroom counter, and I read it. All it said was 'I don't want to sell cars. I love you. Goodbye.' All this over selling cars?"

"What did you do?" Pamela asked.

"I called 911, and they sent an ambulance and four policemen. They told me over the phone to raise Nate's arm and put pressure on the gash to slow the bleeding. Then the responders arrived, not the same group who were there the last time. Everything was a blur. They rushed Nate out of there and brought him here to the hospital. God, it all seemed to happen too fast. It was like a bad dream. It was a nightmare. Nate seemed very weak to me. God knows how much blood he lost."

"But they say he's going to be okay?" Pamela asked.

"That's what the nurse told me."

"Can we see him?"

"The nurse said soon. She said they might have to transfer him to a mental hospital. I told the nurse he was under the care of a psychiatrist, and I gave her Dr. West's name and phone number. She said they were going to give him a call."

"What a mess," I said.

"I thought he was doing so much better," Emily said.

"So did we," I said.

When we finally got to see Nate, he was in a hospital bed, in his own room, recovering. The nurse said he was mildly sedated because he was so agitated when they first brought him in.

"I was hoping not to have any visitors," he said.

"There's no way to keep us away," I said.

"I feel like such an ass."

"Don't feel bad, son. You're just having a difficult time. We all have difficult times in our lives."

"Just know that we love you," Pamela said.

"We love you no matter what," Emily said.

"Looks like you're stuck with us," I said.

Nate laughed feebly. "So I see."

"They're talking about taking you to a mental hospital again. Dr. West is trying to talk them out of it."

"I just want to go home," Nate said.

"We know."

"I'm sorry," Nate said.

"Sorry for what?" I asked.

"For putting you guys through this."

"Don't worry about it," Emily said. "You just need to know that we're all here for you."

"After that dinner … everything came to a boil."

"You don't have to explain."

"Do you still like Dr. West?" I asked. "Maybe we should find a different psychiatrist."

"I like him."

"But is he helping you?"

"He's helped me a lot. This wasn't his fault. It was my fault. It was all my fault."

"Okay," I said.

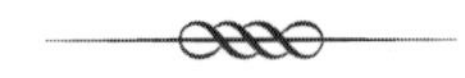

Two weeks later, Nate was back at it, selling cars in Riverside, wearing long-sleeved shirts to hide his bandaged wrist. If you could say anything about Nate, it was that he was resilient. But this didn't keep me out of his life. I called him every evening, trying to get a feel for his moods, talking to him about what I had learned in life. Granted, I've never gone out on a limb the way that Nate did, and I've never experienced a serious failure in anything I've pursued. Still, I think our talks were helpful to Nate, if not for any other particular reason, at least to let him know how much I cared. His brushes with suicide chilled me to the bone. Not sure *what* I would do if the boy actually did kill himself. I think the pain would've been unbearable.

How much of Nate's problems were my fault? I couldn't get myself to stop thinking about this. I felt responsible for his lot in life, maybe more so than ever before. Seriously, if I had been a better father, would Nate now be a car salesman wearing long-sleeved shirts to hide his bandage, to keep the world from knowing his inner turmoil? And how much of that inner turmoil was still festering inside of him? He seemed okay, but he seemed okay earlier before bloodying up that bathtub. There are parents who cut their kids loose at eighteen and say, "It's up to you now. I've done all I can do." I've seen parents like this. They are able to draw a line, give their offspring a hearty shove, and let them go. Why couldn't I do this? I felt so much responsibility. Was this healthy—or was I going too far? My boys were both adults. But? Always with the buts.

And what was going to happen to Zach? The exhibition at the Beverly Center was only going to be for another month or so. What then? Was he just going to be a flash in the pan? A fad? Here today and gone tomorrow? And I was spending so much time with Nate that I really wasn't concentrating on Zach. Did I need to be concentrating on him too, were things going to work out, or was I going to have *two* sons crashing and burning?

Of course, there was also Mom. She seemed to be doing okay, but was this just the calm before the storm? And Pamela? I was ignoring her completely. Good old steady-as-she-goes Pamela. When was she going to burst into flames?

And there were others.

Bartholomew called it "fortune-telling." He said, "Now you're worrying about things that haven't even happened when you have no idea *what's* going to happen. You're looking into your distorted crystal ball and expecting the worst."

"How do I keep from doing that?" I asked.

"You tell me."

"Me? Tell you? If I knew, I wouldn't have to ask you."

"But who am I?"

"You're Bartholomew."

"So you've given me a name. You call me Bartholomew, but who am I actually?"

"I don't know what you're getting at."

Bartholomew just laughed. It was infuriating, and I felt like punching him right in the eye. He was laughing at me? What a pig.

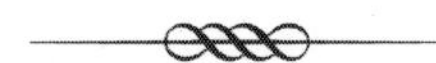

Life goes on, right? I mean, no matter what happens, no matter what you're facing, life just keeps moving forward. Relentlessly and despite it all. Like a steamroller with an endless supply of fuel, flattening everything in its way, spewing black clouds of exhaust.

In four months, I was going to retire. It would be my sixty-fifth birthday, and I didn't make any secret about my plans for retirement. I gave everyone fair warning. This included telling some of the people I'd been doing business with on behalf of John Wiley: "Anything you need me for, ask me now, because four months from now, I'll be gone." They didn't exactly line up at my door with requests or questions. They figured John would have all the bases covered. I did, however, get a call from Bill Collins, a building contractor who had built several of my projects. I liked Bill. He seemed honest, and he always had a positive attitude. He was about twenty years younger than me, but he always seemed mature for his age. He wasn't a fast-talker or a hotshot. Bill wanted to take me to lunch.

I always tried to keep my relationships with contractors on a purely business level. I always tried to avoid being their buddy, but I accepted Bill's offer for lunch. He wasn't currently working on any of my projects, and like I said, I liked the guy. We met at a little café on Lido Island, and we took a seat in one of the booths.

A waitress who I would guess was about my age showed up at our table with our menus and said, "Let me know when you're ready to order."

"Thanks, ma'am," Bill said. That was Bill. Always with the sirs and ma'ams. He was raised in the South where people were taught to show each other respect, and I liked that. Not like California.

We ordered lunch, and then Bill said something that surprised me. "Do you remember the Akermans' house? Back during the Great Recession? It was one of your projects. I think it was the first project I built for Wiley & Associates."

"I remember it," I said.

"Did you know that job nearly put me into bankruptcy?"

"The Akerman house?"

"I lost my shirt on that job, and I didn't have anything else going on to make up for it."

"I had no idea," I said.

"Do you remember the framer?"

"I don't," I said.

"His name was Clarence Tuttle. He gave me a very low price for the rough carpentry, a price I used to calculate my bid. Without his price, I probably wouldn't have gotten the job. Everyone was bidding projects so low back then. There just wasn't any work. It was dog-eat-dog."

"The recession was rough," I said.

"I knew Clarence's price was too low when I signed him up. And I expected him to complain about it during the project. But he'd worked for me for several years, and he always came through. I trusted him, and all of us were in the same boat back then, all expecting the economy to improve soon. Who would've guessed the recession would last as long as it did, putting so many people out of business? Anyway, I don't know if you remember, but Clarence walked off the job and filed for bankruptcy about one week into the project. He left me holding the bag. Not only was I responsible for paying for all the lumber he had delivered, but I would have to find someone to finish his work for the low price he had agreed to. I had already paid Clarence a ton of money. Seriously, the guy burned me good."

"Jeez," I said.

"I called everyone I knew, and no one wanted to finish the job for the money I had left to pay. I got some prices, but there was no way I could afford any of them. Meanwhile, I couldn't very well stop work on the job. I had a schedule to meet and a contract to live up to. So, I hired my own carpentry crew, and I put them to work on the house. It was a big risk, but I had no choice. I was caught between a rock and a hard place. Well, all said and done, the framing cost me even more than if I'd hired a subcontractor to complete. It was completely out of control. There was only one thing I could do, and that was to rewrite my cost breakdown for the bank. I increased the framing budget and took the money out of the rest of the line items. This covered the framing, but now I didn't have enough money to complete the project. I wasn't just off by just a few dollars. I was off by a mile."

"Weren't you also off with the fire sprinklers?"

"That was a whole new story. Somehow, when I bid the project, I completely overlooked the note about the fire sprinklers. It happens. But it couldn't have happened at a worse time. Now, not only did I not have enough money for the balance of the trades, I had nothing for the fire sprinklers. But I kept moving forward, incurring costs, getting the job done. By the time we were finished, I was completely upside down. I had no new jobs on the boards—and no income to offset the losses. It was a mess."

"I never knew any of this," I said.

"I kept it to myself."

"Jeez," I said.

"I could've just gone belly-up and left you guys to sort things out."

"But you didn't."

"I remembered something my dad told me. He said there would be times in my life when things went sour, when everything would seem impossible to handle. But he said, 'There's always a way. There's always a way because there *has* to be a way. Life doesn't pause for problems.'"

"Wise words," I said.

"Now here I am, a successful contractor. I've never walked off a job in my life. The work is good, and the money is good. And I've learned a few things on the way. I learn more and more each day."

"But that doesn't explain it," I said.

"Explain what?"

"It doesn't explain how you were able to pay off all your subcontractors. I would think there would've been lawsuits and mechanic's liens flying all over the place."

"Ah," Bill said.

"Ah, what?"

"That's the beauty of it," Bill said. "Like my dad said, life doesn't pause. Life moves forward because that's the only direction it knows."

CHAPTER 27

THE BELT

The waitress brought out our orders. Bill ordered a bowl of chili, and I ordered a club sandwich. I was also working on a cup of coffee, and I had the waitress pour me another.

"That's quite a story," I said. "But you still haven't told me how you were able to make things work."

"I just did what I had to do," Bill said.

"Which was?"

"I met with each of my subcontractors for the job, and we figured out how much I owed. I then explained the jam I was in and told them there was no way I could pay them. But I also offered a solution. I told them I could make monthly payments for a period of two years. This way, they would be paid what they were owed, just not right away. I explained the alternative was for me to file bankruptcy and walk away from the whole thing without owing a dime. I told them I didn't want to do this. Sure, if I filed bankruptcy, they could lien and sue the owner, but they would also have to hire an attorney and go through the court process. I told them the owner would fight them tooth and nail and that they were better off accepting my proposal. Of course, I didn't want them to feel like I was screwing them over, so I apologized profusely. I said I hoped they would see that I was trying my best to fulfill my obligation. I said, 'I feel terrible about this, but it's the best I can do.'"

"And?" I asked.

"Some of the subcontractors were furious. They said they'd rather take their chances suing the owner. But many of them reluctantly agreed to my proposal. Some of them even thanked me for not filing bankruptcy. Enough of them agreed to the payment plan so that I was able to keep the ship afloat. Of course, the economy began to improve, and I began to sign up more work. My new jobs helped me to keep my monthly payments current. Eventually, I paid every dime I owed. It took me two years to get back on my feet, and I was off and running—with all new problems to solve and fires to put out."

"I would never have guessed," I said.

"Life doesn't pause."

"No, it doesn't," I said.

Bill's story made me wonder how many people in the world did I know closely or casually who were on the brink of disaster? A few? A lot? Or was the whole world teetering on the edge of a crumbling cliff—all of us too embarrassed to admit it, all of us too proud to reveal our *real* circumstance? All of us acting and pretending like everything was okay, like events were all unfolding as we planned, like there was nothing wrong with our lives?

After Bill was done telling me his story, he asked, "So, do you have any children?"

"I have two sons," I said.

"How old are they?" Bill asked.

"One boy is twenty-nine, and the other is thirty-two."

"How are they doing?"

"They're doing great," I said. "The younger boy, Zach, is an artist. He's got a big show right now up in Los Angeles at the Beverly Center. He does sculptures, and his work is selling like hotcakes. I don't know much about art, but I've been told his work is groundbreaking. My older son, Nate, is nothing like his younger brother. Nate graduated with a business degree, with honors, and he's an entrepreneur. My wife, Pamela, and I are always excited to see what project he comes up with next. He's a very clever kid."

"No other architects in the family?"

"Nope," I said. "I'm the only one."

"I have one son," Bill said. "His name is Edward. We named him after his grandfather, my wife's dad. We were planning on more kids, but the doctors told my wife she couldn't have any more children. And we don't want to adopt, so Edward is going to be it. He's twenty now. He wants to be a building contractor like me. I'll tell you, it was a struggle just to get him through high school. He hated school. He told me, 'No one is going to care if I graduated from high school when they pick me to be their contractor. Has anyone asked you to show them your high school diploma? Does anyone care if you graduated?'"

"How'd you answer?" I asked.

"I told him he was right, but that I still wanted him to get his high school diploma. I didn't have a good reason why. I just wanted him to get it."

"Did he graduate?"

"He did, but it was like pulling teeth."

I laughed.

"What's he doing now?" I asked.

"Edward is working as an assistant superintendent on one of my projects. My wife and I were kind of hoping he'd go on to college and be a professional. If you know what I mean. Like a doctor or a lawyer, or even an architect like you. Construction is such a rough and dirty way to make a living. I mean, it's been good to me, but I hoped for better for my son. We all want our kids to do better than us, don't we? Look at your kids. Aren't you proud of them?"

"I am," I said.

"A successful artist and an entrepreneur."

"Yes," I said.

I felt so guilty! There I was, sitting with a guy who was telling me the truth about himself and his family, and I couldn't do it. I couldn't reciprocate. I couldn't tell him the truth about my own life. What did that say about me? Was I a liar and a phony? I think the answer was yes, but admitting this to myself didn't make me feel any better. When was this charade going to end?

I've told you already about my father and his leather belt. The dreaded *strap of discipline*. Looking back, there weren't all that many times that the belt was used on me, but I can remember three days for sure when dad bent me over his knee and let me have it. There may have been more, but if there were, I don't remember them. The first time was the most memorable—and the most painful. I was in the first grade, which would have made me about six or seven. I got in trouble at school. My first-grade teacher was a woman named Mrs. O'Connell. I didn't like her. Actually, I don't think anyone liked her. Why she became a schoolteacher, I'll never know. She was mean and spiteful, and to her way of thinking, children were the shittiest little things ever conceived by God above.

Every morning, Mrs. O'Connell would arrive at class right on time. She'd hang her coat on her coatrack and then take a seat at her desk. She'd remove her binder from the top drawer of her desk and set it before her. She glared at us as we all entered the room, and when the bell rang, she'd open her binder. "Roll call," she'd say. Then she proceeded to read our names out loud in alphabetical order. Each kid was to proclaim his or her presence in class by saying, "Here." If you were late, you'd get a black mark by your name, and if you accumulated three black marks, it was a trip to the principal's office. And the principal? He was even worse than Mrs. O'Connell. Trust me. You did *not* want to go to the principal's office.

After roll call, class would begin. Always referring to her binder, Mrs. O'Connell would proceed with the curriculum. The woman was about as creative as dirt. Right, left, up, down, one subject to the next. My first-grade class was about as exciting as a trip to the dentist. In a way, I felt sorry for the woman. She didn't seem happy. In fact, she seemed downright miserable. On the other hand, I resented her—and I wanted to make her even more miserable. If that was possible. Every day when lunchtime rolled around, she would close her binder and dismiss the class for recess when the bell rang. And off we'd all go to eat our lunches and play in the schoolyard.

During one of these lunch breaks, I had a brainstorm that would introduce me to my dad's belt. I was playing in the grass field with the other kids when I noticed a pile of dog crap near the chain-link fence. A light bulb lit up over my head. Why not? Why not make old Mrs. McConnell as unhappy as she was making the rest of us? I still had some food left in my lunch sack: half a bologna sandwich and an apple. The sandwich was wrapped in wax paper, just the amount of paper needed. I dumped what was left of my lunch in the trash can near the playground, saving the sheet of wax paper, and returned to the chain-link fence.

Carefully, I picked up a hunk of the dog crap with the wax paper. I then folded the paper and made my way back to the classroom. Sure enough, Mrs. O'Connell had not yet returned—yet her binder was still sitting on the top of her desk. I opened the binder, looked around to be sure I was alone, and then smeared the smelly dog crap on the papers in the binder.

I crumpled the wax paper in a ball, left the room, and deposited the soiled paper in the nearest trash can. Ha! I couldn't wait to see the old woman's face when she opened her binder. I was so excited about it that I told a couple of my friends. "You can't tell anyone," I said, and they promised to keep the secret. When the bell rang, we all filed into the classroom and took our seats. My friends and I looked at each other, smiling.

Well, class started, and Mrs. O'Connell opened her binder on the desk. She looked at it, and then she sniffed. "Good Lord," she said. Steam was practically coming out of her ears when she said, "I'll be right back." She took the binder out of the classroom, and a couple minutes later, she returned without it. "I don't know which one of you little monsters thought this would be funny, but nobody's doing anything—and nobody's going home—until I find out who did it."

Well, most of the kids in class had no idea what she was even talking about, but my friends and I knew.

"If you know about this and don't tell me, it's as good as having done it yourself," Mrs. McConnell said. "I'm going to call each of you, one by one, out into the hallway for questioning. By hook or by crook, we're going to get to the bottom of this before any of you is allowed to go home. I'll punish the whole class if I have to."

I hadn't thought of this. Punish the whole class? Long story short, I ended up confessing. It was one of the hardest things I'd ever done. I knew I was in trouble. I knew I would have to deal with the principal, and I knew he would tell my parents. And when my dad found out? It would be the belt for me.

"What the hell were you even thinking?" Dad asked me.

"I guess I wasn't thinking," I said.

"Have you got some kind of death wish?"

"Death wish?"

"Pull down your pants."

There was no getting out of it. I don't know if it was just the fear of it or the actual pain, but I sobbed like a hysterical baby. Then I was sent to my room to think about what I'd done.

"You think about it," Dad said. "Think long and hard—and think about what you're going to say to your teacher tomorrow."

Say to her?

What would I say? Something like, "If you weren't such a mean old battle-ax, this probably would never have happened?" No, I wouldn't say anything like that. I would apologize. I would tell her I was stupid. I would be a kid.

But being a kid wasn't easy. The second time I would feel the wrath of my father's belt, I was eight. It was around Christmastime, and everyone on the street had their Christmas lights up. It was festive, but for a kid my age, the best thing about this time of year was the easy access us kids had to Christmas light bulbs. Here was the thing about the bulbs. You could throw them like little hand grenades, and they would explode when they broke. Pop, pop, pop! Usually, my friends and I would go to one of the neighboring streets to steal the bulbs—just in case we were seen. We didn't want anyone to recognize us, and we could run *fast*.

One day, I was playing in the front yard, and the temptation was just too much for me to resist. The family across the street had strung Christmas lights all over the front of their house. Their last name was Cooley. This was a weird family. They had kids, but they didn't like kids. And they were known for calling the police when anyone in the neighborhood misbehaved. My dad said they were "kooks," and he warned me to stay away from their house. Well, that warning didn't stop me. Like I said, the temptation was too much to resist, and I walked to the front of their house. One by one, I unscrewed their light bulbs and stuffed them into my jeans' pockets. I probably had seven or eight of them tucked away before I heard Mrs. Cooley's voice.

"Hey, you," she said. "What do you think you're doing?"

Busted!

I turned and ran. I didn't know what else to do. The woman had curlers in her hair, and she looked like a real-life Medusa. I didn't dare look at her! I ran into our house and made a beeline for my bedroom. I proceeded to empty my pockets, and I hid the stolen light bulbs under my bed.

Then, the doorbell rang, and my mom answered it.

Mrs. Cooley, hair curlers and all, told my mom about what I'd done.

My mom called for me, and I came to the door. It was no use. I admitted to the theft, and I went to my bedroom to retrieve the bulbs.

When Dad got home from work that night, Mom told him about the event.

My dad blew his top. “Didn’t I tell you to stay away from that house?”

“Yes,” I said.

“Bad enough that you’re out stealing, but to be stealing from the *Cooleys*?”

“I’m sorry,” I said.

“You’re lucky they didn’t call the police on you.”

“Yes, sir.”

“Pull down your pants. You know the drill.”

Damn.

This second whipping wasn’t as bad as the first, but it was bad enough. When Dad was done, I ran to my room to hide.

Ralph opened the door a crack and poked his nose in. “How does it feel?” he asked.

“Horrible,” I said.

“You’re an idiot.”

“Shut the door and leave me alone,” I said.

The last time I remember getting whipped, it was for shoplifting. There was a market not far from our house, and I would go there with my friends to buy Cokes on hot summer days. Mom would give me a quarter, and we’d ride our bikes to the store. The store owner was a nice man named Mr. Parsons. I remember him. He was bald, and he was always wearing a green apron. Anyway, my friends and I entered the store, and we pulled our drinks out of the refrigerator at the rear of the store. To get to the checkout counter, we had to walk down the candy aisle. Jeez, old Mr. Parsons had a lot of candy—everything a kid could ever want. You should know that my parents were against candy. Candy caused cavities, and fillings cost money, but they allowed me to buy Cokes. Go figure.

Anyway, one day, I decided to shoplift some candy. My friends chickened out, but I was determined to be brave. And I wasn’t going to steal just a regular-sized candy bar. I was going for one of those big Hershey bars, big enough to feed an entire family. It was no easy task. I would have to tuck it up under my T-shirt and pretend it wasn’t there. Well, kids are stupid.

When we came to the cash register to buy our Cokes, Mr. Parsons immediately noticed the shape of the big Hershey bar in my shirt. “Out with it,” he said to me.

“Huh?” I asked.

“In your shirt,” he said.

Busted again.

Mr. Parsons told me that ordinarily he would call the police, but since he knew my mom, he would just call her. And he did.

Fifteen minutes later, Mom came to get me. She apologized to Mr. Parsons, and she made me do the same.

“I was a kid once,” Mr. Parsons said. “I know what it’s like.”

My dad, however, was not so forgiving. When Mom told him what had happened, and how she had to come to the store to get me, off came the belt.

CHAPTER 28

THE KNIFE

I realized something while talking to Bartholomew. All my life, I've longed for perfection. It's crazy, isn't it? But it's the truth. Good luck and perfect judgment. A clear head. Always doing the right thing despite the Sirens' enticing songs calling me to the rocks.

"Your life is the cabin in Santa Cruz," Bartholomew said. "The toilet in the neighbor's front yard is reality. I don't know how I can make it any clearer. And if it wasn't the toilet, it would be something else."

"Does that mean I should just accept reality?" I asked.

"Of course not. Acknowledging it and accepting it are two different things."

"Then I should be upset?"

"Not upset. Maybe *proactive* is a better word."

"Proactive?" I asked.

"Taking action," Bartholomew said. "And knowing that by taking action, you may or may not obtain the results you're seeking. And *then* you accept the results either way. Success. Failure. Maybe just progress. Know that the world doesn't care one way or the other. Time marches on."

I thought about this and then said, "There are a lot of toilets in the world."

"There are a lot of them," Bartholomew agreed.

Was my poetry improving? I had no idea. I didn't know anyone who was much of an expert, and my audience so far was comprised mostly of just Bartholomew and me. And I suppose it could be argued that Bartholomew *was* me. A figment of *my* imagination. An extension of *my*

limited wisdom and expertise. Further, did it even matter? It wasn't like I planned on submitting or publishing any of my poems. I wasn't looking for an audience, critics, or fans. All my life, I had been performing 24-7 for audiences: family, friends, clients, employers, engineers, and city and county plan checkers. The poetry was for me. It was the one thing in my spread-out life I could call my own.

Was I just selfish?

Maybe it was. Or maybe I was just insecure. Insecurity breeds selfishness, does it not? We're not sure of ourselves, so we keep others at bay.

It was with these thoughts in mind that I wrote the following poem. I titled it "To My Sons," and it was written to Zach and Nate. This was the first poem I wrote with the actual intention of having someone else read it, but it was no less honest—and no further from my heart—than any other poem I'd written. In fact, upon writing it, I wondered if I should give it to my boys. Maybe it was too honest? Maybe it revealed too much? I'll let you be the judge. The poem went as follows:

To My Sons

Was I right, or was I wrong?
That is the song
Every parent sings while
Watching their children grow.

When I look back, I can see
Those things that we
Did with all the best of
Intentions. Now I ask

Myself, would I go that way
Now and today,
Or would I do it all
Very differently?

Hindsight is twenty-twenty,
Errors plenty.

But what is done is done,
And what is said is said.

Still, I can't help but wonder
If the thunder
Of your troubles could have
Been somehow avoided.

Here is what I tried to do.
My aim was true.
I wanted you to chase
Your dreams to the far edge

Of the galaxy. That star
So very far.
A star you could call all
Your own. Map it, name it,

And compose music to it.
Then you can sit
One day and tell your own
Children all about the

Star you saw and conquered.
And when they've heard
Your story, they too will
Reach out into deep space.

What was the alternative?
To sit and live
Like me with dreams dull and
Going nowhere, going

To that place where all dreams go
When they have no
Heart. I have spent my life
Living in this dim place

Like my father before me.
One, two, and three,
And the line just grows long,
And the days pass, and I

Go nowhere. Paying the bills,
Hiking up hills,
Saving up enough cash
So I can retire.

I have learned that trouble is
Better than this.
And I admire you both
For all you've done, and for

All you're doing.

I thought about it for several days. I gave the matter due consideration, and I decided *not* to give this poem to either of my sons. When I was writing it, I hoped they would understand it. It made perfect sense to me, but would they really get it? I thought, *Well, at least it might make them think about their lives. At least it might shed some light on what I'd tried to do as a father.* On the other hand, maybe I should've written more. Maybe I should've been more specific. Maybe I should've just written a letter. And maybe I should've addressed each of them individually rather than as a pair. No, too many maybes. I kept the poem to myself, unread. *Maybe I will give it to them someday, but not today. Why do today what you can put off until tomorrow?*

When Bartholomew read this poem, he was disappointed that I kept the poem to myself. He stuck his thumbs in his armpits and flapped his elbows like a chicken. "Cluck, cluck, cluck," he said to me.

"Maybe," I said.

"Maybe or what?" Bartholomew asked.

"Maybe I'm not a chicken. Maybe I'm just concerned that I'm giving them both another excuse to keep banging their heads against a wall."

My dad liked proclaiming truths. Do you know what I mean by this? Think about it. Do you have anyone in your life who does this? They don't necessarily ever give you specific advice about anything, but they like making blanket statements about life. Often, they'll resort to age-old adages. "A stitch in time saves nine," they might say, or, "Don't put all your eggs in one basket." My dad said these sorts of things often because he liked boiling wisdom down to its essence. One of the things my dad said often was, "Never get into a fight that you can't win." I liked this one. It made sense to me, and I went on to make a life out of it, choosing my battles and quests carefully, never taking any foolish chances.

My body of work as an architect is a perfect example. I've worked for a lot of clients in my day at Wiley & Associates. I've been in charge of the design of their homes, and I've had a slew of opportunities to *do* something. Not necessarily outrageous, but something above and beyond the bar set by conventional wisdom. I've had ideas. God, I've had a million of them. It's not that I'm not creative, intelligent, or even cutting-edge. What is it that's held me back from promoting my ideas and talking my clients into something other than slate roofs, dormers, flower boxes, and picture windows? It's fear! Fear of losing. Fear of being laughed at. Fear of being thrown off the job. Was Frank Lloyd Wright afraid? Or was he just more of a man than me? Cluck, cluck, cluck—was that me?

Failure is a black mark, a stain, a demerit, a pimple on your forehead, a chink in the armor, a fly in the ointment. Failure is the ultimate imperfection. Failure is what you risk when you try to do something different. You want to know the truth? I didn't actually admire my sons. What they were doing terrified me and went against everything my father taught me. They were going against the grain, God forbid, and they'd been paying the price—and they were probably about to pay an even bigger price. Oh, I know the things they say, that you learn from failure, that failure makes you stronger, that you don't get anywhere by fearing failure, but weren't these really all just rationalizations for something everyone dreaded—the knife of failure.

When I was a kid, I used to have a recurring dream about a man with a knife. The man was tall, thick, and dark. He had oily black hair and a couple days' beard growth. He had eyes like a shark. In these dreams, I was always outside, trying to get into my house. It was night and difficult to see. I could see the lights on in the house, where it was warm and yellow, but I could not get in. The man wouldn't let me enter. In his hand was a silvery butcher knife, stained with red blood, and on the damp front lawn lay the bodies of his victims, people I didn't know. Or maybe I did know them. Maybe they were neighbors—or maybe they were friends. Sometimes they would be children, and sometimes they would be adults. But they were always dead.

Our car was always in the driveway, and I would sneak around the side of the car, trying to keep away from the man with the knife. He would say, "I can see you, Rick. I know where you are. You are mine!"

I was his *what*?

What did that mean, exactly? Did he mean I was his next victim? The man was evil. That was obvious. He was evil, and much stronger than me. His arms were like tree branches, and his hands were like vises. If he got ahold of me, it would be all over for sure!

"I'll do whatever you say," I'd say.

The man would laugh.

"Just tell me what you want."

"I want *you*."

It's funny. I've even had this same dream as an adult. In the dream, I am always a kid, and I never really get a good look at the man's face. If you were to sit me down with a police sketch artist, I wouldn't be able to describe him. He was just mean, murderous, and evil. He had heavy eyebrows—I do remember that. And a furrowing forehead. And beard growth, lots of bristly black beard growth, but not an actual beard.

And he had shiny white teeth. I could see them when he opened his mouth to speak. Teeth cut and polished clean when he gnashed into the bloody flesh of his victims. He was a cannibal, not in the African sense of the word, but just a devourer of human beings, eating them for the fun of it. Like a zombie, except he wasn't anything like a zombie. He was more like a car mechanic, greasy and gritty. And I remember something else. His belt was a heavy galvanized steel chain that jingled a song of death every time he moved. Musical in a way, but not really musical.

But enough about the man. It wasn't really the man who terrified me. It was the knife. My mom had one just like it in the kitchen, a long silvery butcher knife with a smooth wood handle. There was always blood on the knife, and blood trickling off the man's large knuckles. Why me? Why was the man after me specifically?

"Come out from behind the car," he would say. "I can see you. Don't make me come and get you. It'll be worse for you that way."

Then I would wake up, and I would always wonder, *Why do I keep having the same dream? What was it all about?* Never an answer. Just relief that the dream was over with, relief that the man was gone.

CHAPTER 29

MY LONG HAIR

When Zach's exhibit at the Beverly Center was winding down, I asked Zach what was next. He said a friend of Ernest Patterson had several galleries in San Francisco and was considering showing some of Zach's pieces there. Zach's sculptures were selling, maybe not like hotcakes, but there was a market for them. It was a matter of keeping them in the public's eye, and to do so, Zach needed them to be on display. "Nothing is for sure yet," Zach said. "But I'm keeping my fingers crossed." I guess the good thing was that Ernest was going to keep several of Zach's sculptures on display at a couple of his Southern California galleries. They wouldn't be featured like they were before, but they would be there.

Zach's moment of success lit something of a fire under him. He was working hard to create new pieces, thinking that they were going to sell like the others. As far as his marijuana use went, I wasn't really sure how much Zach was smoking. It was hard to tell if his month in rehab had done anything for him at all. I was glad that Zach had a successful exhibit at Ernest's gallery, but I was also disappointed. Was this brush with success encouraging Zach to continue on with a life that was, in all likelihood, going to take him nowhere at all? *A flash in the pan*. That's what I kept thinking to myself. My son—a flash in the pan and then what? Working in construction to pay his bills, smoking weed and playing video games during his off hours?

"Worry, worry, worry," Bartholomew said. "Always looking into that distorted crystal ball of yours."

It was early in the morning. I'd been writing a poem about an artist when Bartholomew appeared. It wasn't a poem about Zach. It was a poem about an older artist who was dedicated to his paintings, but his paintings were giving him nothing in return. They weren't selling. No one wanted to hang them on their walls. He was unappreciated. And I wondered how many artists in the world lived like this, pursuing their passion, thinking that one day someone would come along and say, "Wow, look at these paintings. So much talent! Such skill! Where has this guy been all these years? Did *he* cut his ear off? Did *he* abandon his family to live on an island? What's the story behind this fascinating man?"

I have a friend who's an artist. I guess the poem I was writing was inspired by him. His name was Roger Guest, and he lived in San Diego. We met in college when he had aspirations of becoming an architect, but during his senior year, he decided to pursue painting instead. It was his true love. Here's the thing about Roger. His parents were wealthy, and they set up a trust fund for Roger that would pay him a modest but steady income for the rest of his life. So, he didn't have to work if he didn't want to. He could spend his whole life painting, which is exactly what he decided to do. He was a full-time, lifetime artist. He didn't marry. He stayed in San Diego. He never seemed very happy. He lived in a rental in an older part of town, bought his clothes at thrift stores, and got around in a fifteen-year-old piece-of-junk car. Like I said, the poem I was writing was inspired by Roger.

Bartholomew read it a second time and said again, "Worry, worry, worry."

"This isn't a poem about Zach," I said.

"Of course it is."

"It's about my friend, Roger."

"Roger is Zach, thirty years from now."

"You think so?" I asked.

"I know so," Bartholomew said. "I know how you think. I'm familiar with your crystal ball."

"You keep saying that."

"Who are you to choose your son's future? Who are you to say what he'll do? Who are you to guess what Fortune will lay at his doorstep? And why are your outcomes for him always so depressing? I remember when you were younger. I remember when you were so optimistic."

"Experience teaches us."

"Bah," Bartholomew said.

"You disagree?"

"Experience is not a teacher. It just is. What you take away from your experience is up to you—not up to it."

"I don't even know what that means," I said.

"It means yes, you've had experiences, but those experiences can be interpreted in all sorts of ways, depending on what you're looking to get out of them. You think your friend Roger is unhappy because no one appreciates his art, because he hasn't been a success selling his art to the public. And you? You think that you're a success, giving the public what it wants and causing them to open their checkbooks and pay for your services? You're a success, stifling your creativity in order to make your clients happy? I haven't got the impression that this makes you especially happy at all. Am I wrong about this? Who's happier: the man who sticks to his guns and pursues his passions or the man who whores out his talents to please the passions of others? Since when is Roger unhappy? Have you asked him if he would be happier painting things that he knows people will want to hang above their sofas or in their foyers?"

"I guess I've just made an assumption. I am assuming that he would feel good if people liked his paintings."

"In lieu of truly expressing himself?"

"I don't know," I said.

"Sure you do," Bartholomew said.

We learn so much when we're young. We're like hungry little sponges, soaking up the sopping wet world we live in. I remember those days, and I remember what it was like. The lessons were heady and plentiful. All you had to do was to pay attention.

I remember middle school. Back then, we called it junior high. I'm not sure when they stopped calling it junior high or why. It was junior high when you were being prepared for the people-making machinery of high school. It *was* people-making machinery, wasn't it? They molded us into future good citizens and taught us self-discipline, responsibility, social order, a hearty respect for the American flag, and good manners—all of it shoved down our throats with a special emphasis on achievement. Grades were so important if you wanted to go on to college. Of course, you could opt out of college and be one of *those kinds of kids*. But I was good. I was one of the kids who fit in. In junior high, I was not necessarily super popular, but I got along with others, got good grades, had friends, and my teachers liked me.

There was a girl I liked in junior high. Her name was Samantha Henry. I wouldn't say I had a crush on Samantha, but I liked her. It wasn't so much because she was pretty, even though she was. And it wasn't so much because she got good grades, even though she did. I admired the heck out of Samantha because she was so talented at art. She was in my art class, and I couldn't believe how good she was at drawing and painting. Seriously, everything she did looked like it was done by an adult with years of training. Every line, every shadow, every shape, and every hue—always just right, right down to the smallest detail. This girl was a true artist. Samantha was *going places!*

Art class.

Our art class was taught by a woman named Mrs. Chowder. She was a mean old prune of a woman. She was probably in her sixties, and she always had a chip on her shoulder. It was as if no one took her classes seriously, being art and all, and being that art wasn't really a subject. Art was whimsy. Art wasn't like math, business, or science. Art was a bunch of kids taking an hour off from their more important subjects to horse around with paintbrushes and pencils. But if you thought you were going to take Mrs. Chowder's art class for an easy A, you were mistaken. She'd make you work for your grade. She didn't tolerate goof-offs. She had rules, and God help the student in her class who didn't follow these rules.

One of Mrs. Chowder's rules was that peace signs were strictly forbidden to appear in any of our projects. I don't know why she had such a hair up her butt about peace signs, but she did. And peace signs were popular back then, but if a peace sign appeared in anything you turned in to Mrs. Chowder, it would come back graded with an F. It was understood. We didn't like it, but there was nothing we could do about it. It was 1968. The war in Vietnam was raging, and hundreds of thousands of people were being killed in an effort to maintain capitalism in a tiny country halfway around the world where the people were about as excited about being capitalists as they were about a prospect of becoming Southern Baptists. It was a travesty of huge proportion. Destruction. Fear. Stupidity. There was nothing good that could have been honestly said about this war, yet there we were, shooting, bombing, maiming, and killing as if our lives and freedoms depended on it. It was in the middle of this that Mrs. Chowder handed out our latest art assignment. We were to create an artwork using the medium of our choice to reflect our feelings on a topic of world significance. I don't know what the old woman expected, but I know what she got from Samantha—and she didn't like it.

Samantha did a colored pencil drawing on a huge piece of paper, and the drawing was about the Vietnam War. The bottom half of the drawing was of people. A crowd of people. The crowd filled the entire bottom half of the drawing. There were all kinds of people in the jam-packed crowd, like a human collage of everyone that was being affected by the war. There were soldiers with guns, some of them on crutches, some of them bandaged, some of them healthy. There were Vietnamese people. There were children and babies in their mothers' arms. There were hippies and anti-war protesters, parents of soldiers who had been killed in battle, and parents of soldiers who were still overseas. There were all kinds of people—all with distressed expressions on their faces—and all of them were reaching toward the sky.

What were they reaching for? They were reaching for a huge yellow sun. They were reaching for the sunlight. They were reaching for a common goal: for the sun to shine upon their horrid wartime circumstance. The sun was like a god. The sun would bring love and understanding to their blood-and-guts-drenched world. But it was this sun that would seal Samantha's fate in the eyes of old Mrs. Chowder. The sun! For right in the middle of the sun, bold and as plain as day, in defiance of Mrs. Chowder's rule, Samantha had drawn a giant peace sign! She titled the work *Sun of Peace.* It was a masterpiece. It really was, well, except for the peace sign.

I remember thinking, *Why did she do it? Why did Samantha deliberately break Mrs. Chowder's rule?* It was no surprise to any of the rest of us. Mrs. Chowder gave Samantha an F for the project. All that work, and all that thought, and the drawing came back with an F. A big, fat F. Samantha's family moved away at the end of that semester. I never had a chance to talk to her about the project or about how she felt about getting an F. I didn't know her that well, but I did want to talk to her. I just never got the chance. After her family moved, I thought about her. I still couldn't quite process why she had been so rebellious, and I wondered what her new school was like. I wondered if she was making any friends. I wondered what she was drawing. I wondered if her new art teacher had any rules. She was such a curious creature. She isn't an enigma to me now, but back then, back in Mrs. Chowder's class, she really had me wondering.

I remember telling my parents this story shortly after it happened. I brought it up at the dinner table, and my dad just shook his head and said, "Rules are rules."

"Did Mrs. Chowder give her a chance to erase the peace sign?" my mom asked.

"I don't know," I said.

"What an idiot this girl must be," Ralph said.

"I don't think she's an idiot."

"No?" Ralph asked.

"I think she believed in what she was doing."

"We have rules in a society," my father said. "They don't always coincide with our wishes, but they are there for a reason. Without rules, you have anarchy. You have mayhem."

"Your father's right," my mom said.

My dad had his own rules. Did he ever. Rules for Ralph and me to live up to. Ralph was the first of us to dare to defy Dad's rules, probably because he was three years older than me, and I watched to see where it got him. I told you before that Ralph started to flounder during his senior year of high school. By flounder, I mean he began bringing home lousy grades, and that was one of Dad's rules—no son of his was going to get lousy grades in school. No son of his was going to forgo a college education. It just wasn't done, but Ralph did it. I can't tell you how many arguments Ralph and Dad had about school about the importance of a good education and about how essential college was. It was no use. Like Dad finally said, "You can lead a horse to water, but you can't make it drink."

There was hope for me. I always got good grades in high school, and I had every intention of going to college. I didn't need to be coerced. I *wanted* to go to college. Dad paid for the whole ball of wax, the tuition, the books and supplies, and the room and board. It was costing him a small fortune, and how did I repay him for his goodwill? Yes, I got good grades. But I also grew my hair long, against one of Dad's other rules, the one that said no son of his was going to be a long-haired hippie. Hippies were fags, subversives, and good-for-nothing pot smokers. Hippies were shit. Was I really being all that rebellious? Was my long hair *my* peace sign? I'll tell you the truth. Everyone was wearing their hair long when I was in college. My dad was just behind the times. I wasn't being any more rebellious than he was when he wore penny loafers to high school. I was just fitting in. That was me, always trying to fit in. I just wanted to look like everyone else my age.

It's funny because I don't think Dad could ever quite get over it. He'd introduce me to his friends as his daughter. Ha, ha, ha. He thought it was funny. "Meet Rick," he'd say. "He's too ugly to be a cheerleader, and he's too dumb to be a valedictorian."

Dad's friends would always laugh. Don't get me wrong. I knew Dad still loved me, and we did have some interesting conversations during those years when we were by ourselves. Dad was proud of me for choosing architecture as a major, and I would fill him in on the things I was learning. We talked about other subjects as well, and it amazed me how much my father knew. He was a smart man. He was a loving father. He just didn't like the long hair, and maybe it *was* my peace sign. Maybe if I'd known my dad didn't care, maybe I never would have grown out my hair at all. Who knows? If it was an act of rebelliousness, I got it out of my system. By my senior year, by the time I married Pamela, I had cut my hair short again.

Dad was grinning from ear to ear. "You look like a human being," he said. "Welcome back to the human race."

Chapter 30

Stubborn

Bartholomew liked to say, "You've been alive for nearly sixty-five years. It's amazing how much you've learned—and how little you know." I understood this, and he was right. I had learned a lot, yet I was still unhappy. Happy on the surface, maybe, but deep down, I was disappointed and worried. What was to become of me? What was to become of the people I cared about? Is this what life was about—or was I missing something?

Two months before my sixty-fifth birthday, I was watching football on TV. It was a Sunday, and Pamela was working in the garden. She was planting some new flowering plants in the flower beds adjacent to the house. She told me she liked working in the yard. Good thing because I didn't like it at all. I made myself a cup of coffee and turned on the game. I liked watching football. I mean, I wasn't a fanatic about it, and I would forget each game a couple days after I watched. And I was only vaguely aware of where the teams were in the standings. But football is a lot of fun to watch, especially when the underdogs put up a good fight. I always rooted for the underdogs, and it made me feel good when they won.

Bartholomew showed up while I was watching the game. "Where's Pamela?" he asked.

"She's out in the yard," I said.

"That gives us some time to talk."

"I guess it does," I said.

"Do you mind me interrupting your game?"

"It's not a problem."

"You like watching football?" Bartholomew asked.

"I like seeing the underdogs win."

"Ah, don't we all?"

"We all *feel* like underdogs, don't we?"

"Even the champions feel like underdogs."

"Why is that?" I asked.

"It's human nature. Everyone feels like the odds are stacked against them—even when the odds are in their favor."

"But sometimes people are confident."

"Even confident people are insecure," Bartholomew said. "There's always the story of the tortoise and the hare, the story of David and Goliath, the story of Ulysses and the Cyclops. There are thousands of them. Nothing is ever a sure thing. It's not over till it's over."

"Yes," I said, laughing.

"The question is, do *you* have a chance?"

"A chance for what?" I asked.

"A chance to be happy."

"There are so many variables," I said.

"Not really," Bartholomew said.

"No?" I asked.

"It isn't up to all the things you can't control. It's up to you."

"What does that even mean?"

"It means that the answer is you."

"And what is the question again?" I asked.

"The question is, do you really have a chance to be happy?" Bartholomew said. "The answer is you. How you perceive the world—and how you perceive yourself."

"Go on," I said. I said this because I figured Bartholomew had more to say, and I was right.

At first Bartholomew laughed. Then he said, "For each of us, the world begins and ends with ourselves. All that we see, feel, hear, smell, and taste. It's all in what we experience while we're alive, and how we interpret those experiences. It's in how we file them away, and finally what we do. *That* is humanity. And that's all it is. Nothing less, and nothing more. Some of us get a bag full of gold to work with, and some of us get a bag full of crap. It doesn't matter. It just is what it is. *Que será será*. The question is what are you going to do with the bag that God placed in your care?"

"I—"

I said no more. Bartholomew vanished, and Pamela stepped into the room. "Come see what I've done," she said.

"Jeez," I said.

"Come on. You can miss a few minutes of your game. It isn't going to kill you."

Surprise!

It *was* a surprise. I didn't expect it. Zach said he had an announcement to make, and he came over to the house to make it. It was early in the evening, and he brought Mary Ann with him. Do you remember Mary Ann, the girlfriend with the pink pigtails and the nose ring? She was now tagging along wherever Zach went, so we didn't think much of the fact that she was with him that evening. The two had become inseparable, and Pamela and I both liked Mary Ann. Good thing—because the two of them were now planning to get married. That was the announcement. I would've paid good money to see the look on my face!

"Married?" I asked.

Mary Ann showed us the engagement ring on her finger. "He asked me last night."

"And you said yes?" Pamela asked.

"Yes, a thousand times over."

"This is so sudden," I said.

"I kind of expected it," Pamela said.

"How long have you two known each other?" I asked.

"Almost a year," Zach said. "That is, if you're counting. Certainly, long enough to know we're in love."

"Wow," I said.

"Have you told anyone else?"

"You're the first," Zach said.

"We're going to tell my parents tomorrow," Mary Ann said. "We're having dinner at their house."

"I don't know what to say," I said.

"Congratulations," Pamela said.

"Yes," I said. "Congratulations."

"Where are you going to live?"

"At the Costa Mesa house," Mary Ann said.

"What about school?" I asked.

"This will be my last semester," Mary Ann said. "I'm going to take my mom up on her job offer. I'll probably have to lose the nose ring. I don't think the execs at Taco Bell are crazy about nose rings. And I'll have to do something different with my hair. You know, to look more normal."

"Of course," I said.

"I think she should dye her hair black," Zach said.

"It would go with my eyes."

"And what about you?" I asked Zach.

"The timing couldn't be better," Zach said. "My boss said the guy in charge of his small projects and customer service is quitting to work somewhere else. My boss thinks I'd be perfect for the job. I think I could handle it. And I'd get a pay raise. Of course, it would be full-time rather than part-time."

"And your art?"

"That deal in San Francisco fell through. I'm kind of at a standstill, but I can still work on my sculptures in my spare time."

"No college?"

"You know that I tried it. It wasn't for me. I have to be honest with myself. Computers? I don't even know what I was thinking. I have to be a realist."

"Sounds like you have it all figured out," I said. What was I supposed to say? I thought back to when Pamela and I were first married. I remembered telling my parents about our engagement. Pamela and I were both still in college, without any income, busy with our classes, but we had the whole thing under control.

My dad asked, "What are you going to do?"

I told him that we were both staying in college and not to worry about either of us dropping out.

"We're both going to get part-time jobs," I said.

"Doing what?" my dad asked.

"I have a drafting job lined up with one of my professors," I said. "He has a practice in Oakland. And Pamela has a job lined up answering phones for an attorney in Fremont. We can get to both jobs using BART, so we don't need a car. And we can use the money you're paying now for our dorms plus what we make at our jobs to get a nice little apartment somewhere. We've looked into apartments near school, and there's a couple of them we like. It's all doable."

"You're going to be very busy working part-time jobs and going to school."

"We like being busy," Pamela said.

I remember that first year we were married, and we were very busy. But it was great. I think I've said it before. Those were some of the best years of my life. They were meaningful. They were euphoric. They were nonstop, and I looked at Zach and his fiancé, Mary Ann, and I wondered if they were going to experience the same joy that I did during my first year of marriage. I hoped so. Or did I?

On one hand, I felt happy for Zach, getting married to the girl he loved, working a full-time job, and being responsible. On the other hand, I felt grief, like someone had died an untimely death. Zach the artist. Zach the spirited boy with his head in the clouds, tied to a string and being pulled down to earth where the rest of us lived. One day having his art exhibited at an art gallery in Los Angeles, and the next day, working eight hours a day for a contractor, organizing jobs, mollifying customers, bossing people around for his weekly paycheck. Taxes withheld. Health insurance to pay for. Trash to take out. Lawns to mow. Cars to wash, and eventually, diapers to change. Zach as a father? It was hard to imagine, but the time was coming.

What's that they say on the radio stations? They say, "The hits just keep on coming." Two days after Zach and Mary Ann announced their engagement, Pamela and I learned that Nate's wife, Emily, was pregnant. So weird, right? I mean, one day Nate was trying to take his life, and the next day, he and his wife were bringing a new life into the world. I didn't ask if the pregnancy was planned. It seemed like kind of a rude question. I did ask, "Are you guys ready for this? Babies change your life. Everything is going to change."

"We're ready," Nate said.

"It's so exciting, isn't it?" Emily asked.

"It is," I said.

"Have you thought of names?" Pamela asked.

"If it's a boy, we're going to name him Evan. If it's a girl, we're going to name her Evelyn."

"After anyone in particular?"

"We just like the sound of those names."

"That's as good a reason as any," I said.

"I had a girlfriend in college named Evelyn," Pamela said. "She was cute. Boys were always trying to date her. She was fighting them off all the time."

"I had a boy in my chemistry class in junior high named Evan," I said. "He was a smart kid."

When I told the news about Zach's marriage and Emily's pregnancy to Bartholomew, he laughed. "Life just keeps on rolling forward," he said.

"Seems so," I said.

"Does your mom know?"

"Both the boys gave her the news."

"Was she pleased?" Bartholomew asked.

"She seemed happy."

"And you?"

"The truth?" I asked.

"Why would I want to hear anything else?"

"I'm worried."

"Worried about what?"

"I'm not sure," I said.

"Worried that your sons are both disappearing into the distant horizon of everyday life?"

"The horizon?"

"The flat years—remember?"

"Maybe so," I said.

"Flat as a pancake? Boring? An endless stream?"

"Is that what's happening?"

"It will only happen if they let it happen. They have their whole lives ahead of them. The paths they take? It will be up to them."

"Look at the paths *I* picked," I said.

"And what's wrong with them?"

"Nearly everything," I said.

"It's just your distorted thinking again," Bartholomew said, and he laughed. "It's your misguided quest for what? For perfection? Is that what it is? Study your history. Study your science. Study your philosophy. Study your psychology. If there's one thing you will learn with any education, it's that perfection only exists as an ideal, as an unattainable goal, as a pipe dream, as something that will never be. To expect it, or to demand it, is childish and foolhardy. Take stock. Yes, many things have not gone your way, but so what? Many things *have* gone your way. That's why the wise man with the long white beard says, 'Count your blessings.' It's a cliché, but it's a good one. There's nothing wrong with repeating a good cliché now and again. The truth is the truth."

During one of our conversations, Bartholomew told me I was as stubborn as a mule. Was he right? I had never pictured myself as a stubborn person. I had pictured myself more as a person who was *too* cooperative. A crowd-pleaser. A performer. Even a circus geek, doing some of the strangest things just to fit in with the world. So, what did Bartholomew mean when he said I was stubborn? Me? Stubborn? Then, in a moment of clarity, it came to me. I wrote a poem that I titled "Stubborn," and it went as follows:

Stubborn

I dig in my heels,
Refusing to budge.
Hold out a carrot,
And give me a nudge.

For all the good it
Will do. I'm going
Nowhere. Standing here
Eating and mowing

The grass at my feet,
Brushing away these
Flies with my tail,
Nibbling at the fleas

In my mangy hide.
Why can't I see that
A few steps forward,
A tip of my hat,

A nod of my head,
A click of my tongue,
Is all I need to
Accept what I've done

And what has come my
Direction in life.
I have two fine sons
And a loving wife,

And a job the puts
Food on the table.
I am a healthy
Mule, strong and able.

I have a conscience
And a heart as big
As Farmer John's good
Old prizewinning pig.

I don't like to lie,
And I am sincere.
I have values and
Mores that I hold dear.

Loan me a dollar,
And I'll pay you back.
Tell me your needs, and
I'll give what you lack.

So, why won't I budge?
And why am I so

Convinced I am left
Of right? I don't know.

My friend, he calls it
Distorted thinking,
And maybe he's right.
I should start talking

To my thoughts, rather
Than giving in to
Them. What do you think?
And what would you do?

Okay, okay,
Maybe I'll move!

When Bartholomew read this poem, he said, "Every day, you move a little closer. Good thing because I'm not going to be around forever. Yes, I've been visiting you, but I have no intention of taking up permanent residency. I'll tell you the truth. I debated coming here in the first place."

"But you came," I said.

"I did," Bartholomew said. "Now, if you don't mind, I have a poem for you."

"You wrote a poem?"

"Why not?" Bartholomew asked.

"I don't know," I said.

"You want to hear it?"

"Sure," I said.

It was a short poem. Short and to the point, and I got it. I understood what Bartholomew was saying, but it was like having the air let out of my tires. I could hear the air leaving, hissing, thin streams of rubbery wind. How would I get around? I had come to depend on our conversations. Granted, half the time, I didn't know what he was talking about, but I knew he was right. He was right because he was Bartholomew.

Bartholomew pulled a sheet of paper from his back pocket and unfolded it. He snapped it taut, took it over to the light, and read the poem to me. He wasn't smiling, and he wasn't frowning. The poem went as follows:

I'm here today,
But not for long.
I played my lute,
And sang a song.

Gave you a chance
To love your life,
To love your sons,
To love your wife.

Showed you how to
Cherish your tears,
And therefore how
To love your years.

It is all as
It ought to be.
Now take flight and
Enjoy your free—

Dom.

CHAPTER 31

QUICKSILVER

Freedom is a funny word. We say, "Give us freedom," but we say it meaning freedom from what? Freedom from oppression? Freedom from restrictions? Freedom from unjust laws? Freedom from silly social mores? How about freedom from ourselves? That is the *real* freedom, isn't it? Freedom from devouring our own tail and becoming just another ouroboros.

Guilt is an awful thing, yet aren't we all guilty of one thing or another? Maybe all of our transgressions aren't made public, but they are transgressions for each and every one of us. And I do mean all of us. Out of eight billion souls on the planet, not a single one of them is perfectly innocent. Try them in court, and you're going to get a guilty verdict for every Tom, Dick, and Harry who breathes the air, who walks and talks, who lives in a house, who drives a car, who pulls a handle on a slot machine. They are all guilty of *something*. Guilty of harming their loved ones, their neighbors, or even strangers, in one way or the other. You can rationalize all you want, but when the crops are finally harvested, it is what it is.

Bartholomew was right. When you realize the omnipresence of guilt, you have a better shot at being happy. When you are guilty, you are not alone. You have a lot of company, from the lowest forms of human life right up to the most respected icons and heroes. Everyone. From the life-in-prison convict to the most admirable do-gooder on the planet. From Ted Bundy to Martin Luther King Jr., from Lee Harvey Oswald to Florence Nightingale. Guilt is acquired and deserved—and all-pervasive. Guilt is the inescapable by-product of living, the smoke belching from our factories, the toxic chemicals being dumped into our rivers, the nuclear waste being buried in our earth. At the end of the day, there is no escaping it.

Guilt.

I'll tell you another story that I told Bartholomew. This story concerns my job at Wiley & Associates. I'm telling you this story in confidence because if word ever got out about what I did, well, let's just say it's best that you keep this story to yourself. I'm not proud about what happened, yet it did happen. And I am ashamed. I was in my late thirties, a little too ambitious, perhaps, and not very wise.

First, you need to know that John Wiley trusted me, and I did several things to earn that trust. I understood John because I had put myself in his shoes. It isn't easy running a small business, and there is a lot of trust and dependence involved. You have to trust your employees, and you have to be able to depend on them to work with your best interests at heart. It's more difficult than it sounds because the truth is that most employees have their own interests at heart. Their employer is just that—an employer, the guy who dishes out the work, watches the work being done, and writes the payroll checks twice a month. I didn't understand a lot of things when I was in my thirties, but I understood this. And I understood that an employee who earned the trust of his employer was gold in the eyes of that employer.

The first thing I did to earn John's trust involved a batch of blueprints I ordered from the print shop for one of our projects. I was an assistant designer at the time. The client was anxious to get his project out to bid, and he called the office to order twenty sets of drawings. When he called, the lead designer, Tom Andrews, and John were out of the office, so I was kind of in charge of things while they were gone. I knew this client wanted the drawing right away, so I jumped at the chance to fulfill his request, ordering the twenty sets of plans and telling the printer to deliver them to the client as soon as possible. What I didn't know was that there was a five-page list of final revisions that still had yet to be incorporated into the plans. No one had told me. When it was discovered that the prints delivered to the client were all no good, that I had jumped the gun, I immediately went to John's office and told him it was my fault.

"I should've checked with you or Tom before ordering the prints," I said. "I just assumed the drawings were ready."

"Jeez," John said.

"It was my fault," I said. "I was trying to do the right thing, but I guess I really messed up."

"You can say that again."

"I'll pay for them," I said.

"Pay for them?"

"You can take it out of my next paycheck. And I'll call the client to apologize."

I don't think any employee ever offered such a thing to John, to pay for a mistake, or to apologize directly to a client for a mistake made. He gave me the oddest look, and then he said, "No, no, that isn't necessary. So long as you don't do it again. So long as you've learned."

As it turned out, it was Tom who apologized to the client, and the cost of the wrong plans was not taken out of my paycheck. But I had still accomplished something that day. John Wiley was impressed with me and my willingness to take responsibility for what I'd done.

The second thing I did to earn John Wiley's trust was to get caught working on a Sunday. One of the projects I was working on was behind schedule. It was not my fault that the job was behind schedule, but I took it upon myself to work the entire weekend on it. I worked Saturday, and I came in Sunday. John came into the office Sunday to catch up on some paperwork when he found me at my drafting table. I was being paid salary, not by the hour, so the extra hours I was putting in were basically for free. "If it has to get done, it has to get done," I said. "I didn't have anything planned for this weekend anyway."

"You're a piece of work," John said, smiling.

"Just doing my job," I said.

And I *was* just doing my job. At least, that's how I saw it. I was just being a good employee, but it made me feel good to be caught by the boss going the extra mile.

"You're going to go far in this firm," John said.

"Yes, sir," I said.

There were other things I did at Wiley & Associates that put me on the good side of John Wiley. I don't want to give the impression that I was some kind of brownnoser; I was just doing my job to the best of my abilities. I was proud of the work I did at the firm, and I was proud of my behavior there. If John liked me for it, that was just icing on the cake.

Anyway, years passed, and the next thing you knew, I was leading my own projects. Along came the Watanabe project. Brian Watanabe and his wife, Andrea, had come to John Wiley to design their mansion in Laguna Beach. This couple had some serious money, and they were high-powered socialites. Everyone in Orange County knew who they were, and more than anything, I wanted to be picked for their project. There was only one thing in the way of me being picked for the job, and that was another designer in the office named Frank Barron. Frank was a couple years older than me. Frank had a master's degree from Harvard, and I hate to admit this, but Frank was more talented than me. His house designs were nothing short of amazing.

I was also friends with Frank. We got to know each other well, and we often had lunch together. And, like me, Frank was a devoted employee. I think we liked each other for this reason. We both respected each other. We avoided office games and just hunkered down to get to business every day we came to work. I learned a lot about Frank from our lunch conversations, and we shared a lot of personal information. I told him stories about Pamela and my sons, and I told him stories about my childhood with my parents. I shared my fears, and I shared my successes. And Frank reciprocated, but then he told me something that surprised me. When I asked if he ever planned to get married to some woman and have children, he laughed and said, "Fat chance."

"Why do you say that?" I asked.

Frank paused for a moment, and then, softly, so no one else but me could hear, he said, "I'm gay, Rick."

Well, I was floored. "You?" I asked.

"Always have been," Frank said. "And always will be."

"I had no idea," I said.

"This is just between you and me."

"Of course," I said.

"You're a friend."

"Yes," I said.

"I shouldn't be embarrassed about it," Frank said. "In fact, I'm not embarrassed. I just don't want it getting out. Some people will take it the wrong way. The world isn't exactly kind to gay people. Maybe someday, but not today."

"Sure," I said.

"How do *you* feel about it?"

"I'm a little surprised. But to each their own, right?"

"To each their own."

"How long have you known this?"

"Since I was in high school."

"Wow," I said. "I never would have guessed."

And I was being honest. I never would have guessed. And I was as open-minded as the next guy, but I'll also tell you that it made me feel a little weird.

I kept Frank's secret, and I continued to be friends with him. We still had our lunches, and we still talked about the people in our lives. Everything was fine until the Watanabe project came up. That damned Watanabe project! I wanted it so bad, yet I knew Frank was the most likely employee John Wiley would pick to lead the project. Frank with his Harvard degree. Frank with all his talent. The guy was a shoo-in, and I was sure of this.

I knew something else. I knew that Brain and Andrea Watanabe were homophobes. Everyone and their brother knew about the couple's drive to have one of the teachers fired at their son's elementary school. Why? It was because the poor guy was openly gay—and for no other reason. Mrs. Watanabe was especially vocal about it. She was on the TV news and in the local newspaper. Of course, not everyone agreed with her, but that didn't keep her from speaking her mind until the teacher finally resigned and left the school on his own. It was a shame, I thought, but it also gave me an opportunity to be picked for the Watanabe project rather than Frank. I now admit it. I was wrong, but here's what I did. I met privately with John Wiley, and I told him I had information that was extremely important.

"You can't tell anyone that I told you this," I said.

"Okay," John said.

"I was told this in confidence."

"No one will know," John said.

"It's about Frank. I know you're considering him for the Watanabe project. I know you'll be making a decision soon. I'm not telling you this so that you'll pick me. I just have the welfare of the firm in mind. I don't know how to say this, except to come right out and say it. Frank is gay."

"He's what?" John said.

"He's gay," I said. "He told me so. I promised I wouldn't tell anyone, but here I am, telling you. You can't tell Frank that I told you. Please. The two of us are friends. I'm just trying to avoid what could be a disaster."

"Yes, yes," John said, and he rubbed his chin. "You know this for sure?"

"I do," I said.

And that was all I had to do. Three days later, the Watanabe project was assigned to me. I've never told anyone this story—not even Pamela.

You know, I didn't feel guilty about it when I did it. I felt like I was doing what I had to do to get ahead in the world. By hook or by crook, I was not going to be left behind. But a year or so later, I began to notice something. It was Frank who was now being left behind. He was not getting any plum assignments, and he was being passed over for designers in our firm who had half his talent. It was obvious to me that John Wiley was sending a message to Frank that it was time to move on. I was guessing that John had no more use for gays in his firm than Mr. or Mrs. Watanabe had use for gays in their son's elementary school. This was not what I'd intended to happen, but it happened. A couple years after I told John about Frank being gay, Frank quit and joined up with another firm in Los Angeles. I haven't seen him since.

But I think about Frank often, and I think about what I did to him. He thought we were friends—and we were—but when push came to shove, I betrayed him. The things we do. The things we do to get ahead in the world. The things we do to convince others we are worthy. The things we do to frame our lives the way we think they ought to be framed. The efforts we make to manipulate people. The trusts we betray, and the lies we tell.

"It's so depressing," I finally said to Bartholomew.

"It shouldn't be," he said.

"Why not?"

"It's only depressing when you're expecting perfection. Drop the expectation of perfection, and it's just par for the course. Forget perfection, and it's all wonderful."

"Wonderful?"

"With all its flaws and troubles, life is delicious, a wondrous recipe of the good and the bad, of pride and shame, of the sour and the savory. A little of this, and a lot of that, all mixed up together and thrown in the oven. Light the candles, and set the table—it's a feast of missteps and successes. Unforgettable and incomparable. In that meal, you will find the joy of living."

I still owed Bartholomew a tenth story. So far, I had only told him nine. Actually, I had told him way more than nine, but only nine, formally. I wanted my tenth story to be memorable. I wanted to prove that I'd been listening and learning. It's sort of silly, isn't it? Wanting to impress an imaginary friend? But I had to be honest—it *was* important to me. I sat down at my desk and thought.

I had told him how I rescued Max from the freeway and how we had taken him into our home. This was a good story. It was about me being a good person, but I also had to be honest. I was kind of making myself out to be a hero. In a way, I was bragging about what a good person I'd been, and I didn't think this was exactly what Bartholomew was looking for. No, I wanted a story that exemplified how I'd been good simply *because I was good*. Have you ever tried to come up with a story like this about yourself? If you're anything like me, it isn't easy. I don't know why, but the negative stories always seem so readily accessible while the positive ones are not. It's like trying to pick up mercury from a broken thermometer. Quicksilver. You learn that they call it that for a reason.

Chapter 32

Salesman of the Month

I got up at eleven. I showered and dressed, and then I called John Wiley. I told him I would be a couple hours late for work. I told him I was taking Nate out for lunch.

"Good for you," John said. "You *should* be taking him out to lunch. The more time you spend with your family, the better."

I agreed with him and then left the house. Pamela was at work, and since she knew about my plans, there was no reason to call her or leave a note.

The drive from Irvine to Riverside was always iffy. The 91 was a freeway that could back up at the drop of a hat. But today it was clear sailing, and I arrived at Nate's car dealership even earlier than I'd planned. It was a slow day on the lot, and Nate was ready to go when I got there. We hopped in my car, and I followed Nate's directions to a little restaurant called Emile's, which was on the first floor of a large office building in downtown Riverside. Nate had eaten there before, and he said they had good food.

Nate seemed like he was in a good mood. When we sat down to look at our menus, Nate told me a joke that one of the other salesmen had told him. "A blonde girl is speeding down the road in her new Mustang. She passes a blonde cop who sees her whiz by. The blonde cop hits her lights and siren, and she pulls over the blonde girl. She steps to the driver's door, and the blonde girl rolls down her window. The blonde cop then asks the girl for her license and registration. The blonde girl starts looking through her car and says, 'Darn, I forget—what are they again?"

"'I need to see your license and registration, ma'am,' the cop says.

"'What does a license look like?' the girl asks.

"'It's that little thing in your purse with your picture on it,' the blonde cop says.

"'Oh yeah,' the blonde girl says. She reaches into her purse, pulls out a little compact mirror, and hands it over to the blonde cop.

"The blonde cop opens the mirror, looks inside for a moment, and hands it back to the girl. 'I'm sorry, ma'am,' she says. 'If I knew you were a cop, I wouldn't have pulled you over.'"

I laughed.

It was good to hear Nate telling jokes. It was good to see him laughing again. I asked him how Emily was doing, and he said she was doing fine so far. She'd experienced a little morning sickness, but it was nothing to be alarmed about. I then asked how things were going at the dealership, and he said they were going very well. Nate was in line to be named salesman of the month, having sold more cars than anyone else.

"Your grandfather will be so proud of you," I said.

"Grandpa was right about this," Nate said.

"Right about what?"

"Selling cars isn't such a bad life. And there are lots of perks. Health insurance, a 401(k), and I get to drive a new car to and from work each day. So long as I make the sales. And selling cars is a lot easier than I thought it would be. I mean, it's easy for me. Not so easy for some of the other idiots who work here. But if you do your research and pay attention, it's a good way to make a living."

Bartholomew would've been proud of me. Why? Because I told Nate that Pamela and I were proud of him. "Have you seen Grandma recently," I asked.

"Not recently," Nate said.

"You and Emily should pay her a visit. She would love seeing you two."

"You're probably right."

"She's getting up there, you know?" I said. "Not to sound morbid, but she could drop dead any day."

"Jeez," Nate said.

"I'm just saying you should get your time in. She's got nothing to do all day except muddle around that assisted-living facility, and her family means a lot to her. You mean a lot to her—and so does Emily. An occasional visit from you guys would mean the world to her."

"Okay," Nate said.

"Zach and Mary Ann saw her last week. It meant so much to her. She couldn't stop talking about them."

"I get it," Nate said, smiling.

"Better sooner than later."

"It will be sooner," Nate said.

"Tell her the joke about the blondes," I said. "Mom loves a good joke."

"Since when did you and your mom become so close?"

"Close?"

"You were never close to Grandma. Not even to Grandpa when he was alive. I always sensed that there was a distance between you guys."

"Maybe there was," I said.

"And?"

"A person learns things as he gets older."

"What did you learn?"

Nate was putting me on the spot. He didn't mean to be doing this. I think he was just genuinely interested in what caused me to have a sudden change of heart. "I was the victim of my own distorted thinking," I said.

"What does that mean?"

"I think I was doing what most people do. I was wanting the world to be perfect. Don't we all want the world to be perfect? We want to get our way. We want things to work out. We want people to behave the way we want them to behave so that everything will be just right so that all the puzzle pieces fall into place, but life is not like a jigsaw puzzle. There are many pieces that don't fit anywhere. They're the wrong color and the wrong shape. They're the wrong size. And as you get older, if you're lucky, you learn that there's nothing wrong with this picture. I know it sounds kind of trite, but life just is what it is. Sometimes it's a symphony, and sometimes it's just noise. Sometimes up is down, and sometimes down is up. Sometimes right is left, and sometimes over is under. What we need to do if we want to be happy is acknowledge what life is rather than what we want it to be. Sometimes, we just need to say, 'Hey this *is* okay. Everything is as it ought to be.'"

"Okay," Nate said.

"When it came to my mom and dad, I came to the realization that I wanted them to be perfect parents as I imagined perfect parents would be. I wanted them to say the things I wanted them to say, and I wanted them to behave as I thought they should behave. But what right did I have? First, who's to say that I knew anything about parenting? And who's to say that I had a lock on what was right or wrong? Me? I was just another human being with my own selfish needs, flaws, and misperceptions. Who died and left me in charge? No, my mom and dad had every right to be who they wanted to be, to make their own decisions, to follow their own hearts. And I did know that they loved me. And that's all that should've mattered. That's all that ever did matter. That's all that ever will matter."

Nate just stared at me. Truthfully? I wasn't sure he'd heard a word of what I'd said. He'd asked me a question, and I answered it—but did he hear me?

Suddenly, there was applause. I looked to my left, and Bartholomew was seated in the chair beside me. He was clapping his hands as he shouted, "Bravo, bravo!"

I gave him a look.

"Don't worry," Bartholomew said. "Only you can see or hear me. But that was quite a speech. I just couldn't resist cheering you on."

I'd been wondering, what would my father have to say about Nate and the direction his life was taking. Salesman of the month? Really?

My dad. He always wanted the best for me. He always wanted me to succeed, and he always wanted me to achieve great things. "You have advantages," he would say to me. "You have a good head on your shoulders. You're healthy and smart. You've had a good upbringing. There's no reason why the world can't be at your beck and call." Those were the words I heard, but Dad was also a realist. The words I didn't listen to? He also used to shake his head and say, "You've got to take the bad with the good," and that was the advice I should've given more weight to. Maybe Dad was just like me, struggling between the two ends of life's spectrum, doing your best to achieve great things versus being proud of what you were actually achieving. Dreams versus realities. The air versus the earth.

Maybe my dad had dreams. Did he? You know, we never talked about them. We talked about many things, but we never talked about his dreams, the things that he deep down wanted out of life. Where did he see himself when he was younger—before the world had made an office supply CEO out of him and before the ocean waves had smoothed him out with their constant churning and their obligation to reality? Did my dad want to be an artist? Or a musician? Or a world-renowned entrepreneur? Or maybe a famous writer? Or some kind of one-of-a-kind expert?

It's something I've come to regret, never talking to Dad about his youth. I mean, we talked about some things, but not the things that truly mattered. I think he deliberately avoided the subject, and I was too dumb and inexperienced to ask probing questions. My dad? Who cared? I was selfish, young, and all those things that come with being selfish and young. If Dad was still alive today, I would ask, "What about you? What did you envision for your future? What did you want to be? What were *your* dreams, aside from making a lot of money, marrying Mom, and having children? Surely there was a distant star in the sky that caught your attention."

Maybe Dad wanted to be an astronaut. Maybe *he* wanted to be the first man to walk on the moon. Maybe *he* wanted to make President Kennedy's promise a reality. "One small step for a man, and one giant leap for mankind." Leaving footprints in the lunar dust and installing an American flag. Or maybe he wanted to be a famous music composer. Dad always did have a soft spot for classical music, and maybe he wanted to write music for symphony orchestras, music that would awe the public, music that would carry people to the moon without the assistance of NASA and all its engineers. The next Mozart? Or the next Beethoven? Or maybe he wanted to become the next Picasso, astounding the art world and the public with his artwork. Scribble some doodles on a piece of paper, and they would become worth thousands. Everything he touched with his hands—turning to gold.

How should *I* know what my father dreamed about? But don't we all have dreams? Here's the kind of conversation I remember having with him. It won't be word-for-word, but you'll get the general idea. We'd be in the front yard, and Dad would be mowing the lawn while I washed the cars. Let's say I was a freshman in high school, and let's say I'd just recently received a report card. Let's also say I got a B– in math.

"A B– is almost a C," Dad would say. "It's not like you don't have an aptitude for math."

"It's boring," I would say.

"It's important."

"That's what my teacher says. But what if I don't use it for the rest of my life?"

"Everyone uses some math."

"Everyone?"

"Almost everyone," Dad would say. "What do you plan to do with your life?"

"I have no idea."

"There, see? You don't know."

"Do you use math in your job?"

"All the time," Dad would say.

"Geometry?"

"No, not geometry. Well, maybe a little. The point is to leave all doors open."

"All doors?"

"You need a foundation. You can't build a house without a good foundation."

"What if I wanted to be a writer?"

"A writer?"

"Does a writer do math?"

"Since when have you shown an interest in writing?"

"I get good grades in English."

"Very few writers make a good living at it."

"Money isn't everything," I'd say.

"Some people say that. Usually, people who have plenty of it—or people who don't and are just trying to rationalize their poor choices."

"I won't need money to be happy."

Dad would laugh at this. "You don't know what it's like to be without it. You're talking through your hat."

"My hat?"

"You and your brother have always had what you needed and what you wanted. I think you take it for granted. I'd bet if you lived in a family that had very little money, you'd have a firmer grasp of just how important money is."

Money.

Isn't it interesting what a major role it plays when we are making a decision as important as what we plan on doing with our lives? At least, as far as my dad was concerned, and consequently as far as I was concerned. Other people were making decisions about their lives with no regard to how much they were going to be paid, but they were foolhardy. At least that's what my dad would've said when I was growing up. And I wonder if I'd asked Dad about this when he was older, would he still believe the same thing? Didn't Mom say he had taken up painting during the years before he passed away? Painting? It was a hobby and not a way to make a living, and he seemed to get no satisfaction out of it. But maybe *that* was the dream. And maybe by taking it up when he was older, he was able to prove to himself that he made the right decision when he was younger, telling himself, "See? You're no damn good at this. You could never have made a living at it. Then again—"

I don't know. And I never will know because I never asked Dad the right questions. Again, it was on me.

CHAPTER 33

THE TRUTH

She did it. She had her nose ring removed, and she died her hair black. She also had her hair nicely styled—no more crazy pigtails. And Zach? He took the job his boss was offering, and he was now working full-time as a construction supervisor. Zach and Mary Ann set a wedding date that was far enough off to give them time to plan a big wedding and to give Mary Ann time to finish off her last semester at USC.

It was crazy. So much was happening so quickly. Pamela and I finally got to meet Mary Ann's parents in person. We all went out to dinner together, and Mary Ann did most of the talking. It was amazing how this girl could talk. She was never at a loss for words. Mary Ann's father's name was Jacob, and her mother's name was Sarah.

I wrote a poem about our meal together. I titled it "The Dinner," and it went as follows:

The Dinner

There we all were at our
Table, a family soon to be.
Mary Ann, Zach, Jacob,
Sarah, plus Pamela and me.

I knew as much about
This family as I knew of
Quilting or atomic
Nuclei. Right? But it was love

That brought us all to this
Restaurant to eat and talk. We

Said hello and shook hands,
Smiling and pretending to be

At ease with everything.
"Nice to meet you." "How do you do?"
"Have you ever eaten
Here? I've heard they have good food."

Mary Ann says that the
Beef stroganoff is to die for.
Zach says the prime rib is
Too. "You'll finish it, wanting more."

The waitress's name is
Elaine, and she hands out menus
And brings us buttered bread.
Then she announces the good news,

That there are specials in
Addition to the everyday
Items on the menu.
She speaks and we listen. "Sounds great,"

Zach says. "I think I'll order
The fettuccini Alfredo,"
And Mary Ann laughs and
Says, "I think I'll order that too."

When Elaine comes back to
The table, we all order our
Food. Pamela orders
Some white wine. Me, a whiskey sour.

Jacob and Sarah don't
Drink, so they each order coffee.
Zach and Mary Ann ask
For beers from some other country.

"Well, well, well," Jacob says,
"Here we all are at last, the six
Of us together." And
I begin to feel kind of sick.

It's not that I don't like
Mary Ann's parents. But here we
Go again, lying as
If two plus two equals a three.

I make much more out of
My job than it ever deserved,
And I bend all the flat
Boxes into circles and curves.

I play the same game I've
Been playing with others for years.
Exaggerating the
Smiles and ignoring all the tears.

Sarah and Jacob do
The same. Life is great, and their work
Is interesting, and
Jacob plays golf, and Sarah cooks.

We're getting along well.
They like what they hear, and I like
What they say. We're all the
Best ever to come down the pike.

The crap is so deep here,
And my boots are soaked and leaking.
My socks are wet, and my
Sweaty, calloused feet are stinking.

"Ha, ha, ha, that was a
Good one. Have you ever heard the

One about the blonde cop
And the blonde driver. This is one

I heard from my son Nate."
I tell the joke, and everyone
Laughs. The next thing you know,
We're all full, and dinner is done.

We don't know any more
About each other than we did
When we first met.

Nowadays, that's about as real
As it gets.

When Bartholomew read this poem, he laughed. "You know what your problem is?"

"What?" I said.

"You're confusing a right to some privacy with objectionable deceitfulness."

I thought about this, and then I said, "I don't know what you mean by that."

"Somehow, you've got it in your head that people should be honest with each other all the time. And if they're not honest? You say they're deceitful. You say they're phonies, but nothing could be further from the truth. Honesty isn't always the best policy. When it comes to being honest, you need to pick and choose, wisely and carefully. Sometimes it pays to be honest. Sometimes it's appropriate, but often, it isn't appropriate at all. Shying away from honesty doesn't make you a bad person. It just means you're exercising your right to a little privacy. Sometimes you lie to protect yourself. Sometimes you lie to avoid hurting others. Sometimes you lie just because there's no law that says your life has to be an open book to everyone."

"So, it's okay to lie?"

"Of course it is. Since when do you owe everyone the truth about everything? If we all walked around telling the truth to each other, can you even imagine the mayhem?"

"Mayhem?"

"Yes, mayhem. It'd be like throwing a lit match into a fireworks factory."

I laughed at this.

But was Bartholomew right? When I was younger, I saw a movie about a man who could read minds, and I wondered about the subject. What if we were all able to read each other's minds? All privacy of thought would be long gone, and then what? The glue that was holding society together would disintegrate, and we'd all be at each other's throats within seconds. The glue? It was a perfect analogy, and that glue was the lie—that simple, much maligned perversion of the truth that we all claim to despise and avoid, cross our hearts and hope to die. Do you swear to tell the truth, the whole truth, and nothing but the truth? No, but it would be great if you accepted my lies as truth. It would work out much better for all of us.

I'm not perfect, and neither are you. Why make all our flaws and deceits public to an audience that is always expecting us to *be* perfect? Why should we be punished and ostracized for being human?

"So, where does this leave honesty?" I asked. "Is it without value?"

"On the contrary," Bartholomew said. "Honesty sparkles like a brilliant star."

"Meaning?"

"Honesty is sincerity, and sincerity is a thing to be valued and treasured for being what it is. And what is it? It is rare. It is uncommon, but it is also beautiful. But make no mistake about it, it would have no meaning without all the lies and deceit that surround it in such plentiful abundance. It is a once-in-a-lifetime sunset over the ocean. It is a girl so beautiful that she literally makes your heart skip a beat. It is a hibiscus bush in blood-red bloom. It is a brand-new Ferrari on a showroom floor, a tree full of singing songbirds, and two lovers taking a stroll for no other reason than to be together. It's a walk-off home run in a World Series game. But without the muddle and confusion of deceitfulness surrounding it, sincerity has no shine. Truth needs deception like a bright star needs the blackness of a night sky to truly sparkle."

The year was 1975. I was still blazing my way through college at Berkeley, and so was Pamela. We had met earlier that year, and we'd been seeing a lot of each other lately. I remember a few things about the year. Stevie Nicks and Lindsay Buckingham joined Fleetwood Mac, and Mitchell, Ehrlichman, and Haldeman were all found guilty of their Watergate charges. In response to the energy crisis, daylight saving time commenced two months early. Bill Allen and Bill Gates founded Microsoft in Albuquerque, New Mexico, and *Monty Python and the Holy Grail* was released in the United Kingdom.

Lots of things were happening that year—but none as significant as what happened between Pamela and me. It was a cool fall day, and the two of us met for lunch at a little café on Telegraph Avenue. I ordered a club sandwich, and Pamela ordered turkey. We each ordered coffee.

"I should never have taken this logic class," Pamela said.

"Don't you like it?"

"It's entirely illogical."

This made me laugh. "How can that be?" I asked.

"None of it makes any sense to me."

"Have you talked to your professor?"

"No, the man is a lush."

"A lush?"

"He comes to class half drunk, and then he scribbles a bunch of nonsense on the chalkboard. He may as well be writing in Martian."

"Is there a teacher's assistant for the class?"

"No," Pamela said.

"There must be someone who can help you."

"I think I'm going to drop the class."

"Won't your parents be upset?"

"My parents?"

"I mean, dropping a class?"

"My parents don't even care if I go to college. This is all for me. And you know what? Logic is *not* for me. I don't know what I was even thinking. I thought, *Logic? That sounds good. I'm a pretty logical person.* Was I ever wrong!"

"If I dropped one of my classes, my parents would throw a fit."

"If I dropped out of school completely, my parents wouldn't care one way or the other. Haven't you ever had a class you wanted to drop? Surely, you can't like *all* your classes. No one likes *all* their classes."

I didn't know what to say. In fact, I thought I *did* like all my classes, and surely, I would never drop a class. Pamela was unique. She was new to me, and I admired her honesty and her ability to say, "Enough is enough." Me? I would struggle through this logic class no matter how difficult it was and no matter how often the professor showed up drunk. Did that make me a better person? I decided no, not at all. It just meant that I didn't have the courage to admit I'd made a mistake by signing up for the class to begin with. And did I truly like all my classes? Not really, but you would never be able to get me to admit this. My parents had trained to be a good student and get good grades. Hold up the hoop, and I'd jump through it—no questions asked.

Pamela changed the subject. Enough about her annoying logic class. She wanted to talk about her best friend back in Oregon, a girl named Judy McGuire. Pamela and Judy were friends all through middle school and high school. Judy applied to Berkeley, but she wasn't accepted. She didn't have the grades or SAT score to get in, but she was accepted to Oregon State University. The two girls kept in touch often. They did not want their friendship to suffer just because they were going to college in different states. Pamela told me she had just received a letter from Judy. That's right, a letter. You have to remember that this was when long-distance phone calls were expensive, and email and texting were nonexistent. The stone age.

In Judy's letter, she talked about school. Then she told Pamela a story that Pamela wanted to tell me. The story was about Judy and her boyfriend, Paul. Judy liked Paul a lot. Paul had told her that his father was a stockbroker in Portland, and he modestly told Judy about how much money his dad was making. He grew up in a big house in an affluent neighborhood. He told Judy that he always had trouble finding a girl back home who wasn't interested in his money, who loved Paul for himself. He said every girl he dated had dollar signs in her eyes and that he had been looking for a girl who just loved Paul for himself. "Someday, I'm going to inherit a lot of money," Paul told Janet. "I don't want that to be the reason a girl has latched onto me. The money? It means nothing. A marriage should be built on love. Trust and love."

Well, this was great. Judy agreed that a good relationship should not be based on money. And theirs wasn't. She liked Paul because he was Paul. He was sweet and caring. He was reasonably good-looking, and he had goals in life: he wanted to become a stockbroker like his father. Judy told Pamela that the two of them had been going together for months, and Judy also said that they were beginning to get serious. They told each other about their lives, and they revealed secrets to each other. "I could really picture myself marrying this boy," Janet wrote. "You know how it is? We seemed to be on the same page about everything. I kept thinking, *Maybe this is the one.*"

Well, long story short, Janet found out that Paul was lying. He was lying about everything. His dad wasn't a stockbroker at all, and he stood to inherit nothing. His dad was a handyman, and his mom was a babysitter. Each month, they struggled to make ends meet. Sure, they lived in Portland, but they lived in a shitty little rental in a shitty neighborhood. Judy learned about this from one of Paul's ex-girlfriends. Paul had told *this* girlfriend that his father was a doctor, making money hand over fist. Janet was furious, and she dropped Paul like a hot potato. She told Pamela it wasn't because he wasn't rich. Although that would've been nice. She dumped Paul because he'd lied to her.

Pamela said, "Can you blame the poor girl?"

"No," I said.

"I can't even imagine."

"He had to know she'd find out eventually."

"He was an idiot," Pamela said.

"I feel kind of sorry for the guy," I said.

"Not me," Pamela said.

We continued to eat and sip our coffee. We didn't talk for a minute or so.

Then, Pamela set her sandwich on her plate and leaned forward. "I love you," she said.

Did I hear her right? "I love you," I said—without even thinking about it. It just seemed like the right thing to say.

"I mean I *really* love you," Pamela said.

"I really love you too."

Well, hell. There you had it. We both finally said it, and then the strangest thing happened. Everything in and around the café became brilliant, the colors, the sharp edges, the light. I don't know exactly how to describe it. The world was beautiful. Everything was overwhelmingly right. And I swore I heard music, a harp. No, a hundred harps, all playing together to the beat of a hundred timpani drums!

It *was* love. There was no question about it. I was having lunch with the girl of my dreams, the girl I would marry. No lies. Not yet, anyway. The truth, the whole truth, and nothing but the truth.

CHAPTER 34

SIXTY-FIVE

I was still stewing over what I was going to tell Bartholomew for my tenth and final story. I didn't want to tell him another story about what a rotten person I'd been. I'd told him enough of these, and I also didn't want to make myself out as a hero. I wasn't in the mood for patting myself on the back. So, what *did* I want? I wanted to tell a story that showed I had been listening, that showed I accepted my world as it was, that showed I was okay with being a human being. The problem was my distorted thinking. I had spent so much of my time looking for perfection—demanding it of myself and demanding it of others—that I had lost sight of what life was all about. Then it occurred to me that maybe I didn't even have this tenth story.

Instead of telling another story, I would write a poem. Why not? What better way was there to express myself at this point? Okay, maybe I wasn't much of a poet. Maybe I was just a bricklayer, but I would lay each brick carefully, one atop the other. I would search for the truth about the world and the truth about myself. I would do my best to avoid my distorted thinking and come up with something that proved I had been listening. I would prove that I had been listening to Bartholomew. I would show him that his words were not falling upon deaf ears. Regrets? I had plenty of them, but I would try to weave them into a tapestry of hope, of life, of the future. I would celebrate what it means to be human, in all its imperfect glory.

I sat down and wrote. I worked on this poem every morning for a week and a half, and when I finished it, I spent another couple days making revisions. Was it perfect? Of course not. But wasn't that the whole point? I titled the poem "Almost Sixty-Five," and it went as follows:

Almost Sixty-Five

The sun has been afoot all day,
And it's headed toward the horizon.
It won't be setting soon,
But it's thinking about it. One

Life, one day, spring, summer, autumn,
And winter. Over and over,
Almost sixty-five years.
Lightning flashes, and clouds hover.

Rain falls, winds blow, and snowflakes melt.
Flowers bloom, trees grow, and insects fly
About and crawl and live
And die and people wonder why

It's happening. Created by
A perfect God. Everything He
Does here is right and just,
So why all the trash in the sea,

And smoke in the air, and toxins
In the rivers, and blood on the ground?
And why does He insist
Lines are curved and rectangles round?

Why did He curse us with a love
Of perfection, a longing that will
Never be satisfied?
We push the boulder up the hill,

Day after day, season after
season, year after year. Does He smile
Or does He cry when He
Watches us go the extra mile?

It seems cruel to me, but then
Who am I to question His motives?
I'm just trying to survive
Like every other man who lives

On this planet. There are those who
Compare life to walking a tightrope,
Despair on one side, and
On the other side, there is hope.

It's a balancing act to be
Sure. A tricky trek by anyone's
Definition. Keep a
Watchful eye on the traveling sun,

As it will set before you know
What even happened? Were you happy
Or were you troubled by
How far you fell short? I think we

Are all in the same boat, dying
Of thirst on an open sea. Praying
For salvation, singing
From the good book and all saying

That we did our best. Do you
Know what really irks me? It is that
No matter how much food
I put in their dish, my two cats

Are always hungry for more. And
No matter what I do, my efforts
Are always lacking, and
The results? They are always poor.

Then

Along comes my friend,
And he speaks and sends
Me down a new road.
He lightens my load
And opens a door,
And the lions roar,
And the sunlight shines,
And the church bells chime,
And, for once, I see
That He is for me.
He never did say
All would go my way.
Imperfection is
The art of the miss,
And what a fine haul
It is, after all.

He laughs and sings,

"I beg your pardon,
I never promised
You a rose garden."

It's taken me so long to learn
The simplest things. It's not that I am
Stupid. It's just that I
Am human. It's not that I ran

Away from the truth. It's just that
My legs only run so fast. So, I'm
Okay. I'll cut myself
Some slack. I'll give myself some time.

I'll give myself the benefit
Of the doubt. I'll count all my blessings.
If I do all these things
With sincerity, I'm guessing

God will welcome me with open
Arms and say, "It's nice to have you here.
Where have you been all this
Time?" And I'll say that I was near

But far,
And that it's nice to
Finally wish upon a star.
"Star light, star bright,
First star I see tonight."

Now I stand alive,
Almost sixty-five

With God at my side.

When Bartholomew read this poem, he smiled and said, "So, you are now comfortable?"

"I think I am," I said.

"You are cutting yourself some slack?"

"Yes," I said.

"It's taken us a long time to get here."

"It has," I said, laughing.

"Then my work is done."

"Done?"

"You brought your car in to be serviced. The engine now idles smoothly. The windshield wipers work. The brakes don't squeak. The air conditioner operates flawlessly, and the tires are full of air. The bugs have been cleaned from the front grill, and the rattle in the dashboard is gone. It's time to give your car a spin, around the block, and off you go to wherever it is that you have to be. Yes, my work is done."

I slept in that day. When I woke up on the morning of my sixty-fifth birthday, the sunlight was pouring in through the window. Pamela was already awake and out of bed. I could hear the birds singing in the trees, and I stayed in bed for a few minutes to collect my thoughts.

It was a Saturday, and I had chores to do. They were the same old chores I always did. No news there. But I have to tell you that I did feel different. I felt like I'd been in a violent and relentless tempest, like the previous day was nothing but storm clouds, rain, hail, lightning bolts, and thunderclaps. The wind had been howling all day and night. The ground was soaked to the bone. Broken tree branches and twigs were everywhere. There were newly formed lakes and streams, a carpet of wet pine needles and leaves. There were tipped over trash cans, dripping downspouts, and clogged rain gutters. But now? The sky was clear, and the morning was calm. The yellow sunlight was warming and drying everything in sight, and the birds were all out, happily talking about the storm that had come and gone. Of course, this scene was all in my mind.

My mind.

What an amazing thing the mind was—that mysterious organic contraption that was as capable of causing distress as it was capable of coming up with a cure.

As I remained in bed, I could hear the clanking of dishes, coming from downstairs in the kitchen. Pamela was emptying the dishwasher and putting all the dishes away. In a way, I felt sorry for her. She knew nothing about Bartholomew. I had kept him secret from her, and for good reason. No doubt she would've thought there was something seriously wrong with me, and it would've upset her. And the last thing I wanted her to do was worry about me. Both of us had enough on our minds. Can you imagine if I'd told her I'd been carrying on every other day with my childhood imaginary friend? "You need to see a psychiatrist," she would've said, and she would've talked me into it. I would've gone for her sake, for her own peace of mind.

No, Bartholomew was my secret. He was all mine, and only mine. True, he could be annoying, but at the end of the day, I trusted him. We were on the same wavelength, and he understood me. If I'd tried to have the same sort of conversations with Pamela that I had with Bartholomew, they would've led nowhere. Listen, I loved her, but she was not Bartholomew, and she was not me. She was different. She was simple. I don't mean simple as in stupid, but simple as in that none of the things that were bothering me would've made any sense to her. I didn't hold this against her. In fact, there have been times when I would've given anything to be more like her. Circles were circles, squares were squares, and triangles were always triangles—and every shape had a mate.

I got out of bed. I brushed my teeth, combed my hair, and put on some clothes. I then looked at myself in the mirror. "Sixty-five—and you're well into the twenty-first century." It was kind of cool. When I was younger, I used to wonder if I'd even reach the twenty-first century. Back then, being forty seemed old, and now here I was, at sixty-five, fit as a fiddle. I did have some aches and pains, mostly in my back, but they were nothing to be complaining about. Oh, yes, and there was the cataract surgery, but that wasn't really a big deal either—and my health insurance company paid for most of it. Now I was going to be on Medicare. I would need a supplemental policy, and as I looked at myself in the mirror, I wondered how much that was going to cost. No doubt, I would be paying less than I had been paying. It was another thing to be grateful for.

There was so much to be grateful for, so many things to be happy about, and so many major and minor times in my life where I could point to myself and say, "You're a good man!"

I walked downstairs to the kitchen. Pamela was done with the dishes, and she was now getting ready to run the vacuum.

"Need any help?" I asked

"I'm fine," Pamela said.

"I don't mind helping."

"It's your birthday. Just relax."

"I'm sixty-five."

"I know that."

"It's a milestone age," I said.

"You made it. How does it feel?"

"Kind of weird."

"If you could take out the trash?"

"Sure," I said. I opened the trash compactor, and the thing was full. "We sure generate a lot of trash for two people."

"We do," Pamela said.

I pulled the trash bag out of the compactor and set it to the side. I then put a new bag in and took the full bag outside to the trash can. It was a nice morning. Not too cold, but not hot. A perfect day for a birthday.

When I came back inside, Pamela was running the vacuum. It was the sound of progress. The sound of maintenance. Keeping things up and keeping them going. That was Pamela. The maintenance queen, always keeping the ball rolling. I poured myself a cup of coffee, stood in the kitchen, and drank it.

When Pamela was done with the vacuuming, she put the machine in the pantry, in its spot by the pantry door with the brooms and mops and dustpan.

"I still think we should hire a maid," I said.

"We tried that," Pamela said.

"And?"

"All they did was break vases and rearrange things. It was very annoying. They were more trouble than they were worth."

"I guess you're right."

"Are you going to mow the lawn this morning?"

"As soon as I'm done with my coffee."

"You don't have to if you don't want to. The grass doesn't look that bad."

"I'll do it."

"The guests are going to start arriving at three."

"Is everyone coming?"

"No one said they weren't."

"How's my mom getting here?"

"Ralph is going to give her a ride. I've got everything covered."

"It will be good to see Ralph. I haven't seen him for a while. I don't think I've seen him for a year."

"It hasn't been that long."

"No?" I asked.

"But his kids are coming."

"That will be nice," I said. "I wonder how they've been doing."

"You'll be able to ask them."

"Right," I said.

CHAPTER 35

A SHINY SIDE

I'd been in charge of mowing lawns ever since I was eight years old. First at my parents' house. That was my job. Then at the first house Pamela and I rented in Santa Ana—and at every house we've ever lived in since. I was now sixty-five years old, and I'd been mowing lawns every weekend since I was eight, which, knocking off the four years I was in Berkeley, added up to almost three thousand lawn-mowing ventures. That's a lot of lawn mowing any way you look at it—a whole lot of blades of grass. I now had a gas-powered mower that I kept in the garage. I went to the garage to get it, and I checked the fuel level in the tank. There was plenty of gas. I then pushed the mower to the front lawn and fired it up. As I mowed our lawn, I thought about the first house Pamela and I rented. We had just come to Orange County from Berkeley, and while we both had jobs, we were making next to nothing. The house we lived in was a dump, but it was all we could afford. Part of our agreement with the landlord was that I mow the front lawn.

My mom and dad didn't like the place we lived in, and Dad offered to subsidize our income so that we could afford a nicer house. But I turned down his offer. Not that it wasn't tempting, but it was important to me that Pamela and I were self-sufficient, paying our own way. It wasn't really a pride thing. It was more just a commitment to responsibility, if that makes sense. I wanted to be responsible.

The last time Bartholomew and I talked, we discussed responsibility. I said something to the effect that, "Despite my flaws and faults as a human being, at least I am responsible." I said this with some satisfaction. I was expecting Bartholomew to agree with me and pat me on the back.

Instead, Bartholomew laughed and said, "It's pointless, trying to be responsible."

"Oh really?" I asked.

"One can be *held* responsible. But actually being responsible? I don't think so."

"Meaning?"

"As in responsible, as in doing what you should do?"

"Yes," I said. "I've always worked for a living. I've always done what it took to put food on our table. I've always done what it took to pay our mortgage, car payments, utility bills, medical bills, and the costs for everything else associated with living a decent life. My family has never been without. I've never put us at undue financial risk. With only a few exceptions, I've always chosen the straight and narrow path, and I've been a good husband and father. And a good son. When push came to shove, I always had my family's best interests at heart, and there hasn't been anything I wouldn't do to protect and care for my family. I love my family. All said and done, I've been very good to them, very responsible."

Bartholomew laughed again, and I asked him what was so funny. "You haven't been responsible," he said. "You've been nothing more than a scaredy-cat."

"What does that even mean?"

"We like to *think* we're responsible. It makes us feel better about ourselves. And when we do screw up, we like to think of our screwups as the exceptions that prove the rule. But honestly? Being human is all about fear. We can't help it. It's in our DNA. Do you want to know what the real motivator is in the behavior of the average human being? And as such, of yourself? The real motivator is fear of failing—and being held accountable for your failures. The *real* motivator that keeps you more or less on the road that is straight and narrow is the fear of stumbling and falling flat on your face. What if you did fall? People would laugh at you. They would point at you, shake their heads, and make you feel ashamed. Shame, shame! Who did you think you were? Where did you ever get it in your head that you could do something with your life that was—extraordinary?"

"There are people who do extraordinary things," I argued.

"But you and 99 percent of the population are not among that group."

"But I *have* been responsible."

"You've been acting out of fear. You've been doing your best to play it safe. And face it. When you saw your sons going out on a limb to chase their dreams, it frightened you. You envisioned the worst for them. You encouraged them, yes, because, down deep, you admired them for their nerve, but all the while that you were encouraging them, you were scared to death. And when they didn't achieve their dreams, your biggest fears came to fruition. You didn't tell either of them to get back on their feet and keep fighting the good fight. You basically said, 'God favors responsible men.'"

"But He does, doesn't He?" I asked.

"Does He?" Bartholomew asked.

"Now you're confusing me," I said.

"How so?"

"You've spent the past year convincing me that I should be happy with what I am, and now you're telling me that I've thrown my life away."

"Thrown your life away?"

"Being, in so many words, a coward," I said. "A coward is afraid to fail. A coward is afraid to take chances. A coward plays it safe and calls it responsibility."

"I'm just being honest," Bartholomew said. "You can lie to other people until the cows come home, but if you really want to be happy, and if you really want to be content, you need to be honest with yourself."

"And admit that I'm a coward?"

"That's your word, not mine."

"Then what is your word?"

"If I have an apple in my hand, and I'd rather have an apricot, what happens when I tell myself that I have an apricot? Does that apple turn into an apricot? No, of course not. An apple is an apple. It doesn't matter what you wish it was. It's red. It has seeds and a stem. Coming clean with yourself and admitting that you're afraid of failure is no different from saying, 'You know what? I *do* have an apple in my hand. Apples are apples, and apricots are apricots.'"

"And there's nothing wrong with an apple?"

"Nothing at all."

"And if I'd rather have an apricot?"

"Then look for an apricot tree."

Bartholomew was right. Bartholomew was always right. This shouldn't have come as a surprise to me, but it did. It was a revelation—and a good one. When one is honest about oneself, and able to accept that honesty, not as a criticism or belittlement, but as a giant step forward, one really has a chance at true happiness. It's like science, right? Science is a search for the truth. Science means discarding make-believe notions and stepping forward into the sunlight of *what actually is.* Me? I was a man. I was a flawed and frightened construct of bones, flesh, organs, blood, and hair, doing my best to survive in a world that sometimes made perfect sense and sometimes made no sense at all. Lost in space, doing my best. And sometimes not doing my best. Making every effort, and sometimes not trying at all. A *human being.* And this was okay!

"What if I'm not satisfied with what I am—and what if I want to improve?"

"There's nothing wrong with that."

"But?"

"Just don't seek perfection. You'll never find it no matter how hard you try. Reach for the stars if you must, but be happy if you get a handful of tree leaves. Cut yourself some slack. You are a man. There's nothing wrong with that. The experience of living should be enough for you. Grade each assignment and move on to the next one. Learn from your past, assess in the present, and move on to your future. And know that no matter how miserable you may be, there is always hope, and there is no gift you will ever receive as precious and valuable as the life you've been given."

When I was done mowing the lawn, I put the lawn mower back in the garage. I then got out a broom and swept the sidewalk and the driveway. I put the broom back in the garage. Near to where we kept the broom was a box, and in the box, there were several baseball bats and gloves. We hadn't used them for years. When the boys were young, we used to practice in the front yard. Throwing the balls. Hitting them. Pitching. Catching flies and grounders. It was a lot of fun, and I felt a strong desire to turn back the clock, back to those days. Life was a lot simpler then, and I recalled my own childhood. I took one of the gloves out of the box and put it on my hand. I remembered when I played baseball. I wasn't very good at it, but my dad put me on a Little League team when I was in seventh grade. It was daunting, but at least we had a coach who was kindhearted. The man didn't have a mean bone in his body, and I liked that.

I remembered one game. We were playing against the best team in our division. The coach put me out in right field, thinking that not many balls would come my way. I remembered standing out there on the grass, hoping that I wouldn't have to do anything. I watched the clouds change shape overhead, and I watched the birds flying in formation. Then I kept my eye on the batters—just in case they hit a ball to me.

"Heads up!" the coach yelled to me, and for good reason. The boy coming up to bat was Henry Gable, the other team's best hitter. I ignored the clouds and the birds and concentrated on Henry. Sure enough, on the fourth pitch, Henry blasted a ball to right field. To me! Jesus, I tried to keep my eye on the ball. Then it came falling out of the sky like an asteroid.

I held up my mitt with one hand, shielding the sun from my eyes with my free hand. It was falling, falling, falling, and then *whack*! The ball landed in the heel of my glove, and before I could close the webbing on it, it bounced out and landed on the grass, at my feet. It was my one chance to be a hero, and I blew it. I could hear the crowd in the bleachers moan as I leaned over to pick up the ball. I don't know what I was thinking. I threw the ball toward first base. The throw wasn't even close, and the ball rolled to the left of the first baseman and toward the opposing team's dugout. "You should've thrown it to second," I heard one of my teammates yell, but it was too late. Henry Gable was rounding second and on his way to third. It was a triple, and it should've been an out. My one chance to be a hero, up in smoke. A dropped ball and a bad throw.

After several runs were scored by the opposing team, the inning was finally over. We all came back to the dugout.

"I can't believe you dropped that ball," one of the boys said to me. "It was right to you."

"My grandmother could've caught that ball," another kid said. "And she's half blind."

"That's enough," the coach said.

So much for my memories. I put the glove back into the box, and I closed the garage door. There were better things to do with my morning. Besides, that was just one memory. I actually went on to become a pretty good ballplayer. Maybe not great, but good enough to hold my own. And I was a better person for that bad experience. When other kids made mistakes, I did not insult them or rub their noses in their errors. I was a good teammate. I was a good kid. And, yes, all things considered, I was a pretty good adult.

Sixty-five? That's a lot of years. Plenty of mistakes, but even more successes. We like to belittle Pollyannas, but they have a good point, don't they? All coins have a shiny side. And there is always hope. And the person who concentrates on all the mistakes he's made and all the dog crap he's stepped in really misses the whole point of being a human being. True, it may take some effort to look back and find all the good things that have come your way—all the lessons you've learned and all the triumphs you've earned—but it *is* worth the look. You might be surprised at what you find. There may *be* a pot of gold at the end of the rainbow.

When I went into the house, Pamela was busy cleaning the kitchen counters and the sink. "If there's nothing else you need me to do, I'm going to my study," I said.

"You mowed the lawn?"

"I did," I said.

"The garage needs to be swept," Pamela said. "But today's your birthday, so you can do that later. Go enjoy yourself. As soon as I'm done here, I'm going to the bakery to pick up your cake."

"Okay," I said.

"They make the best red velvet cakes."

"They do," I said.

"Do you want me to pick up anything else?"

"I can't think of anything," I said.

"Do you need beer?"

"There's plenty in the garage refrigerator."

"We might need more milk."

"You're in charge," I said.

"I think we have plenty of coffee. People like either milk or coffee with their cake. I guess I should pick up some cream. Some people like cream in their coffee."

Details, details. That was my wife, Pamela. "Sounds like you've got it covered," I said. And she did have it covered. Pamela always had it covered.

CHAPTER 36

I HATE GOODBYES

One last story. It's a short one. I didn't tell this story to Bartholomew, but I can guess what he'd have to say about it. Why didn't I tell him? I guess I ran out of time.

This story took place about twenty years ago, while I was working full-time at Wiley & Associates. I was in the middle of designing a new home for the Richards family. First let me tell you about this family in order to give you an idea of what I was up against. Joe Richards owned a commercial security company, the second largest company in the US. The guy was worth millions, and to date, he and his family had been living in Palm Springs. They wanted to build a summer house in Newport Beach, on the bay. The lot was located on Balboa Island. It wasn't actually a lot. It was a charming little cottage that Joe planned to have razed to make room for his new house. Out with the old—and in with the new. I was put in charge of the project, and I had spent a lot of time with the Richards family coming up with a design. I just about had all the final design drawings done; the project needed about one more day's work.

I was supposed to meet with the Richards family on a Friday, the morning before they were to leave for a trip to Italy. It was important that I have the drawings done because their trip to Italy was scheduled to last three weeks. This would be my last chance to get their approval of the design and move on to preparing the construction drawings. It was Thursday, and I started to work on the drawings. I figured I would have plenty of time to get them done by evening, thus by Friday morning, but then Arnold Witherspoon came into the picture. Arnold was about seven years younger than me, and he was still a little wet behind the ears. John Wiley had put Arnold in charge of the Gabriel house as Arnold's first project. It wasn't the first project he'd worked on, but it was the first time he'd been assigned as a lead architect.

Arnold came into my office that Thursday morning, and he asked me if I could help him. He was supposed to make a presentation of his preliminary design to Mr. and Mrs. Gabriel on Friday afternoon.

I went to Arnold's drafting table to see what he'd done to date, and I looked over his design.

"It's not working," he said, and he was right. His design was a mess. This surprised me because I'd always thought of Arnold as being a capable designer. "It's all wrong," he said. "I can't make anything come together. There's no way I'll have this done by tomorrow."

I could tell by the tone of Arnold's voice that he was panicking. It wasn't any more complicated than that. His first project. His first chance to prove himself, and his mind was reeling. I knew the feeling. I'd experienced the same thing when I was handed my first project by Mr. Wiley, and I felt for the guy.

"Let's see what we can do," I said.

"Any help would be appreciated."

"It's no problem," I said.

I don't know what I thought I was doing. I had my own project to work on and my own deadline to meet, but I sat at Arnold's table and went to work with him. One hour passed. Then another, and then another, and the next thing I knew, it was five in the evening. We came up with a pretty good design. In fact, it was an excellent design. I was confident that it would make Mr. and Mrs. Gabriel happy, and Arnold was extraordinarily grateful. He must have said thank you to me five times. He then put on his coat, and he went home for dinner. Me? Well, I was screwed. I hadn't done a thing on the Richards project all day, and the only way I would have the drawings done in time for our meeting was to work all night on it. I called Pamela and told her what had happened, and I told her I would probably be in the office all night. And I was. I turned on my radio to a jazz station, and I worked until nine the next morning. My eyes were burning, and my head was spinning.

All said and done, both the Richards and the Gabriels were pleased with the drawings Arnold and I presented to them. And me? I was a mess. With a stomach sloshing full of coffee, and a thousand details swirling in my head, I finally drove home at the end of the day on Friday. The first thing I did was eat dinner. Then I plopped on the sofa and fell asleep. I never did tell John Wiley how I'd helped Arnold. I let him think that Arnold had done everything on his own. And I didn't tell Arnold that I had to work all night because of him. I wasn't looking to score any points with anyone. So, why did I help the guy? I guess it was because I knew what it was like to panic. It's a horrible feeling. You can have all the talent in the world, but when you panic, you are suddenly paralyzed. Unable to work. Unable to think. Helping Arnold just seemed like the right thing to do.

Yes, it was the right thing to do. You know, we have opportunities throughout our lives to do the right thing, to lend a helping hand. Even at our own discomfort. Even at our own inconvenience. Even at our own loss. And we *do* help, maybe not always, but often enough to make it significant. I've seen this in myself, and I've seen it in others. It exists. It's not like I risked my life or anything like that, but it was important. It was important to Arnold, and therefore, it was important to me. It was a small difference, but I did make a difference.

Life.

It is complicated. We misbehave. We do the right things. Sometimes we think of others, and sometimes we think only of ourselves. Sometimes you'd swear that we don't think at all. Sometimes we're ingenious. Each of us takes our own path, and no two paths are the same. They literally go all over the place, through valleys, jungles, plains, deserts, and over hills and mountains. Left and right. Up and down. Over and under. Some of us fly, and some of us burrow. Some of us seek the shade, and others seek the warmth of the sun. Who's to say if one path is any better than the other? They all have their pros and cons, and they all lead to *somewhere*. Somewhere good? Somewhere bad? I guess that depends on your perspective. And what exactly is perspective?

Bartholomew told me several times that I was suffering from distorted thinking. Wasn't this another way of saying that I had a defective perspective?

Do you feel guilty—or do you feel proud? Do you feel confused? Are you happy—or are you blue and sad? Are you energetic—or do you always feel run-down and tired? How much of what you feel is up to you—and how much is the result of outside forces? Did you feel better when you were younger—or do you feel better now that you're older and wiser? I think these are all questions that we ask ourselves sooner or later. And how do we answer them? When we examine our perspectives, do we get emotional or try to be objective? I've been lucky of late; I've had Bartholomew to talk to. I'm convinced that everyone ought to have their own Bartholomew.

Maybe the most important thing that Bartholomew taught me is that perfection doesn't exist, anywhere. This seems so simple and obvious, but it isn't. We all expect perfection out of life, and we are disappointed when we discover there simply is no such thing. We expect perfection from others, but we never get it. We expect perfection from ourselves, but we don't cooperate. We expect perfection from the world, but it doesn't come. It simply doesn't exist unless you redefine the word to mean perfectly imperfect, and in which case, you will have described everything. We live in a perfectly imperfect world. Others misbehave, we do stupid things, and the world is misshapen and cruel. News flash. Everyone and everything are in on the conspiracy. Don't try to ignore it. You won't be successful. You may as well beat your head against a brick wall.

Here's what I've learned about myself, what I've learned about others, and what I've learned about the world. Life is a great big recipe of betrayal, goodwill, evil, indifference, greed, love, jealousy, hate, altruism, anger, humor, fear, contentment, dishonesty, and a hundred other human ingredients, all mixed up in a bowl, poured into a giant baking pan, glazed with hail, sunlight, rain, snow, and sleet, and baked at 450 degrees. That is the beauty of it, a little bit of everything, a flavor for every taste bud, a concoction of aromas that will make your sleepy head spin like a planet in orbit around a sun. Life. It's both unique and astounding. There is nothing like it in the known universe. I get out of breath just thinking about it.

Everyone is eating their cake. Some are washing it down with milk, others with coffee. Pamela was right when she said we would need milk *and* coffee. She was also right about the bakery. They did make the best red velvet cakes, and this cake is delicious. Even my mom likes it, and she isn't much of a cake person. "This icing is amazing," she says.

Some of us are sitting, and some of us are standing. Bartholomew is still seated across the room, away from the crowd. He isn't eating any cake, of course.

Ralph decides to liven things up by telling a couple of his jokes. That's the good thing about Ralph. He always has a joke for every occasion. "What do Australians call an upside-down cake?" Ralph asks. He can't wait to get to the punch line.

"What do they call it?" I ask.

"They call it a cake," Ralph says.

Everyone laughs.

"Why do we put candles on top of a birthday cake?" Ralph asks.

"Why?" Pamela asks.

"Because it's too hard to put them on the bottom," Ralph says, and he laughs at his own joke.

"That's dumb," I say.

"That's what makes it so funny," Ralph says.

The spotlight is suddenly off of Ralph, and everyone is striking up their own conversations. Somehow, I wind up with Ralph, and we are talking about Hawaii. Ralph is planning to take his family to Maui this spring, and to hear him talk about the trip, you'd think they went there every year. But I know they've only been there once. Ralph took his family there eight years ago, and I think the trip nearly broke him. Thank God for credit cards; otherwise, Ralph would never have seen the island at all. It probably took Ralph eight years to pay down the credit debt so he could afford this second trip.

"There's so much to see here on the mainland," Ralph says. "The national parks. The cities. And we usually prefer to drive. I've always liked to drive, and we like to camp. But hey! Once in a while, it's good to hop on a plane and fly. Once in a while, it's nice to stay in a hotel. The weather should be perfect."

"You'll have a good time," I say.

Then we start trading lies. His kids have been doing great, and so have mine. Ralph *loves* his work, and I'm looking forward to retirement. But am I? All that free time ahead of me, and to do what? Write poetry and do chores? He doesn't share his fear that he'll be working for the rest of his life, and I don't share the fear that I'll soon be bored out of my mind, paying attention to things that I never used to care about just because I have nothing else to do with my time. I think we're both uneasy, but we don't talk about it. Not at all. We're brothers, but we may as well be total strangers. We talk about Hawaii, and then we talk about football teams. Then we talk about hockey teams. Then we talk about cars, and then we talk about lawn mowers.

Zach and Mary Ann join us.

Ralph congratulates the kids on their engagement, and Mary Ann shows Ralph the ring. "That must've set you back a pretty penny," Ralph says to Zach.

"I bought it on time."

"So, now you *have* to work," Ralph says.

"I guess so," Zach says.

You know who I miss? I miss Max, my dog. Max, who I rescued from the freeway all those years ago. He didn't have a mean bone in his body. All he wanted was to be loved. All he wanted was to play fetch, have his belly rubbed, and eat. My God, that dog could eat. Meals. Table scraps. Treats. He was always hungry, but he never gained a pound. Losing Max was one of the worst days of my life, worse than when I lost my dad. You know what it is about pets? They're not complicated. They have no reason to lie. I like everyone who showed up for my birthday party, but you'll be hard-pressed to squeeze the truth out of any of them. Except maybe my mom. She pretty much says what's on her mind. But even Mom has her personal secrets. Oh, yeah.

Bartholomew is still sitting away from the crowd. He is looking out the front room window, thinking. He doesn't seem to be paying much attention to the rest of us, like he has heard it all before.

I feel an urge to leave the party. I want to sneak off to my study. I've been working on a poem for the past week, and I want to finish it. Not much left to do. Just a few more lines ought to do it. I excuse myself, go to my study, and close the door behind me. The poem is on the computer monitor, just the way I left it. And I read it. Then I begin to write. I spend about a half hour on it, until it is finally done. It is a goodbye poem. As a rule, I hate goodbyes, but that's what it is. I titled the poem "Friend," and it now went as follows:

Friend

Invisible,
Inscrutable,
You walked back into my life with
Your doctor's bag, needle and thread,

Here as a friend
Able to mend
My misguided psyche. Able
To arrange the pieces into

Something that makes
Sense like those lakes
That settle so nicely into
The low points of a rational

Landscape. Never
Mind the weather.
Never mind the forces trying
To tear the world asunder.

You bring reason
To all seasons.
What's that they say? "I was lost, and
Then I was found?" That's what I say

Now that you have
Applied your salve
To the wounds that foolishness have
Inflicted on my bone and flesh.

Laugh at the pain,
Shelter from rain,
Warm fire in the fireplace
Soothing my extremities. The

Misdirection
Of perfection
Is a thing of the past for me.
You have blown the squall from the sea.

It's clear sailing.
Sirens wailing,
They missed their opportunity
To bring me to their rocky shores.

I know that you
Are leaving soon,
But it breaks my heart to see you
On your way again. But I know

The next time I
Focus my eyes
On the confusion that is life,
I will see, because I will be

Talking to me,
And because we
Are one; you are me, and I am
You. Still, I will miss your voice

Like crazy. I
Will surely cry
When you say goodbye. So please leave
As stealthily as you arrived.

I am going to miss Bartholomew something terrible. Not everyone has such a friend—even if that friend is himself. Why is it that I was so afraid to talk to myself? Why did I have to invent an imaginary friend to fill the role? Maybe I didn't trust my wisdom enough to believe in myself as my best advisor. Like Bartholomew said, over and over, it is not a perfect world we live in. Never has been—and never will be. Not ever.

When I finish this poem, Pamela knocks on my study door. Then she opens it. "Here you are," she says. "What are you doing in here? Everyone is wondering where you went."

"I was working on a poem," I say.

"Come on," Pamela says. "We're going to play charades. It was Zach's idea."

"Sounds good," I say.

"Well?"

I turn off my computer and stand up. I follow Pamela down the hall and into the front room. Everyone is seated on the sofas and chairs, waiting for me. Bartholomew is gone. He left while I was in my study. Gone, gone, gone. He vanished, gone for good.

"Are you all right?" Pamela asks quietly.

"I'll be okay," I say.

"You look sad. You look like you're going to cry. Are you sure you're okay?"

"I'm fine," I say. "Where do I sit?"

"You can sit on the floor with me."

"Good," I say. "Charades, you say? Let's play. What do we do next?"

Made in United States
North Haven, CT
28 March 2022